Mountain Murder

By Ida Vincent

MOUNTAIN MURDER
First published in the United States in 2016

Cover design by Michelle Hobbs
Edited by Gary Smailes

Copyright © Ida Vincent, 2016

ISBN: 978 1 53715 716 0
ISBN: 1 53715 716 7

PART I – Pacific Northwest

"Life is an adventure or it is nothing at all."
– Marie Curie

Chapter 1

"Come on, we are going to be late. Marta, hurry up."

I am transfixed. Something has caught my eye and I can't speak, walk, or for that matter hurry up. The entire wall of the town hall is covered in a poster of high peaks, it shows an American flag flapping in the wind and a weather-beaten face raising an ice axe high in the air. Below the scenic shot a caption reads '*36 years since THE SUMMIT*'. But what has captured me is the face barely peeking out behind the smiling celebrity climber; I know that face, I have seen it before, but where?

Sonia grabs my arm and yanks me back to reality. "We are going to be late."

I shake my head, look at my watch, and let out a little yelp, allowing Sonia to drag me along the sidewalk towards the town hall entrance. She has me by the cuff as we enter the foyer, which is buzzing with excited people clad in Gore-Tex and Patagonia sweaters.

"I guess we aren't the only climbers here," laughs Sonia.

"Nope," I smile back at her. "I think the entire Mountaineers community has shown up for this one. I guess we aren't Mr. Hawkins' only fans."

"Guess not."

Sonia squeals as we enter the auditorium and points towards the front of the room. Mr. Hawkins is already seated and ready to start. We have to push our way through rows of people before finding two chairs next to each other and not too far from the stage. We have become accustomed to our hero being a grey-haired and bearded man, large in stature and personality, eyes always glinting with life. But the man up on the stage today looks terribly sad and old. His eyes look despondent and he is slumped in his chair. Despite his tall frame he looks frail.

"What's this all about? It feels like we have arrived at a funeral," whispers Sonia.

I nod in agreement; my eyes are still fixed on our hero. Something is off. The microphone whines and his voice, normally strong, but now dry and cracked, fills the room. I suddenly realize I have been sitting on the edge of my seat, and I relax back to listen to the stories told many times before.

"It has been 36 years since I stood on the summit of K2..." Mr. Hawkins pauses, the microphone lets out another whine as he draws a deep breath.

"K2 may only come second in height, but in difficulty I have never met its match. I have climbed many mountains since and not one can compare to K2. I have always believed that uncertainty and risk creates bravery, and that death is a small price to pay for living a full life. I have lost many friends to avalanches, rock fall, altitude, and hidden crevasses. But perhaps the price paid to summit K2 was too big." He looks out at the audience. The room is dead quite.

"To be the first American to summit K2 has shaped my life and allowed me to pursue my dreams as a mountaineer. I first attempted to climb K2 in 1953. We hoped to summit via the Northeast face, it is a bold route with a long heavily-corniced ridge. In 1953 it proved *too* bold of a route. The only reason I am here today is because in 1953 I was a rookie and much slower than my two teammates. When the cornice they stood on gave way creating the most furious avalanche I have ever witnessed, I was so far behind it did not take me with them. I was saved by my own inexperience."

I know this story well, I have read every book, watched every documentary, and turned over every stone there is about mountaineering history and the early mountaineers pioneering new routes in the high Himalayas. In my mind I have climbed there next to them, slept at high camp, weathered out snowstorms so fierce they threatened to rip the tents off the mountain, and gasped for air at high altitudes. But in reality I have never even left the state of Washington.

"I went on to climb many other mountains before I finally got a chance to return to K2 some twenty-five years later. We had already missed out on being first on the summit, the Italians set that record on 31st of July in 1954, but we hoped to be the first Americans on the summit. I still had my mind set on the Northeast face, I had seen the route in 1953 and thought it doable, and it was still unclimbed. This time I went for the summit alone, my teammates wanting to wait for a better weather window. That decision cost me two toes to frostbite. Storms moved in and I ended up spending a night bivouacking 500 feet below the summit. One of the highest bivouacs in history. I guess that means I set three records on that climb, first American on the summit of K2, first and to date only ascent of the Northeast ridge, and the highest bivouac at the time. That last one has been beaten a couple of times by now. But all up worth losing a couple toes for." Mr. Hawkins gives his trademark wink.

There is his spark, I think to myself. But as he finishes up his presentation the spark is all gone. No more jokes or cheeky winks. He is back to looking sad and old.

"If you want to purchase a signed copy of my book *K2 – dreams, distress and disaster,* which covers both my first failed attempt in 1953 and then my successful summit in 1978, I will be signing copies at the back of the room."

People applaud for a long time, even a couple of loud whistles bounce through the room, and as Sonia and I get up to leave people are pushing and shoving to get to the back of the room, to get their copy of his book signed. Normally I would be there with them, but this time I take Sonia's arm and we sneak out a side door. I can't shake the sad look on Mr.

Hawkins' face.

"I think he's broken his back," I say. "That look on his face is the same look my dad got after he broke his back, I think he has given up on life just like Dad did."

Chapter 2

The red letters of the alarm clock announce that it is 3:22 a.m. I am awake. I was dreaming, there is something that Mr. Hawkins said that is nagging me, but I can't make it float up to the surface. His tired eyes, the twitching at the edge of his mouth. I try to bring the dream back into focus, but I am unable to sharpen the picture. Instead I hop out of bed and open up my laptop.

I open a new browser and type in *1978 American climb of K2*. All the results show up in purple, indicating that I have read all the articles and studied every account of this monumental achievement. I click the *Images* tab and the first image to show is the poster for yesterday's talk. I click on it and it fills my screen, again I am drawn to the person barely poking out behind my hero. I zoom in and the feeling of recognition is overwhelming. Where do I know this guy from?

I jump when the air is pierced by my alarm clock. Six a.m. already. I have been sitting staring at the same picture for over two hours willing my mind to connect the partial face to my memory. I close the laptop lid and realize I am shivering with cold. I hadn't noticed the cold morning air finding its way in through the window that I had left cracked open last night. Through my kitchen window you can glimpse Puget Sound, and when the windows are left open the air fills with the salty aromas of the sea. I claim to once have seen an orca from my kitchen window, but I am no longer sure that is what I saw. I have considered downgrading my tale to a harbour seal, but that is about as exciting as a seagull, so I am sticking with orca.

The wind is brutal as I hurry down the hill from my tiny apartment in Queen Anne towards work. It is cold, and I am tired and hung over. Sonia and I went out for gin and tonics and endless Guitar Hero contests at Shorty's Pinball bar after the talk. I am definitely not in the mood for dealing with domestic abuse victims at the women's shelter where both Sonia and I work. I grit my teeth and force my mind to think positive thoughts. When I round the corner of Bell Street I almost collide with Sonia, who looks terrible.

"I take it you are feeling a little worse for wear today too," I say laughing, "perhaps five G & T's wasn't such a good idea after all."

But Sonia doesn't laugh with me. She stares at me for a couple of seconds. "Haven't you heard the news? He is dead, they found him last night after the show."

I am not sure what Sonia is on about, but she is visually upset and tears are threatening in the corners of her eyes, so I bring her inside. The women's shelter is in an old building, not old enough to be charming, more like a left-over eyesore from the 60s. It is a wonder it hasn't been torn down and made into fancy apartments like so much of this part of town. I sit Sonia down in the large staff kitchen, it has always seemed unnecessarily large considering we are only twelve employees, but I am not complaining. It is bright and spacious, a nice place to escape from our often not so uplifting work. I take out two cups and fill them up from the coffee pot that is always on, 24/7, before sitting down next to Sonia.

"What on Earth are you going on about? We saw him signing books as we left, how could he have died between now and then?" I say.

Sonia is shaking her head at me, her trademark smile is nowhere to be seen. Sonia is the prettiest woman I know, maybe not in the conventional way, but there is something ridiculously charming about her freckle-covered face and her wild smile that makes her dark blue eyes turn into little slits. At this moment, however, she looks upset.

"He was found dead after the show. Heart attack. But

there was something else Marta, I think he was hiding something and I think he was scared, something is not right about this."

"Well, right or not we need to get to work," I say, trying out a smile.

Sonia gives me a deflated smile back. "Lunch at noon? At the usual? They have TVs, so perhaps we can get some updated news?"

I give her the thumbs up as I walk out the door heading down the corridor towards my office. At my desk I try to concentrate on today's list of things to do, but I can't focus. Endless times I end up back on Google, searching the news for any information about the death of our hero. The information is slim at best, *Seattle Times* reports that a heart attack caused the elderly man to die, and that he was found dead in the men's bathroom by the cleaners. A knock on my door stops me in my tracks.

"Come in," I call.

"Hello Ms. Bartowiak, I have a lady in need."

I recognize the deep voice before I look up from my computer screen; it sends little shivers down my spine. "Hello to you too, Officer Johnson. Who is the damsel in distress this time?"

"You have got to stop calling me Officer Johnson, just Jose will do. It is Barb again; he won't stop until she is dead."

I let out a deep sigh. Barbara is one of our regulars, whom despite being beaten blue by her boyfriend on a regular basis seems unable to leave him behind for the new life and secret identity we repeatedly offer her. It seems to be pretty typical of the women we get at the shelter. Once Barbara's boyfriend cracked her skull with a baseball bat, but as soon as she sobered up she stopped screaming bloody murder and insisted on having fallen down the stairs, yet again. This time will undoubtedly be no different.

"She called us at four this morning. Jonny had given her a thorough work over this time. We took her straight to Swedish Hospital, luckily the damage is all superficial. Jonny is being questioned down at the station."

"Did you take her to the sign-in desk?" I sigh. I know that by today's end she will have withdrawn her complaint with the police, signed herself out of the shelter, and will be on the bus back home. Home where her boyfriend will swear never to lay a hand on her again... Until next time. I have seen it so many times before.

"Umm... yes, yes, but of course, she is all signed in. I just thought I should let you know, you know, in case there was something you wanted done differently this time..." He trails off and looks at his feet. Before I get a chance to say anything, he starts off again, "Oh and did you hear about that old mountaineer getting murdered last night?" Jose nods towards the picture frame behind my desk, it is a large print of me and Sonia on top of Mount Rainer smiling widely, arms stretched up towards the sky, each of us grasping an ice axe and leaning towards each other to not be blown over by the fierce winds. It is the highest mountain I have ever climbed, the highest mountain in Washington.

"Murdered? The paper said it was a heart attack?"

Jose looks confused. "Uh, I am pretty sure it was murder. I assumed it would be all over the news by now. Three stab wounds to the torso and blunt force trauma to the head. Still looking for the murder weapon, or weapons. Not sure what it is we're looking for, blunt force trauma was square, and the stab wounds were circular, so not a knife." He stops, perhaps realizing he has said more than he should.

"Black Diamond Venom Ice Axe Hammer." The words come out of my mouth as a whisper, I am thinking aloud. "That is the murder weapon, it has got to be. I mean, surely it would be too coincidental for it to be something else. Blunt force trauma caused by the hammer, and stab wounds by the pick."

Jose looks puzzled by my forensic deductions. "He was sponsored by Black Diamond, and was the poster boy, well poster old man I guess, for the Venom ice axes, his tools of choice. It fits. Why aren't the media all over this? Are there any suspects? Why would someone want to kill one of America's all-time mountaineering legends?"

"No bloody idea, some cabrón got to him after the show. Wait, hold on, what are those ice axes you are talking about?"

Despite the upsetting news I can't help but smile at the anger in Jose's voice as he uses the Mexican slang word for asshole. The first time I heard him call someone a cabrón was after Barb's boyfriend had cracked her skull. I didn't know what it meant at the time and was too embarrassed to ask Jose, whom I had never met before. I Googled the translation, which came up as castrated goat. I thought it a peculiar insult until a friend explained that in Mexico the understanding of the word is asshole rather than its literal meaning. Jose's mom is Mexican and his dad American. Resulting in a son with olive skin, black hair, and light green eyes. Dreamy green eyes.

I write down the name of the Venom ice axes for Jose. He takes the slip of paper and smiles. "I'll check this out." He gives me a quick smile and a wave as he steps out my door and closes it behind him.

***

"Marta, are you ready?" Sonia is at my door. It is already lunch time and I haven't managed to do any work all day.

"You were right, he was hiding something, he has been lying all along." Sonia looks confused. "I'll tell you over lunch, let's go."

We walk down the street arm in arm towards the corner bar and café that we favor for lunch. I am deep in thought and Sonia for once does not pester me for information until we are seated at the well-worn bar with glasses of ice water in front of us and club sandwiches ordered from a disinterested waitress that ends each sentence with love. *"What can I get for you love?"* *"Is that all love?" "Thank you love."*

"So, are you ever going to tell me what is on your mind?" Sonia is looking at me.

"Yes, sorry. Well, there are two things. First of all, it was no heart attack. Mr. Hawkins was murdered."

Sonia gasps.

"Jose told me. Blunt force trauma to the head and stab wounds to the torso. They found him in the men's bathroom."

"Oh my God. That is horrible. Why would anyone want to kill Mr. Hawkins?"

"Yeah. There is this other thing though. It is even worse…"

"Worse?"

"Yeah. Mr. Hawkins was a liar."

"No way Marta."

"Yes way. Something has been nagging me since I saw that guy in the poster of Mr. Hawkins yesterday, it only came to me just before lunch. Mr. Hawkins said he summited K2 alone."

"Yes…"

"So why is there someone else in the summit photo with him?"

Sonia opens and closes her mouth several times before finally replying. "Are you sure? I didn't notice anyone else in the photo."

I get my phone out and open Google Images, I enter *Mr. Hawkins 36 years since the SUMMIT* in the search window. As we wait for the images to load on my screen a picture of Mr. Hawkins appears on the TV behind the bar.

"Hey, could you turn up the volume?" I holler at the waitress.

"Sure love."

The newsreaders are still saying that Mr. Hawkins died of a heart attack.

"Wow, how long do you think they will be able to keep this from the press?" asks Sonia.

"I guess we don't give the police the credit they are due," I say with a smile.

"Oh, oh, you only feel that way because Jose was in earlier. Tomorrow you will be back to bitching about how the police are useless, and unable to protect the lower social layers of our fair city," Sonia says, laughing.

I ignore her and look back down at my phone. "What the…" I tap on my phone, searching the images Google has brought up for me. "Sonia, I can't find the poster from last night. It came up as the number one hit just before…"

"It is that stupid smart phone of yours, you can't trust them." Sonia still has her old-school Nokia phone. "Let's get back to the office," she says, whilst stuffing the last of her sandwich in her mouth. "We can look at it there."

As soon as we walk in the door at work I can hear loud shouting and I rush towards the sign-in desk. I had forgotten all about Barb, who is now shouting at Lisa behind the desk, hair on end and a wild look in her eyes. I leave Sonia behind and walk over to Barb. When she sees me she calms down.

"Marta, tell this imbecile to let me go home, it was all a misunderstanding. *She* thinks Jonny did this," she says, pointing at her left eye, which is swollen shut and an angry color of blue. "But I *explained* to her that I simply fell -"

"Down the stairs?" I cut her off.

"NO. I fell in the shower, there was some soap and I slipped."

I lead Barb towards my office and when I look behind me Lisa is mouthing *thank you* at me, I smile and wink at her before heading down the corridor with Barb in tow. I know there is nothing I can do or say to Barb that will make her change her mind, but the law requires me to keep trying. So we will go through the same song and dance again and again. I sigh.

"Barb, how long are you going to put up with this? One day he will kill you."

"I know," Barb whispers, before taking a breath and continuing more confidently. "Oh it was nothing, he got home late and drunk from some job last night, he was dirty and we showered, that is when I slipped."

"Uh-huh," I say.

"I have got to go home." Barb's voice is shaky and I think she may burst into tears.

This is unusual; the normally angry Barb looks vulnerable and scared.

"Barb, we can offer you protection. We can help you, give you a new life."

Barb shakes her head, her eyes darting across the room wide open and scared like a deer caught in the headlights of a car.

"OK Barb. Let's get you signed out." I stand up and open my office door for Barb, who starts down the hallway ahead of me, eager it seems to get home. What for I do not understand.

"Lisa, can you please sign Barbara out?"

Lisa looks displeased but does what I ask, and soon we are both watching Barbara leave through the front doors.

"Next destination; the police station." says Lisa.

We both know this is where Barb is headed next, to withdraw her complaint before boarding the bus back to hell.

Back at my desk I sit for a while trying to rid myself of the feeling left behind by Barb. I take a deep breath and shake my head to clear my brain of the hopelessness lingering like smoke in the air. I move the mouse to wake up my computer and in an instant Google Images is back on my screen from before lunch. But the screen has auto-refreshed, and while an array of photos of Mr. Hawkins on K2 fills my screen, the poster from last night is no longer there. I lift up my office phone and press the little button that says Sonia next to it. Before I even hear a signal go through Sonia picks up.

"I'll be right there."

We spend thirty minutes trying various searches before giving up. Sonia had opened up Google Images as soon as she got to her office while I was dealing with Barb, and had realized that it wasn't my smart phone being dumb, but rather all images of last night's poster have been removed. On the official website the image has been replaced by another picture of Mr. Hawkins, still on the summit of K2, but this time alone and his ice axe is planted firmly in the snow rather than raised in the air. I bring up the contact information for the Seattle Mountaineers Club House on the computer and pick up my phone, dialling the number for the office.

"Seattle Mountaineers, Sue speaking, how can I help you?"

"Hi Sue, my name is Marta. I am a member of the mountaineers and was wondering if you have some of the posters from the talk by Mr. Hawkins at town hall last night?"

"Oh no. A man was here half an hour ago collecting all the posters, I think he was a family member or maybe Mr. Hawkins' manager or something. He came into the office to ask if we had them up anywhere other than the notice board in the foyer, so I gave him the key for the notice board outside. I am so sorry; I guess his family wanted them."

I thank her and hang up. Sonia's eyes are big as saucers,

she has been straining to hear the conversation, and by the look on her face she must have overheard. I pick up the phone again and this time I dial Seattle Bouldering Project, the bouldering gym across town in the International District, where I am a member. I was there yesterday morning and I remember seeing the poster on their notice board.

"Good afternoon, you have reached SBP."

"Hi, my name is Marta. I have a question. Do you still have the poster from last night's talk by Mr. Hawkins on your notice board?"

"I am sorry but a gentleman picked it up about five minutes ago. He took our only copy. Sorry."

"No worries, thank you." I hang up.

"Marta, he was there five minutes ago. He must have gone directly from the club house to SBP, it takes thirty minutes to drive, which means we have a chance to catch a poster before he does."

My brain is all of a sudden working in high gear trying to think of where else the poster may have been displayed. "He would have gone to town hall first. Our best bet will be one of the other climbing gyms... We need a car and we need to get to either Vertical World, Stone Garden, or perhaps the university... Scrap the university," I say before Sonia gets a word in.

"He would have gone there on his way to the club house, let's shoot for Vertical World, I think we still have some time if he is coming from the International District."

I grab my coat and Sonia's arm. "Lisa, give me your car keys," I shout as I get closer to the front desk, "It is an emergency."

Lisa's silver Prius is parked in the underground garage in the building next to ours. I sprint down the ramp instead of using the pedestrian stairs, Sonia hot my heels. As I speed out of the garage I hope no one else is as foolish as me using the ramp on foot. I drive as fast as I dare, skipping red lights, praying I won't be pulled over by the cops. Sonia is clinging to her seat with one hand, the other hand firmly on her seatbelt. Normally she goes on and on about my poor driving abilities and how I go around corners way too fast, but today she sits in silence.

I pull up outside Vertical World and literally jump out of the car sprinting towards the front doors of the gym. I speed past the check-in desk, ignoring the young guy at the counter. I can hear him call out to me. It is empty. The notice board is empty apart from one piece of paper with a picture of a pair of rock shoes that someone is trying to sell. I walk back to the desk and the guy looks at me with a frown on his face. His arms are muscular, a sure sign he spends a lot of his time on the walls and not just behind the desk, and he is sporting a tan, suggesting he has already started climbing outdoors for the season.

"Did someone come to collect the poster from Mr. Hawkins talk last night?" I am trying to catch my breath as I speak. I feel deflated because I know what he is going to say. The guy ignores my question and disappears behind the desk.

He pops back up. "Is this what you are after?" He hands me a crumpled up ball of paper, his frown replaced by a smile.

I open it up and give out a little cheer of delight as I realize it is the poster.

"I just cleaned out the notice board before, it was old so I threw it out." he says.

"Thank you, thank you, thank you." I shout. I could kiss him I am that happy, but instead I head out the door. I jump back in the car beaming at Sonia. "We got it!" I shout. "We beat the bastard here. We bloody well got it." I open up the poster pointing at the face poking out behind our hero number one.

"See I told you so, there was someone else on the summit with him."

"I guess you were right, but what does this mean?"

"I know his face from somewhere, I just can't place where from. Do you recognize him?"

"I don't think so. It is hard to tell, it isn't exactly crystal clear; you can't even see the entire face."

We are deep in thought and I barely register the black Town Car that pulls up next to us. Out of the corner of my eye I can see a man in a black suit get out and walk towards the climbing gym's front doors. Must be climbing during his lunch break, I think. Climbing has become the favorite pastime of every Seattleite it appears, something I have noticed not just in the packed climbing gyms, but also out in the mountains. It seems that each year I run into more and more people in the mountains. I hate it.

"Marta, let's go. I got a magnifying glass back at the office, perhaps I can recognize the man when I get a better look."

I start up the car while laughing at Sonia. "You have a magnifying glass? Who has a magnifying glass?"

"I bet you want to borrow it though," Sonia laughs back at me.

I pull out of the parking lot, spotting the man in the suit exiting the gym through the rear-view mirror, he is sprinting towards his car. He must have forgotten something. I turn on to West Commodore Way and head back towards Belltown and the office.

Chapter 3

Sonia is studying the flyer through her magnifying glass, shaking her head.

"Marta I don't know, it is quite blurry and I don't recognize the guy…"

I snatch the magnifying glass out of her hand and study the photo. I do recognize the man behind Mr. Hawkins despite the picture being blurry, I just can't recall where from. I search my memory but nothing floats to the surface. "I can't quite connect the dots, but it will come to me."

We are crouched over Sonia's desk, the dark wood-panelled walls and cramped space makes it feel like a sauna. It is making me claustrophobic.

"Let me see what I can dig up tonight. I am headed home, it is five o'clock."

Sonia grunts. She believes in working overtime; I do not. I close the office door behind me and head for home, I am tired and in a foul mood. All I want is a hot bath and an early night. Back in my apartment I fill the tub and open a bottle of Rioja before starting up my laptop. While I wait for it to power up I get undressed and pour a glass of wine. Sipping on my wine I sit down in front of my computer. The screen announces five new messages and I sigh, probably work.

Just as I am about to stand up one of the messages catches my eye. It is from Jose. My heart skips a beat and I sit back down. I can't recall ever getting an email from Jose, and definitely not to my personal account.

Marta,

Firstly, you were right, the murder weapon was one of those ice axes you were talking about (perhaps we should be hiring you). However, I have just been told that no further investigations will be conducted. I am not sure why or what is going on, but I thought you might want to know. I still have a copy of the coroner's report, I can't let you have it, but knowing your interest in the case perhaps you would like to look at it with me over a bite?

/Jose

I take another big sip of my wine, unsure of whether I should be dancing around with joy or outraged. Jose just asked me out for a date, sort of. But why wouldn't they keep the investigation going when it was so obviously murder? I type a reply.

Jose,

Yes, how about Annapurna café on Broadway, Cap Hill, tomorrow night 6pm?

/Marta

***

Cold air is hitting my face as I ride my bicycle to SBP. I like to get to the gym at 6 a.m. when they open. At that time I usually get the gym to myself. Today is no different, I get to enjoy the largest bouldering gym in the world with only two other people. I climb for an hour before the 7:15 a.m. yoga class. It is 9:23 a.m. by the time I rush into the office out of breath. Only twenty-three minutes late, that is not too bad, I think to myself as I shake out my raincoat. Sonia waves to me through her open office door as I head down the corridor.

In comparison to Sonia's office mine is a delight. I have a window and the walls are painted white, maybe not very exotic, but much better than wood panelling. As soon as my computer has powered up I check my personal email. My heart skips a beat when I see that Jose has replied. He apologizes that he can't meet me until the end of next week, and after a few emails back and forth we settle on Thursday night at Annapurna Café. Work drones on and soon I have forgotten all about Mr. Hawkins, instead I am perusing the NOAA weather forecast trying to work out where to climb for the weekend. The weather looks bad everywhere.

It has been months since I spent a weekend at home. I feel a nagging sense of guilt, I haven't visited Mom in ages. I call Sonia's office across the hallway.

"Hey, have you looked at the weather forecast? What do you think about climbing for the weekend?"

"Are you insane? NOAA says ninety percent chance of precipitation pretty much everywhere. It is early March, it *will* be wet heavy snow."

The Pacific Northwest is famous for its wet snow that creeps into even the fanciest of Gore-Tex jacket, soaking you head to toe.

"Don't you remember Whitehorse Mountain?"

Once Sonia and I had to emergency bivvy during a spring ascent of Whitehorse Mountain, a formidable mountain right next to my hometown of Darrington. We had summited in whiteout conditions and were on our way down when we got lost in the heavy wet snow. As it got dark, we built a snow cave and hunkered down for the night. We were both soaked to the bone and I have never been so cold in my life; our intention had been to climb it in one long day, and as such had no sleeping bags, stove, or extra food with us. My water bladder had frozen and we spent a miserable night soaked, yet dehydrated.

"Fair point. I guess I will stay in town then." I hang up.

OK, I think to myself, *I will visit my mother.* My visits have become rarer and rarer as her memory has gotten worse and worse, I just simply can't bear it. It breaks my heart having to explain to her who I am, and no matter how many times I tell her she seems unable to comprehend it. She always thinks I am one of the nurses, and as such asks me to help her go to the bathroom. While I would do anything for my mother, I know she would be mortified at the thought of her twenty-seven-year-old daughter taking her to the bathroom, so I never do.

***

Saturday morning, I sleep in until 8 a.m., this is late for me and I am surprised I managed to sleep this long. I open the fridge, but I know it is futile even before I do, there is nothing in there. Instead, I head up the hill to Starbucks, and as I wait for the bus I sip on a piping hot Americano and bite down on a croissant.

The bus is late and it is drizzling. By the time I get to the nursing home, nestled in amongst new apartment blocks and hospital buildings on First Hill, I am soaked and I have spilt coffee on my jeans. Oh, what does it matter, I think to myself, she won't know who I am anyway. But when I enter the large common room with its smell of old people and school kitchen food I am met by a squeal.

"MARTA, oh how I have missed you." My mother races towards me with her arms spread ready to embrace me. Her grey hair tied up in a ponytail and small frame is making her look younger than she really is.

I am so surprised I drop my empty coffee cup on the floor and my eyes fill with tears. "Mom." I choke as she is squeezing me tight. I can almost smell the spent coffee grinds and the aroma of Dad's whiskey, hear the rain hitting the roof, and Dad stomping the beat with his foot as he is playing the accordion, mom dancing in the living room. Happy childhood memories hidden in my mom's embrace.

"Oh come on poppet, no tears." She smiles as we head arm in arm towards her room. The corridor feels sterile with its bright white walls, a stark contrast to my mom's room, which feels homely. It smells of my mother, and the quilted blanket that used to decorate our sofa is now at the foot of my mom's bed. There is a framed picture of my dad on the bedside table, and on the wall hangs a photo from my high school graduation. I wonder who helped her put it up. Probably the same person who placed a vase of fresh flowers on her table. I wish I could somehow thank them. But to be honest I probably wouldn't, even if I knew who they were.

We sit down by the window and she tells me about her week, well, I guess what she remembers of it at least. I can't remember the last time my mom was this lucid and I bask in her love, not quite sure what to talk about. When she runs out of recent memories she starts telling me stories from her childhood in Poland; I am enthralled.

"I wish you could have met your grandfather, he was so much like you with all that mountain climbing," she says.

"My grandfather climbed mountains?" I ask.

"But of course," she says, annoyed that I don't know. "I have told you he was one of Poland's finest climbers back after the war. It was a ticket to get out of the country back then."

I sit with my mouth agape. "Mom, have you got any pictures of my grandfather?"

Her eyes have clouded over and she looks at me as if I am a stranger. She looks confused and I know this wonderful moment has come to an end, my mom has once again disappeared into the land of dementia. I try to take her hand but she pulls away from me.

"Can you bring me a cup of tea dear?" she says, the love gone from her voice.

I stand up and on my way out I ask one of the nurses to please bring my mother some tea.

On Sunday morning I wake to my phone ringing. It is Sonia, she says something about sunshine and snowshoeing and I rub my eyes as I am trying to make sense of it all. I poke my head out the blinds and am met by a brilliant spring sun, all of a sudden my mind is clear.

I scramble around gathering things, shoving them into my backpack.

"I'll pick you up in thirty minutes," Sonia tells me, and I hang up.

I pop two frozen steamed pork buns in the oven while I shower, and pack my bag and grab them as I head out the door. Sonia is already there and soon we are on the I-90 headed towards Snoqualmie Pass and Red Mountain. The city scape is changing as we head out of town, and soon instead of skyscrapers the horizon is dominated by snow-capped mountains that appear to be growing as we get closer to the pass. My pork buns are still frozen in the middle, but I don't care, the sun is shining and I get to go outside and play in the mountains.

We turn off I-90 at Snoqualmie Ski Resort, mountains covered in snow in every direction and evergreens with their branches dropping heavy with snow. As we are heading up towards Red Mountain, our snowshoes sinking in the fresh layer of snow and sun rays dancing across our faces through the wooded path, I tell Sonia what my mother told me about my grandfather. Sonia's eyes are sparkling.

"Marta, that is fantastic. It is in your blood," she exclaims. "What was his name? We can probably find information about him on the Internet."

"Well, Mom's maiden name is Pyszka."

"You don't know your grandparents' first names?" Sonia

asks looking shocked.

"Mom never told me anything about them, I just figured it was too painful for her to talk about or something. They died before I was born."

Sonia looks shocked but decides to not say anything further. Sonia grew up in a close-knit family with four older brothers, and her grandparents on her mom's side lived with them when Sonia was young. To her, my childhood with just me, Mom, and Dad sounds awfully lonely. I never did feel lonely however, I guess the other kids in Darrington gave me enough company and I didn't have to fight for my parents' attention.

It is just before noon when we reach the last steep section to the summit, crampons biting into the icy snow. I place my ice axe one last time before cresting onto the summit and am met by the panorama of the Commonwealth Basin. Its white snow-blanketed peaks shooting up towards the crisp blue sky. I am grinning wildly; I really do live in the best place. Less than an hour's drive away from the city and yet in complete wilderness.

"Let's eat lunch." Sonia has sat down and is busy opening her backpack.

"Oh, I didn't bring any... I will just eat when we get out."

Sonia rolls her eyes and hands me half of her sandwich.

"I think we can still find some information about your grandfather even with just a surname," Sonia says whilst biting down on her half of the sandwich. "If he was as good of a climber as your mom says there must be some information about him."

I smile at her, she is the best person I know.

***

On Monday morning I am at the office early, I feel great after a day in the snow and mountains and I get through a lot of work before Sonia even makes it to the office. I only know she has arrived by my computer announcing a new email from Sonia. It is text copied from Wikipedia.

Category: Polish mountain climbers
From Wikipedia, the free encyclopedia
Zygmunt Pyszka (1931-1978) born in Warsaw
was a Polish alpine and high-altitude climber.
Marta, this must be your grandad, only Polish
mountaineer I can find with the surname Pyszka.
Haven't found any more information yet, but I bet we
can find some.
/S

I smile to myself, only Sonia would be more determined than me to find out about my family history. Sometimes I pretend family is more important to me than it really is, just to make Sonia feel better. She wants everyone to be loved and belong, so I keep my desire to be alone to myself. I am not one for big gatherings and emotional expressions. I once spent Christmas with Sonia's family, right after my mom was placed in the nursing home. The entire day I couldn't wait to get back to the peace and quiet of my own apartment, having a glass of wine, and watching a movie in peace. Instead I was thrust in amongst Sonia's many brothers' wives and children playing board games and singing along to Christmas jingles. The entire day was a nightmare, and I have managed to come up with some valid excuse to not participate in this madness the following years, despite Sonia being on my case each Thanksgiving, Christmas, and Fourth of July.

I look at the email again. This could be correct; this would make my grandfather 23 years old when my mother was born, and he would have perished at age 47, when my mom was 24, some eight years before I was born. I bring up Wikipedia, but Sonia has copied all the information there is, the article gives no clue as to how my grandfather died or of his family. I enter his name in Google, but the only hit is the mention on Wikipedia and some site that is in Polish. I wish I was better at Polish, but my parents, eager to fit into their new American home, never bothered teaching me and I only picked up snippets as a child. My parents only used Polish when they argued or whispered endearments. I copy the Polish article and place getting it translated on my mental to-do list, right below cleaning the apartment, something I never manage to get around to on the weekend.

Chapter 4

"Good morning Barbara. How are you feeling today?" I am not really expecting Barbara to remember much from the previous night.

"Marta, I need that new identity you told me about," she says.

"OK. Take it from the top Barb, what happened last night?"

Barb looks uncomfortable but leans in closer and starts telling the story in a low voice, as if scared that someone would hear us, although my office door is closed. "Last week when I came in, I hadn't actually fallen in the shower."

I give a grave nod, although thinking to myself, 'no shit, Sherlock.'

"Jonny came home and his shirt and hands were covered in blood, he seemed on a high and I asked what on Earth he had done. I think he was high on heroin, but I don't know for sure. He told me to shut my mouth, but when I pressured him he got mad and said it was none of my business, and then he beat me some... Not too hard or anything... Just a little..." She trails off and her eyes fill with tears. "I came in here as you know, and once I had checked out and gotten back home he was real mad with me and told me it was a good thing I had taken back my police report, and that I best keep my mouth shut. But then he has been really strange ever since, getting a lot of phone calls, and I saw him talking to a man in a suit. I mean, when does my Jonny ever meet people wearing suits? He looked real important too, with a suitcase and dark glasses. I asked Jonny about it, but he said to keep my nose out of his business, so I did. But then last night we had a few drinks..."

Aha, a few drinks, I think to myself, Barb still smells heavily of yesterday's bourbon, and I know 'a few drinks' is more like a bottle of cheap knock-off whiskey. She came into our office hysterical and drunk as a skunk last night.

"I asked him about it again and he got real mad and said that if I ever mentioned it again he would kill me too, free of charge."

"Free of charge?" I ask.

"Yes, that's what he said. That he would kill me, 'free of charge.' That was his exact words. He looked real serious, his eyes were black, I never seen them like that before. But I knew he was telling me the honest truth. I got real scared and walked into the kitchen, out the kitchen door, up the road, got in a cab, and came here." Barb stops talking and looks at me, waiting for my response.

I turn on my computer, wait for it to power up, and pull up Barb's file. Barbara Weston is 32 years old, she looks older. She is not a pretty lady, her skin is grey and wrinkly, her eyes blood shot, and her hair bleached blond. Perhaps she had been pretty once upon a time, but alcohol, cigarettes, God knows what other drugs, and years of abuse have made her into this pitiful sight in front of me.

"Marta, I really *really* need that new identity today, now."

I look up from the screen. "Sorry Barb, but you should be going to the police with this, if you actually believe that Jonny has killed someone. That is serious."

"Marta, you know the police won't listen to me. With all my previous reports and withdrawals no one takes me serious anymore, and it would only be my word against his anyway."

Tears start to run down her cheeks and I realize how utterly terrified she looks.

"OK, I will get you that new identity, but this means you can never come back here, no contact with old friends, no phone calls, nothing. OK?" Barb nods but remains silent. "I will have to hand you over to the authorities, they will find you a halfway house while they work out your new identity. But you cannot have any drugs in your system. Have you been taking anything other than alcohol?"

"No, no, only bourbon."

"You sure, you mentioned heroin before, and they will test you."

Barb starts crying again. "No, I swear, I haven't taken any drugs for over a year, not since the brain injury."

"OK, good, let's get the process started then."

It takes me hours to get Barb entered into the system and handed over to the right government agency, and by the time I finally send her away in the car, which will take her to her new life, my stomach is grumbling. I missed lunch, but it was worth it to help Barb; I really do hope she finds happiness.

I look at my watch, it is already three o'clock. Suddenly any thoughts of Barb flee as I realize it is only three hours until my date with Jose. In my office drawer I find a nut-bar and an apple to still my hunger until dinner. Biting into the apple I open up a new browser and start searching for Polish translators. The University of Washington has a language school and I shoot them an email before shutting down my computer and heading out the door. It is only 4.30 p.m., but I need to clear my head before seeing Jose.

I start up the hill towards Capitol Hill and Annapurna Café. The air is crisp and the sun still high in the sky, a sure sign summer is on its way. It always makes me laugh when people mistake Seattle's Capitol Hill for the one in DC, from what I have heard they couldn't be further apart. Capitol Hill here is the hipster neighborhood with bars and restaurants, and the host of Seattle pride each year. It is not uncommon to share the coffee queue with a punk rocker, hipster, millionaire, and homeless man all at once.

I walk past Rumba, a rum bar on Pike Street, and pop my

head in. It is cozy in there and I feel wired from today's events and a little nervous about my dinner with Jose. I step inside and sit down at the bar. The bartender seems pleased to have a guest.

"What can I get you? You are too early for happy hour, it starts in 20 minutes."

"No problem. Could I have a Zacapa, please?"

The bartender lets out a whistle, obviously pleased with my choice. It isn't cheap, but not really expensive either. My love affair with Zacapa, a most excellent Guatemalan rum, started while I was in college. The exchange student in the room next to mine had bottles of it in her room and eager to share a part of her homeland, she was always happy to have me over for large cups of Zacapa and political discussions. She was only there for a year, and we haven't kept in touch, but my love for rum stayed. Preferably Zacapa, but I am not picky, Flor de Cana or Diplomatico will do as well. I sip on my rum as the bartender slides the wooden ladder across the rows of shelves behind the bar, restocking the top shelf with rums so far out of my price range I am scared to even look at them.

"Can I get you another?" The bartender has come down the ladder and is leaning over the bar. I look at my watch, 5:30 p.m. I look in my wallet, this is going to cost me the equivalent of two of the new fancy Petzl carabiners I have been eyeing up at REI.

"Sure," I say with a smile, what the heck, happy hour has now started, and I haven't had rum in ages. It is delicious and I already feel more at ease.

At 5:55 p.m. I drink the last drops of my rum, say thanks, and head out the door, rushing up the last bit of the hill to Annapurna Café. Jose is already waiting outside on the curb, traffic rushing passed him on Broadway and a homeless man leaning against the building next to where Jose is standing. I spot him before he sees me. It is strange to see him out of his uniform, I try to recall if I ever have before. He looks good in jeans and a bright orange rain jacket. When Jose spots me he greets me with a big smile and I can't help but grin back like a love struck teenager.

The set of narrow stairs leading down to the basement is decorated with posters of high Himalayan peaks and traditional Nepalese ornaments. It feels like descending into another world. At the bottom of the stairs we are greeted by a delightful hum, people enjoying the aromatic food and cozy atmosphere, and a soft tinkering of Tibetan bells are escaping from the speakers.

"Table for two?"

"Yes please." I reply.

The waiter brings us over to a table in the corner with a lit candle and a photograph of some tall mountain hanging on the wall above it. The caption informs me it is Annapurna, which seems appropriate.

"Can I start you off with something to drink?"

"Yes, could I have an Everest please?"

"Ha, you only want that because it is named after a mountain," Jose laughs. "I will have Kingfisher please."

"Am not." I laugh back at Jose, but his face has gone somber.

"So this is getting weirder and weirder Marta. I have the coroner's report, but today when I went to look over the file it was missing. I asked the captain about it, but he pretended he didn't know what case I was talking about."

I stare at Jose, "What the... That is so strange. Why would he do that? It was only a little over a week ago."

Jose looks embarrassed. "I know, I don't know what the hell is going on Marta, but I know that right now I am not particularly proud to be a cop. Well, here look at the coroner's report. That is all I have, apart from the fact that both the police and the media seem intent on pretending this one never happened. Not even the guy who usually calls me from the press for information has contacted me, it is creepy."

I start leafing through the coroner's report whilst sipping on my beer.

"It is bloody obvious it was murder," I say.

"Yeah, the blow to the head was inflicted first. Didn't kill the guy, the first stab to the heart did, however. By the way, the murder weapon was one of those ice axes you told me about. Thanks for the tip."

"Any time. Hey, it says here that the first stab to the heart killed him. Why would anyone keep going if the victim is already dead?"

"To make sure, or out of rage, or revenge."

A shiver runs down my spine and I look up at Jose. "This is pretty brutal; the killer must have known Mr. Hawkins. Or why would the killer use an ice tool, surely it can't be the most effective murder weapon?"

Jose nods at me. "Do you know if there is someone who didn't like him?"

"Nah, it isn't like I knew him personally. But from all the literature he seemed loved and actually pretty low key, apart from the Black Diamond advertising campaign."

"Let me look into it some more. I will do some digging at work, and maybe you could send me anything you find out that may be related? Anything that you can pick up in your mountaineering world."

I blush a little, but before I get a chance to reply the waiter sets down a tray full to the brim of steaming hot momos, lamb kofta, chicken tikka masala, and giant naan breads.

The rest of the night we spend chit-chatting about work. I fill Jose in about Barb and he is overjoyed she has finally done something for herself. Which ultimately, unless she falls back into the same trap with another abusive man, will save her. He asks about my mountain climbing, and although we have finished all the food some time ago, we order a third beer and Jose asks me why climbing allures me so much despite being such a dangerous sport.

"Well, I used to think I was invincible in the mountains." I smile, but my face turns serious as I continue. "But last year I lost a friend, well we weren't real close, but I had climbed with him before and he was good. He was hit by a falling rock and didn't survive the impact. Even if he had he wouldn't have survived the consequential fall."

"Geez."

"It shook me, it made me feel mortal, and I have finally accepted that my favorite pastime and happy place is a place which comes with some danger. But it is a risk I am willing to take, because there is nowhere else that makes me feel more alive, vibrant, and happy. But it has given me cause for thought. I feel mortal, I avoid risk more than I used to."

"Wow, those mountains must be something pretty special, maybe you could take me one day." Jose winks and I can feel my cheeks turning bright red.

In the taxi home, another unusual luxury, my mind drifts from Mr. Hawkins' mutilated body to Jose's gorgeous smile. My body is buzzing from the rum and beers, thoughts flitting around my brain like fireflies. I pay for the taxi and start up the stairs, skipping every second step without as much as getting out of breath. Good, I think to myself, I am not totally out of shape after winter. When I get into my apartment, I pull *K2 – dreams, distress and disaster* off the bookshelf and sit down on the sofa. I start reading and soon my mind is as clear as crystal and I can't put the book down.

Chapter 5

All through the book Mr. Hawkins keeps alluding to there being someone else with him, but you wouldn't notice it unless you were looking for it. In fact, the first time I read the book I had assumed that these remarks were an internal conversation he was having with himself. Many high-altitude mountaineers talk of the sense of there being someone else there with them in the mountains as they climb. My initial thought had been that that was what Mr. Hawkins was experiencing. But now having seen the photograph I am not so sure. I highlight sections, no longer caring to keep my signed copy in pristine condition, so I can show Sonia and perhaps Jose. In fact, I even go on a hunt for my yellow highlighter as I don't want to use the pink one, just in case Jose wants to see my highlighted sections. I don't want him to think of me as girly. Silly, I know. At 3 a.m., just as Mr. Hawkins tops out on the summit, I force myself to put the book down, it is late and I need to sleep for at least a couple of hours before work.

I sleep poorly, tossing and turning and wishing I had just stayed up and finished reading the book. At 6 a.m. I give up on pretending to sleep and pull my duvet out on to the sofa and sit back down with the book. It is raining outside. I sigh, always the way, clear weather during the week then rain just as the weekend rolls around. The book sucks me right back in, and despite my usually strict work ethics, I decide to call in sick. After calling my boss Karen, I also call Sonia and ask her to come around to mine once she gets off work. She agrees, and even better, tells me she will bring dinner.

I am still on the sofa under my duvet when I hear three hard knocks followed by Sonia's voice, "Honey, I am home. And I brought along a friend."

Jose's voice fills my tiny hallway. "Hi Marta, sorry to barge in, but Sonia said it would be OK."

I jump off the sofa. "Oh, oh, hold on one second."

I am still in my pajamas, un-showered, and the place is a mess. I randomly grab dirty clothes off the floor and old coffee mugs off the table and shove it all in my bedroom. I close the door and pull on jeans and a flannel shirt, tying my unwashed hair up in a bun. As I exit the bedroom I almost walk straight into Jose.

"Hi. Sorry to come unannounced but I have been trying to get a hold of you all day. I went in to your office just as Sonia was leaving and she told me to come along. I hope you don't mind?"

"No, not at all," I say with a smile. "I just wish I had known, I would have cleaned the place up and showered."

"I hope you are feeling better."

I look at Jose with confusion.

Sonia giggles, her wide smile reaching her eyes, transforming them into almond shaped slits. "Yes dear, how *are* you feeling? Still have that head cold coming on?"

Oh shit. I have forgotten I am meant to be sick. "Yes, I am feeling a little better." I don't want Jose to think I am a slacker skiving off work, so I make a little cough and pick up an empty coffee cup from the table, which I had missed in my dash to tidy. "I just finished some tea with honey in it, and I feel heaps better."

Sonia is still giggling, but luckily Jose doesn't seem to put two and two together and instead says, "I am happy to hear it. You must have been feeling poorly since you haven't replied to any of my phone calls, texts, or emails."

I look at my phone, there are several missed calls and unread messages. I haven't looked up from my books all day and my phone has been on silent. When I had finished *K2 – dreams, distress and disaster* I had moved straight onto Mr.

Hawkins' other books to see if I could detect anything from them. Not reading them word for word, but skimming through the summit push sections. But there had been no internal conversation or sense of there being someone else with Mr. Hawkins on any of his other climbs, which has only strengthened my feeling that there indeed was someone else with him on K2.

"I got take-out Thai, do you have any clean dishes?" Sonia is standing in my tiny kitchen peering out the open doorway into the living room.

"There should still be some." I know the sink is full of dirty dishes and I am hoping that Jose won't venture into the kitchen.

"I am going to pop downstairs to pick up some beers, any preferences?" asks Jose, as he turns back towards the hallway.

"Any kind of IPA," I reply. When I hear the door close I hurry into the kitchen and help Sonia clean up and quickly run around my apartment trying to make it more presentable.

By the time Jose comes back, the various Thai dishes are on the coffee table, a few candles are lit, and I have organized Mr. Hawkins' books into a neat pile on the floor, with *K2 – dreams, distress and disaster* on top. We sit down and start eating, and Jose opens bottles of Mirror Pond Pale Ale for us.

"Yum, Pale Ale." I say.

"Oh shit, you asked for IPA didn't you?"

"Ha, ha, don't worry, I am only teasing." I am laughing. "So, Jose, why is it you spent today trying to get a hold of me?"

He finishes chewing. "A thought popped into my head last night after you left Annapurna Café. You told me that Jonny had said that he would kill Barb, free of charge. Could it be that someone paid him to kill someone else?"

I can feel Sonia's eyes bore into me. It is confidential what clients tell me, I should not be telling anyone. Yet greased by rum, beer, and a handsome smile I had relayed my conversation with Barb to Jose over dinner last night. I feel terrible and am sure Sonia is unhappy with me. But instead I hear her squeal. "Oh my, Jose you are a genius."

"Gosh, Jose that is crazy," I say, "that is way too much of a coincidence. If Jonny killed someone, it is more likely to do with his drug buddies."

"But the dates add up." Jose is looking at me.

"She did say he would kill her 'free of charge.' It was such a bizarre threat. Free of charge, like someone paid him before... But if it was Jonny...who would pay Jonny to kill Mr. Hawkins?"

"Well, I suspect we will never find out. Barb has gone into protection so we can't ask her, and I can't use any of it since it is meant to be confidential. Not that it would matter much anyway," he adds. "Since the case is non-existent as far the head of police is concerned. I went over to Jonny's house earlier. I couldn't really talk to him since there is no case, but I sat in my car outside his place for an hour or so and he is nervous about something. He kept looking out from behind his curtains."

As I stand up to clear the plates I stumble over the pile of books on the floor. Instead of taking the plates to the kitchen, I sit back down and open the K2 book to one of my highlighted sections. "Listen to this, - *as I neared the summit all else fell silent, I no longer struggled to make out the heavily accented words being blown across the snow by the fierce winds, there was no longer a need for words just a deep desire to reach the summit, so that the souls battered by low oxygen and the cold could turn around and head for safe haven...* He is talking of listening to words, and he uses souls, not soul. Doesn't it sound like there is someone with him?"

Sonia leans over my shoulder and reads the highlighted section again. "You're right Marta, it does sound like there is someone with him. What else have you highlighted?"

I hand over the book and turn to Jose, who looks like a question mark. I get the poster we recovered from Vertical World out of my purse and show it to him. "It looks like Mr. Hawkins didn't reach the summit of K2 on his own. Look," I am pointing at the face poking out behind Mr. Hawkins, "there is someone else in the summit photo. He has always claimed that he went for the summit on his own. Clearly not the case."

"Who is it?" asks Jose.

"No idea. I recognize him though, so probably some other mountaineer from the time. I just can't figure out who he is."

"Why would he lie about being on his own?"

"I don't know. Maybe he didn't want to share the glory... But I think it is connected to his murder somehow," I reply.

"Well, I best get home to bed, but I think you are right, this is all connected somehow." Jose stands up. "You want me to take care of the poster? I can make some copies for safe keeping."

I hand Jose the poster and follow him to the door, he gives me a hug and tells me to get some sleep so that the cold won't catch me. My entire body is tingling as he lets go of the embrace. I watch him walk out the door, the poster safely tucked in his back pocket.

Chapter 6

When I walk into the living room it is already daylight outside and Sonia is curled up on my sofa, snoring softly. We watched a movie last night after Jose left. Sonia picked some soppy romantic comedy. She refuses to watch anything remotely scary or that has a sad ending, she likes to see the world through rose-tinted glasses.

"Rise and shine." I holler as loud as I can.

Sonia cracks one eye open and groans at me.

"Come on, I am starving."

"OK, OK, OK. I am up."

"Let's go out for brunch."

"Ha, you don't have anything in the fridge do you." Sonia teases, but she is out of bed, or sofa rather, pulling a sweater over her head.

It is drizzling as we walk up the hill to the main street in Queen Anne. Another grey day. The main street is nothing more than a short stretch of road on top of the hill lined with cafes, restaurants, bars, and boutique shops. We pick our usual brunch place, it is nothing fancy but they serve good eggs. When we enter the brightly colored room we are met by the aroma of bacon and coffee.

"Seat yourselves." Hollers the waitress. She is carrying two large plates of eggs and bacon to a table by the window.

My tummy grumbles. We sit down at a small table lined with at least five different types of hot sauces. We barely get seated before the waitress slams down two cups of hot coffee in front of us. "The usual?" She is looking at me.

"Yeah sure, why not." My usual is easy; bacon, fried eggs over easy, and sourdough toast.

"And for you?"

"I will have the vegetable omelette, egg whites only, hold

the bread."

I can almost hear the waitress roll her eyes at Sonia as she walks away to place our orders.

"Looks like the weather will be bad all day. Why don't you go see your Mom, maybe she can tell you more about your grandfather."

"Sonia, I don't know if..."

"You are going and I am coming with you to make sure."

I know that Sonia is not really coming with me to make sure I actually go, but rather to be there to pick up the pieces if my mom is off in la-la-land. She really is a great friend, despite her poor taste in movies.

"Sonia, you are going to disappear if you continue to eat like that." She has pushed half of her eggwhite omelette to the side of her plate.

"We can't all eat like a man." she retorts.

"Hey, it takes a lot of food to cultivate a belly like this," I say rubbing my belly. I am naturally small and skinny, so I never bother to care about what I put in my mouth, if I am hungry I eat. Sonia on the other hand is a pinnacle of health, making sure calories in match calories out.

"Oh come on."

"Let's go." I smile.

We catch the bus to downtown and walk the last bit up to First Hill. It is still drizzling and my jeans are moist when we enter the white painted reception area.

"I am here to see my mom, Aniela Bartowiak."

"She is in her room."

I sign the guest sheet and we walk down the corridor. Mom is sitting in her chair looking out the window, her white hair in a braid down her back.

"Mom. Mom it is me Marta. Your daughter. Mom, can you hear me."

"Oh hello dear." Mom has turned around and is looking at Sonia. "I can't believe what Ivan said today in class. Petra come sit down." She is motioning for Sonia to come closer.

"Err... Umm... Mrs. Bartowiak, I think you have me mistaken for someone else."

"Mom, this is Sonia, my friend."

"Stop your silliness. Petra come, I have so much to tell you."

"I am sorry Aniela, it will have to be another time." Sonia is smiling at my mom as she takes my hand and leads me out of my mother's room and back out into the sterile corridor, closing the door behind us.

"She must have thought I was one of her school friends or something," says Sonia. "Are you OK Marta?"

Sonia is visibly upset and has wrapped an arm around me. My first instinct is to shrug it off, but I catch myself. I know Sonia will get hurt and read into it, so I let her arm stay slung over my shoulders.

"Yeah," I say with a big audible sigh. "I am used to it, it doesn't really make me feel anything these days."

Just as we are walking out the front doors, one of the staff members calls out to me. I keep walking, pretending I can't hear her. But Sonia grabs my arm and walks me back inside.

"Marta, can I talk with you for a minute in the office?" says the lady whose nametag reads PATTY.

I recognize the face, and figure we must have talked before. Sonia and I sit down in the office and Patty starts up.

"Marta, like I have asked you before, it would be really helpful if you could go through your mom's boxes down in the storage room. It's been over six months since I last asked you, and there are a lot of boxes, and space is kind of tight. It will probably make it easier for you too, if you start sorting through them earlier rather than later..." Patty trails off.

"Sure, no worries. I will try to make time for it, it is just so hard with work. It is pretty demanding." I smile sweetly.

Patty smiles, obviously thinking she has won a small battle, although I have no intention of sorting through my mom's boxes. I might as well declare her dead, and I am not ready for that yet. We stand and shake hands.

"All you have to do is call us ahead of time to let us know that you will be coming in."

"Sure. Thank you." I turn to leave the building for a second time, rain jacket hood firmly draped over my head.

"What are you grinning about?" I ask Sonia, who is sporting one of her trademark wild smiles.

"Marta, you may find out more about your granddad when you go through your mom's boxes, who knows what hidden treasures you might find in there."

"Yeah, only I am not going through my mom's boxes," I say a little sharper than intended. Sonia's face drops.

"MARTA, you have to, what about Zygmunt?"

"What about him? We don't even know if he is my grandfather. My mom's word isn't the most reliable account," I say turning away. Thankfully Sonia doesn't press, instead she remains silent the entire bus journey back to Queen Anne.

We step into my apartment shaking raindrops off our jackets and Sonia finally gives me a smile, "Do you want a cup of tea?" Fight over. That is what I like best about Sonia, she is never mad with me for very long no matter how difficult I am. I stop being mad the instant after I say something rude, but Sonia needs a few moments of silence to collect her thoughts before letting things go. I am sure there is a giant box in her brain where she dumps annoying Marta comments, and then hopefully every now and again she has a burn session to make space for future Marta annoyances.

I smile back. "Yes, and I still have popcorn."

We sit down on my sofa, legs curled up under a blanket and steaming cups of tea in hand.

"I really think you should start looking through the boxes Marta, if not for Zygmunt for yourself."

"Ha, you were the one who told me to keep everything. And now you want me to go through it again and get rid of stuff?"

Sonia doesn't answer she just gives me her *is-that-so* look, and I am left wondering if she has known this whole time how much I wanted to hang on to every single piece of my parents' stuff. How scared I had been of being left all alone. The only time I had desperately wished for a sibling, lucky to have Sonia there to fill that role.

"Ok, I will look at it," I say, giving in to Sonia's pleading eyes. "But it won't be for Zygmunt or me, it will be for you, my dear." I smile and reach into the popcorn bowl stuffing still warm, salty popcorn into my mouth.

"Good, you can call them in the morning, then spend most of tomorrow going through the boxes."

I almost choke on my popcorn. "Sonia, maybe not that soon. I will get to it, I promise."

"Marta, I know you and if you don't start immediately you will never do it."

"But not tomorrow. Give me some time to get used to the idea first."

Sonia gives me a cheeky smile. "OK, but since the weather is bad and you have no plans for tomorrow, you should come with me to my niece Lily's birthday party instead. It will be fun, all the relatives are going."

"OK, tomorrow it is, I will sort through boxes till my… YOUR heart is content," I smile.

***

In the morning I wake early, much too early to call the nursing home. It is still dark outside and it is windy and wet. I go for a long fast run along the waterfront hoping the exercise will settle my jittery nerves. It doesn't work, back at the apartment I feel angry and defiant for no reason. I am playing "Sunday Bloody Sunday" way too loud for 6:30 a.m., no matter how fitting the tune. At 7:30 a.m. I can't wait any longer, I pull on my rain jacket and walk the entire way to the nursing home, arriving just as visiting hours start at 9 a.m.

Patty is not at reception, but a young man with acne kindly locks the front door, leaving a *Will be back in 5 minutes* sign, before taking me downstairs to the storage.

"Your mom's stuff is over in that corner, there must be at least fifteen boxes. They are all labelled Aniela Bartowiak."

Aniela. The formality of using my mother's name makes her feel separate, no longer part of me. Not mama, mom, mommy or mother, the names I know her by. But Aniela, the name given to her by her parents. OK, I think to myself, maybe it is easier to pry into Aniela's life rather than my mom's.

I start by counting the boxes, there are only ten. I make a mental note to correct the guy in the reception on my way out. Yes, I am still feeling defiant. Next to the labels with my mother's name, each box has text written in my mom's neat handwriting in Polish. I don't understand what it says, but there are years on each box. I sort them in chronological order before opening the box with the years 1954-1956 on it. Start from the beginning, I think to myself.

The box contains old withered hospital records in Polish, which I gather is from Mom's birth, a posed black and white photo of what I guess must be my grandmother holding baby Aniela in her arms, a baby blanket, a worn wooden baby rattle that looks home-made, and an intricate white baby dress that I recognize from the black and white photo. It must be from my mom's baptism; both my parents were Roman-Catholic. Although they never actively practiced their religion, I can still hear my mother's voice scolding me for using the Lord's name in vain. The memory makes me smile, my mom scolding but never angry. Her gentle reassuring hugs, her hair smelling of home-baked bread, and even as she scolded a trained eye could have detected the secret bemused smile lingering at the edge of her mouth. I smell the blanket, it smells old and musty like our attic had. I study the photograph, trying to remember if I have ever seen a photograph of my grandmother before. Surely Mom would have showed me these. But the photo triggers no memory, so I move on to the next box, forgetting I am meant to sort out what to keep and what to throw out. Year 1957-1959, by now my mom would have been walking and talking. There is another home-made toy, a sewn doll, more paperwork in Polish, and some old clothes.

My tummy grumbles and I glance at my watch. Eight minutes past two, no wonder I am hungry. I am halfway through box number six. Best pack it back up and find some lunch. So far each box has contained memorabilia from my mom's childhood in Poland. Well-loved toys, the odd photo of my mother beaming at the camera, school work, worn pieces of clothing, and documents I do not understand. This box had a diary in it, my mother's name written in gold on the front. It is locked and I guess it is in Polish anyway, so I don't try to open it. My mom would have been fifteen or sixteen, I bet it is full of secret love stories about boys in class. I giggle to myself. As I reach to put it back in the box a news clipping slides from the diary and floats to the floor. I pick it up, turn it over, and gasp. My body is frozen, eyes fixated on the old yellowed piece of news.

Chapter 7

"Marta, I can't just leave, we haven't had cake yet."

"Sonia, you have to come get me now. This is crazy."

"I don't understand why you can't just tell me over the phone Marta," Sonia's voice is heavily accented with nuisance. She lets out a deep sigh. "I will be there in thirty minutes, this had better be worth it Marta," she hangs up.

Thirty minutes, I think, pacing back and forth in the storage room. What will I do for thirty minutes? It doesn't give me enough time to go through the next box, or even finish the one I am half-way through. Instead, I rummage through the first box again, grabbing the photo of my grandmother and Mom. I shove the photograph together with the diary and news clipping in my bag before stacking the boxes back in the corner, turning off the lights, and closing the door behind me.

At reception I wait while the young guy with acne signs in some visitors before letting him know I have closed up downstairs and will be back soon to finish with the boxes.

"You look like you have seen a ghost. Are you OK?" He has a worried frown on his forehead.

"Yeah, I kind of have," I say and turn, sprinting out the front door. My earlier determination to let him know that there were only TEN boxes has long since vanished. I pace up and down the curb outside the nursing home as I wait for Sonia.

"You look like you have seen a ghost," says Sonia as she opens the passenger door for me from the inside.

"You're not the first one to say that. Truth is, I have."

I hold out the faded news clipping and watch Sonia's face break into a smile.

"I told you your grandfather was Zygmunt the mountaineering hero," she laughs.

"Can't you see it?" I ask.

"See what? I see a photo of a man in the mountains and the name Zygmunt Pyszka, and a lot of writing in a language I can't read. I assume you found this amongst your mom's stuff. So this confirms that Zygmunt is your grandfather."

I shake my head. Sonia's smile is fading.

"I don't understand Marta?"

"That man in the picture is the same man that is in the photo of Mr. Hawkins on K2."

Sonia's mouth opens and closes several times before she says, "Are you sure Marta? I mean it sure looks like it, but neither photo is very good quality…" She trails off sounding like she is trying to convince herself just as much me.

"I am sure."

Sonia picks up her phone, taps the screen, and lifts the phone to her ear. There's a short wait. "You need to meet us now…yes, now. At the Blue Water Taco Grill in lower Queen Anne… Sure, we will be there in fifteen minutes. Bring the poster. Bye."

"Is Jose coming?" I ask.

"Yes. We need to compare the photos and figure out what this means Marta."

I am still pretty shaken up by the time we get to Blue Water Taco Grill, so I order a bucket of mini Coronas to go with my tacos. Sonia gives me a frown when I carry the beer bucket over to our booth. But she doesn't say anything, instead she pops open a beer and hands it to me. She then leaves to get herself a glass of water, and cutlery for the both of us. Each time the little bell at the door jingles I jump. When it is finally Jose setting off the bell some twenty minutes later, I have already finished two and half of the mini Coronas and scoffed down my two *tacos al pastor*. Jose sits down and I hand him a beer.

"You want to order some food?" asks Sonia.

"Nah, I am good," says Jose, fishing out the folded poster

from his back pocket. Sonia hands him the news clipping, which is sitting on the table.

"Hey. That's the same dude," says Jose.

"Aha, see I told you so." I smile whilst looking at Sonia.

"Where did you find this clipping? Do you know who he is?" asks Jose in rapid fire.

"Yes," says Sonia. "It is Marta's grandfather, Zygmunt."

Jose stares at me for a long time. "Marta, why didn't you tell me this before?"

"Because, I did not know," I say before letting Sonia take over, doing all the explaining for me. I hate explaining, this is why teaching never suited me well and part of the reason why I don't volunteer more at the Seattle Mountaineers. Sonia is always trying to get me to come along, trying to coax me into committing a perfectly good weekend to instruct at one of their fieldtrips. I know I should. I am just not very good at it; the first time I tried I made a lady cry —

"Marta, are you even listening?" Sonia's voice interrupts my thoughts.

"Yeah, sorry, what were you saying?" I mumble.

"Marta, this is crazy, there must be some sort of connection between your grandfather and Mr. Hawkins. What else did you find in those boxes?" Jose looks concerned.

"Well, nothing much really, just memorabilia from my mom's childhood," I say as I pull out the photograph of my grandmother and my mom's teenage diary from my bag. It takes Jose less than two seconds to pick the lock on my mom's diary. I feel like a traitor when he hands it over and I slowly open it up.

"Marta, you don't have to," says Jose.

"It is OK. It just doesn't feel great prying into mom's teenage life. If I ever have kids I am burning all my old diaries."

"Good idea," says Sonia. "No future children of yours

need to know that you live off beer and popcorn." She winks at me as I blush, wishing Jose hadn't been here to hear about my unhealthy habits. But then I guess I have a half-empty bucket of beer in front of me, so the secret is already out. Like I had guessed the diary is in Polish. It is all text, apart from one page where the name Jakub is written, surrounded by lots of little golden hearts.

"No more photos or news clippings?" asks Jose.

"Nope. But Mom had a crush on some guy called Jakub," I say grinning, holding up the page with the name for Sonia and Jose to see.

"Look," I say. "We don't even know for sure that Zygmunt is my grandfather. Perhaps he was just my mom's hero. Or a more distant relative."

"OK," agrees Jose, "was there really nothing else in the boxes that could identify him as your grandfather?"

"Well, I didn't get to finish all the boxes. There were some hospital records from my mom's birth, maybe I should have a closer look at those."

"No shit Sherlock," says Sonia.

Jose cuts in, "Well, let's start with what we do know. We do know that Zygmunt Pyszka was a Polish high altitude mountaineer and that he was on the summit with Mr. Hawkins the day he summited K2 in 1978. Right?"

"Right," Sonia and I reply in unison.

"So, we need to find out three things to start with. If Zygmunt is indeed Marta's grandfather? Why Mr. Hawkins never mentioned he summited K2 together with Zygmunt? And who else was climbing K2 that year, and is anyone still alive? Sound OK?"

"Yes," again in unison.

"Marta, you need to get your mom's hospital records and finish going through the boxes. Sonia, why don't you do some research on who else was climbing K2 in 1978? And I will take a closer look at Mr. Hawkins."

"Sure." says Sonia.

Jose and I have polished off another bucket of mini Coronas, and my head is spinning. "I may need to get this little lady home to bed." I say pointing at my chest.

"You want me to walk you home?" offers Jose.

His smile and light green eyes, so stark against his olive complexion, makes my skin tingle. I can feel blood rushing to my cheeks.

"Nah, it is only a couple of blocks," I reply, swaying slightly as I stand up to leave.

***

I arrive in the office out of breath, rushing into the kitchen to grab a coffee before hitting my desk.

"You are only on time when you have a date with the mountains." Sonia is seated at one of the tables in the kitchen eating a croissant, of which she hands me half.

I pour my coffee and sit down next to her. "You are here early." I smile.

"No, I am here on time. Hung over?" she asks.

"Nah, just tired. A little overwhelmed maybe."

"No wonder. Let's get to it." Sonia stands up, offers me her hand, and pulls me up.

In my office I try to push the thoughts of Zygmunt and Mr. Hawkins out of my mind, focusing on the endless list of work emails. I am about halfway through my emails when I notice an email further down from the University of Washington. I click to open it.

Dear Marta,

I am pleased to inform you that we do have a Polish

53

translator that can translate the document for you.
The starting rate is 60 dollars per standard page,
increasing if the document is of high complexity. If
you wish to proceed, please send us a copy of the
document to be translated. We will then provide you
with a more accurate quote.
Kind Regards,
Jonas Nimms
The University of Washington Language Learning
Centre

Sixty dollars per page. Outrageous. I scroll through the text I had copied, it is one and a half pages long, which would mean a minimum of a hundred bucks. I have no idea if this document is complex, how could I know, I can't read it. Hence why I need a translator. I delete the email out of frustration and am about to start back on the work emails when the phone rings. It is Lisa.

"Hi Marta, I am going to be in late today." I smile with relief, it isn't just me sleeping in on a Monday. "Someone broke into my car, the windows are smashed." Oh OK, valid excuse. "I am waiting for the police to arrive. I will be in as soon as I can."

"No worries Lisa, we will hold down the fort. No rush."

I pop my head into Sonia's office on my way to the front desk. "I will be in reception until Lisa gets in. She is late, someone broke into her car. Smashed the windows."

I am thankful for the break. There is obviously a computer in the reception, so I could log in to my account and continue working. But I need a break, so I do another fruitless Google of Mr. Hawkins and K2 images, as well as stepping into Sonia's territory by searching for who had a permit to climb K2 in 1978. I tinker around on the web for some time, checking my Facebook and private email before Lisa gets into work.

"I am so sorry about this." Lisa apologizes as she rushes behind the desk to relieve me of her duties. In my opinion, she gets in way quicker than necessary.

"No worries at all. What happened?"

Sonia has heard us chatting and comes down the corridor to joins us, eager to get in on the gossip.

"It is so strange. I had like eighty bucks in cash in the glove box, but nothing was stolen, even though they had been through my entire car. The police said it looked like they were searching for something and started asking me about drugs. Oh, and there was a typed note on the front seat – *WE NEED THE POSTER BACK.*"

All at once it feels like the air in the room is being sucked out like a deflating balloon and I can't breathe.

Lisa prattles on, "I don't even know what that means. The police sure thought I did though." She falls silent.

The room has gone so quiet you could hear a pin drop. Sonia and I are looking at each other, panic stricken.

Chapter 8

"Hey you two, what's going on?" Lisa looks at us with concern.

"Oh, nothing," Sonia is grabbing my arm and yanking it hard.

"Oh, I am so sorry to hear Lisa. That is really very peculiar. I hope insurance covers the damages," I stammer while Sonia is literally pulling me down the corridor, shutting the door behind us when we get to her office.

"Marta, this is scaring the crap out of me." This is uncharacteristically profane language coming from Sonia, so she really must be scared shitless.

"Sonia, maybe we should just let all this go. Let the dead rest and plan fun climbs for summer instead?"

"No way, we need to figure this out before somebody else gets hurt."

"OK, OK, OK. You're right." My mind is racing. "I have to get some work done first. Dinner at mine after work."

Back in my office I sit for a while letting my head stop spinning before taking a big breath and opening my work emails back up. Amazingly, the rest of the day goes well and I go back out to chat to Lisa, trying to make up for our previously odd behavior. I also work through all my emails and a large stack of paperwork. The anxiety must be giving me spurts of adrenaline, because I get through more work in a day than I did the previous week combined. So at five o'clock when I pop my head into Sonia's office, I actually feel great. Sonia does not look great, however. She looks worried and tired and I feel a prick in my chest. This is all my fault, dragging Sonia into this. But she smiles at me, and when we are hurrying up the hill, the sun peeking out behind the clouds, she fondly grabs my arm; the take-out bag of sushi from Obasan swinging on her arm. She doesn't even tease me for not having food in the house, I did offer popcorn for dinner. Mostly as a joke, but had it been just me that might have been dinner. Neither of us talk until we have sat down with the sushi between us at my tiny kitchen table. I draw a big breath and start out.

"So, what do you think about Lisa's car?"

As soon as I speak it is like a can of worms have been opened and we can't stop talking. Stuffing pieces of sushi in our mouths, swallowing them almost whole to get the next sentence out.

"Whoever was looking for the posters must have seen us in Lisa's car at Vertical World. They think Lisa is the one with the poster."

"I know," I say with my mouth full of sushi.

It is a relief when the plate between us is empty and we can continue our conversation unhindered by raw fish.

"Let me call Jose," I say. "Hi Jose, Marta here. Could you give me a call back when you get a chance? Bye. He isn't picking up. Anyway, I need to get this article translated from the Polish Alpine Club. It mentions Zygmunt, but the University wants over a hundred bucks to do it," I say pointing on my laptop that is on the table between us.

"You call *me* technically challenged," scoffs Sonia. "You can just have Google Translate do it for you for free, silly."

Sonia turns my laptop so it faces her and pastes the text into the translation software.

Archive from the Polish International Mountaineering Organization

Another one of commodity nation's heroes have been lost in the high Himalayan Mountains. Zygmunt Pyszka, 47 years old, disappeared somewhere between High Camp and the summit of K2 on the 6th of September 1978. He leaves behind his wife Luiza, and 24 year old daughter Aniela. Zygmunt participated in the American expedition, after his friend Mr. Douglas Hawkins Zygmunt offered a place on their condition. Mr. Hawkins reached the summit on the day of Zygmunt disappeared, and thus became the first American to climb K2, after five previous American failed attempts in 1938, 1939, 1953, 1960, 1975. Zygmunt was best known for his successful winter expeditions, winter 1959 he climbed all of Tatra's highest mountains, and in 1970 he climbed over 8000 meters on Nanga Parbat during the winter, in order to climb in 1974 Lothse. His climbing Resume is long and it is with heavy within the hearts we take farewell of a true hero.

On 16 October 1978 Wanda Rutkiewicz became the first Pole, the third woman and the first European woman to climb Everest. In Warsaw hailed her success with celebrations...

"Bingo."

"OK, OK. No need to brag." But I am secretly impressed. The translation may not be the best, but all that we need.

I read through the translated text a second time. From what I can gather this website has posted archives from the Polish Alpine Club, which detail significant Polish climbing achievements. Most of the article has nothing to do with Zygmunt. But it is now clear that Zygmunt is indeed my grandfather. I feel both pride and sadness.

***

"Hey, Marta, how did you sleep?" Sonia is leaning in the doorway of my office.

"Like a baby," I reply. Looking up I realize Sonia is looking a little worse for wear. "But you didn't by the looks of things."

"Nah, I have been up all night thinking about all of this. I did some Googling too. There really isn't much about your grandfather, but I got an idea of what it was like being a Polish mountaineer post World War Two."

"So enlighten me." I smile.

Sonia walks into my office, closes the door behind her, and sits down in the chair opposite mine. She looks so grim I can't help but say, "So, who has beaten you up this time, or did you fall down the stairs again?" I actually get a smile before the *ha-ha-very-funny* look takes over Sonia's face.

"Well, in 1949 the Stalin system finally took over, after heavy Soviet government influence since the war ended in 1945. The frontiers closed and there was tightened security. The city of Wroclaw was the industry hub, but seemed to breed climbers. Perhaps they needed to get away from the polluted air, and the proximity to the Tatra Mountains made climbing a feasible escape."

"Wroclaw. But my parents lived in Warsaw."

"Well, this situation wasn't exclusive to Wroclaw, but that seemed to be the hub for climbers."

"OK, go on."

"By the 60s the standard of living was very low, income was a pittance and zloty, the Polish currency, was worthless. Meanwhile the party bosses lived a life of luxury."

"Sounds about right," I interrupt.

"Anyhow, climbers were a source of national pride, and as such they got permits to travel outside of Poland. Something a normal person could not do. So I think climbing was just as much an escape mechanism as it was a passion for these climbers."

"That makes sense. Who wouldn't want to escape poverty and an iron fist? My parents sure did." Suddenly I am wishing I had asked my mom and dad more questions when I still had the chance. I know they escaped for a better life, but never fully understood what life it was they were escaping.

"And... there is this other thing..." Sonia is looking unhappy. "Many Polish climbers actually worked as spies," she pauses, waiting for me to say something, but I stay silent. "Not every Polish climber was a spy, but if you did not agree to spy the government wouldn't issue you overseas permits or allow you on climbing expeditions."

"Wow. My grandfather was not only a mountaineer, but a spy."

"We don't know that. Like I said, not every Polish mountaineer was a spy."

"But it would explain a thing or two," I interrupt.

"Perhaps," Sonia replies.

***

My computer screen is showing five o'clock, that is me, time to go home. But instead of heading up the hill for home I walk through downtown, people are hurrying home after work and clustering around the bus stops. I enjoy the walk to my mom's nursing home, it lets me clear my head. If my grandfather was a spy then I am determined to find any clues. I still can't decide if I feel proud or upset at the fact that he may have spied on the nation I call home. I think I am mostly proud, not at the spying, but at the resolve to get up mountains no matter what the cost. Thinking of the moral aspects of it makes my head hurt, so I push it aside, and when I open the door to the nursing home Patty meets me in reception.

"Hi. I have come to continue with the boxes. Did... hmm... the young gentleman..."

"Peter," Patty corrects.

"Yes. Did Peter tell you I started?" I ask, feeling pleased with myself.

Patty looks annoyed. "It would be helpful if you called first to let us know that you will be coming in."

"Oh, sorry, I forgot," I say feeling sheepish, my pleased feeling gone. *Bitch,* I think to myself. I despise being treated like a child, I hated it as a child and hate it even more as an adult. But I smile sweetly.

"Follow me." Patty takes me down the stairs and unlocks the door to my mother's secrets.

I go straight for the first box and rummage through until I find the hospital records. Despite them being in Polish I manage to find the names of both my grandparents; Zygmunt Pyszka and Luiza Pyszka, as well as my mother's name – Aniela Pyszka. This again confirms that Zygmunt is indeed my grandfather. I also find the word Miasto Katowice multiple times in the document, making me suspect that perhaps my mother was in fact born in Katowice and only moved to Warsaw at some later stage. Despite my eyes searching the document and all the foreign words I can't decipher anything further, so I move my attention back to box number six, year 1969-1971. The one I was halfway through, the one that had contained my mother's diary.

There is nothing else of interest, just old school work and a wooden flute. But as I am about to pile the stuff back in I spot something poking out from the folded over cardboard base of the box. I pull it out. It is a worn piton, an old-school piton. I have never used a piton for climbing, they are not so common these days. But back when my grandfather climbed that would have been the only kind of protection they had, a small metal peg hammered into a crack in the rock to save you from any potential falls. Its weight is heavy in my hand as I inspect it. When I turn it over it has a message inscribed into the metal. It starts with the name Aniela and follows on in Polish. I figure it must be a gift from my grandfather to his daughter, my mom. I feel the cool metal on the inside of my hand as I curl my fingers around it before slipping it into my pocket.

My mom must have been a once-only diary writer, because the next box doesn't contain one. Unless, like I would have, she burned her subsequent diaries. Just a bunch of paperwork from the University of Warsaw, or like the documents say, *Uniwersytet Warszawski*. By now my mom was definitely living in Warsaw. I wish I had paid more attention when I went through the previous boxes, perhaps the school work would give clues as to when my mother moved.

I already know she went to Warsaw University, where she studied electrical engineering, an unusual choice for a woman in her day, and a profession she never got a chance to practice again once she moved to the US. Her Polish degree was not recognized here, she instead became a full-time mother and baker of fresh bread for her husband and child. I sigh at the stupidity of it all. Spending a lifetime studying to be told it was worth nothing.

There is another news clipping, Zygmunt on top of some mountain. Arms stretched out, ice axe in one hand, the typical *I have summited* pose so favored by mountaineers, me included. I scan through the Polish text and by the number of times I see the word Lhotse, figure this must be the mountain he is on top of. I already had an inkling that Zygmunt had summited Lhotse from the poorly translated document from the Polish Alpine Club. I set it aside before moving on to the next box, again no diary.

Only when I get to box number nine do I find anything else of interest. In the bottom of the box is a small wooden box, inside it is a pipe that still smells vaguely of tobacco, a postcard with a black and white picture of K2 on the front addressed to my mother in Warsaw, and another news clipping. No picture, just text. But I recognize the words Zygmunt, K2, and 6 Wrzeisien 1978. His final climb.

Is this it, the life of my grandfather whittled down to three objects, four if you include the piton. I fish it out of my pocket and place it in the wooden box together with the earlier news clipping, and the hospital records, which I have to fold to fit in the box.

The last box is half empty and mainly made up of documents relating to my mom and dad's wedding, which surprisingly appears to have taken place at a courthouse rather than a church, followed by a thick bundle of documents concerning their emigration to America. At least half of these are in English, but hold little interest to me. Nothing about my grandparents. Whatever happened to Luiza, I think to myself? There is no wooden box with treasures dedicated to my grandmother.

Chapter 9

It is dark as I catch the bus home, the wooden box balanced on my knee. Back in my apartment I lay out all the pieces on my table. Three news clippings, one hospital record, one postcard, a piton, and a pipe. All of it needing translation apart from the pipe, and maybe the hospital records. I reason that I have probably already figured out all the important details and I know my mom's birthday. I type the inscription of the piton into Google Translate.

> *Aniela, this piton has been higher than I could have ever dreamed of going, but I never feel as high as when I hold you in my arms. Love Dad*

I feel a pinch in my chest. This is unusual, I don't subscribe to emotional notions and rarely succumb to sadness. I hold the piton to my cheek, the cool metal feels good on my skin. How have I, Marta, the tomboy from Darrington ended up with such an intriguing history? I had fully expected my memoirs' most interesting tidbit to be that I grew up in a town that deemed itself the home of bluegrass music in the northwest. Despite bluegrass originating somewhere in the southeast, maybe it is North Carolina or Tennessee, I am not sure, but either way, some thousands of miles away. Instead the headline now reads, *Dangerous Mountains and Espionage.* I sigh, breathing out all the sad air and steeling myself from my emotions.

"All this sadness leads to nothing," I whisper to myself as I place all the pieces of my grandfather's lost life back into the wooden box, something my mother used to say when I came home from school crying, some kids teasing me, or me falling off my bike. But sometimes, on those days when the air was a little thicker in our house, almost electrified, my mom would whisper those very words to herself, like I am now. It seems to work, all the sadness pushed aside as I go to bed. Dreamless.

***

It isn't until a few days later, when Sonia pops her head into my office asking if I have heard from Jose, that I realize I haven't. Work has been busy; with spring arriving there are so many emotions, so many women being beaten blue when their boyfriends drink too much beer in the first warm sunshine of the year.

"No, not since Blue Water Taco," I reply.

"Me either. I have left him a couple of messages. Maybe you could call him?" Sonia asks.

"Sure, I will try to call him later."

Sonia shakes her head and leaves. I know she thinks I am not actually going to, I often do say I will do things just to please her, with no intention of actually doing them. It is pretty lame I know, but often easier. This time, however, I am just as keen as Sonia, probably even keener, to get a hold of Jose. Screw it, I put down the file I am working on and pick up my phone. I smile when I start typing Jose and two numbers come up, Jose – work, and Jose – private. It makes me tingle a little that I have a private number for Jose, and that is the one I dial. As the signals start to go through I am wondering which number Sonia had called? Work or private? My thoughts are interrupted.

"Hi Marta."

"Oh, hello, Jose, how are you?" I am caught off guard. I had been so sure it would ring through to voice mail.

"I am at work; can I call you later?"

"Sure."

"Or actually, you ladies want to meet for dinner tonight?"

"Yeah, sounds good to me, I think Sonia is free too."

"OK good, I will pick you up outside your office at five-thirty."

"Sounds good," I am about to continue but realize Jose has already hung up. That was brief. I pick up the work phone and dial Sonia's extension to let her know.

I really want to have the wooden box with me at dinner, but I don't have time to go home to pick it up. Instead of getting any work done I end up spending half an hour agonizing over how I can get the box. Realizing I could have gone home to get it in that time, I feel frustrated by the time Sonia comes into my office at 5:15 p.m.

"Jose will be here soon," she smiles.

"Yeah I know. Let me finish up this email."

By 5:30 p.m. Sonia and I are standing outside our office building on the stairs like two school girls waiting for their prom dates. Jose pulls up and hollers, "Hop in."

We dash from under the entranceway into his car, fat rain drops pelting down all around us.

"Another gorgeous spring day in Seattle," laughs Jose.

"Well maybe this rain will stop the bastards beating up their wives," I reply.

Jose looks at Sonia for clarification, but she just shrugs at him as he pulls out from the curb.

"Where to ladies?" asks Jose.

"Could we swing by my place, there is something I really would like to show you guys?" Jose doesn't reply but takes Queen Anne Avenue up the hill towards my tiny home.

Once we finally sit down for dinner, my wooden box propped on the table, my tummy is grumbling. We have driven all over town trying to work out where to eat. I suggested my favorite Mexican restaurant in Fremont, but Jose objected stating that just because he is half Mexican doesn't mean he eats Mexican food every meal. In the end we decide to instead feed his other half with all-American burgers. Smith's up in Capitol

Hill has the best burgers in town and booths affording us some privacy. The restaurant is dark and decorated with vintage knickknacks, making it feel old school, or like we are dining inside a poorly lit op-shop. I like it, it feels like we are secret agents or boot-leggers at a speakeasy. We all order Smith burgers and beers, apart from Sonia who gets a glass of wine.

"I am dying to know what is inside your box." Sonia is leaning over the table to get a better look.

"Shouldn't we fill Jose in about Lisa's car first?"

"Oh darn, I almost forgot. Lisa at work. We borrowed her car when we went to pick up the poster from Vertical World. Her car got broken into a few days ago. They didn't steal anything. But they left a note saying 'we need the poster back.' I think whoever broke in thought the car was ours. They must have seen us at Vertical World. It must be the same person that was collecting all the posters. We need to figure this out before someone gets hurt." Sonia stops talking and draws a deep breath.

Jose looks at us with a grim face. "Only it is too late for that, someone has already gotten hurt. Jonny, you know Jonny, Barb's boyfriend, or I guess former boyfriend now… I mean since she left and all."

"Oh come on, get to it." I am impatient.

"Sorry, yeah Jonny, he is dead. He was murdered."

Both Sonia and I sit with our mouths open as the waitress places our drinks in front of us, sensing a tense moment she quickly moves away.

"It looks like suicide, shot in the head, but a few bits and bobs doesn't add up. The case is closed nonetheless, he wasn't exactly a man on the straight and narrow. So conclusion is that it was something drug related. I beg to differ though."

"Me too." I am angry.

"The rest of the police force does not, however. I tried to

get some support for my theories, but the case is closed. I think the chief of police is purposely shutting me out."

"Holy crap. That is shit Jose."

Sonia a little more sensitive, "Jose, can we help you in any way? This wasn't meant to hurt your work?"

"Oh it is OK; I didn't join the police force to please my colleagues or superiors."

I push the box to the middle of the table.

"So, what's in there?" asks Sonia.

"What is left of my grandfather's life," I smile.

I take out the items piece by piece, saving the piton till last, not yet sure if I want to share it with anyone else. I am worried that the pinch in my chest will return if asked about the inscription. I only get through the pipe and news clippings number one and two before our food arrives. Happy for the interruption I put the box next to me on the bench while we eat our burgers and joke about mundane everyday things to escape the intensity of where we had arrived.

After I have polished off my burger and fries, and half of Sonia's sweet potato fries, I again open the box. I produce the last news clipping and the hospital records, but leave the piton inside.

"Why didn't you tell me about this before?" asks Sonia. "I have seen you every day at work and not one mention."

"I am so sorry Sonia. I needed a little time to digest it all."

She looks hurt. "I will bet my left arm that the news clippings are from each of his big achievements, right?"

"Yes, I think this first one is from when he got higher than 8,000 meters on Nanga Parbat during the winter of 1970, the next one when he summited Lhotse in 1974, and finally his last climb, K2 in 1978," I say.

"Makes sense," Jose chimes in.

"Did you translate them?" asks Sonia.

"No I haven't had a chance; it will take some time to type this."

"Let's do one each." Jose picks up the last article, which is probably about my grandfather's death. I am happy I don't have to translate that one. I keep the earliest article for myself and give Sonia the one from 1974. I want to read the story in which the piton was involved. It makes no sense, but for some reason I want to hold on to that piton for dear life. Keep it my secret.

Jose drops Sonia home first, and when we get to Queen Anne he asks if I want to have another drink. It makes me nervous and happy all at once. We park the car and I run up to drop off the wooden box before we walk up to Hilltop Alehouse. We both order some local IPA, Jose is laughing and saying there are too many local breweries to keep track off. I probably would have thought it was a dorky thing to say if it wasn't that it is Jose saying it. Only during our second round, which Jose insists on paying despite him having paid the first round as well, does Jose ask, "So Marta, what else was in your wooden box?"

I freeze and put my face in my hands for a second, scrunching up my face. This is my fourth beer, I am tipsy, and my guards are down.

"So you saw that, hey?"

"Yes, I could tell there was something else in there. I don't think Sonia noticed, she was on the other side of the table."

"It isn't really anything secret. It is just something I wanted to keep to myself for a little longer. It isn't important to the story."

"Oh no, I didn't mean it like that. I just thought maybe you wanted to share it with someone. But if not, no worries. This is your story." He is looking me in the eyes the entire time.

I am sold.

"Come." I finish the last bit of my beer before ushering us

both out the door. "I will show you," I explain as we are walking down the street. Jose reaches out and takes my hand. Little warm electric shocks are shooting up my arm as his warm fingers wrap around my cold ones.

Chapter 10

In my apartment I pour us wine and we curl up on my sofa. I re-open the box. Jose's hand is resting on my thigh and it is hard to concentrate. But I pull out the piton and hand it over to him. Jose looks confused.

"Hey, what is that face about?" I ask.

"Oh, it is just that this isn't what I saw."

"What? There is nothing else in here."

"Oh, I thought I saw a black and white photo of a mountain. But maybe I was mistaken."

"Oh, shit, shit, shit, I totally forgot about the postcard."

I rummage through the box and pull it out. I hand it to Jose, who has to put the piton down on the coffee table to inspect the postcard.

"I think it was from my grandfather to my mom, sent from his last expedition on K2."

"It looks like it," agrees Jose.

"It is post stamped in Rawalpindi, where is that?"

I type in Rawalpindi on my phone and Google Maps brings up the location for us. "It is a city in Pakistan, close to Islamabad."

"How did your grandfather get to post it there?"

"Oh, porters would have probably taken it out to Skardu," I say, showing off my limited knowledge about Pakistan that I have learned from reading Mr. Hawkins books. "Then it would have had to travel down the Karakoram Highway for a couple of days before reaching Islamabad, or I guess Rawalpindi, where someone posted it." I smile.

"OK, so easy peacy then." Jose laughs.

"Not really. I think he must have sent it with someone he knew to get it safely all that way."

"Probably. Maybe there are still friends of your

grandfathers in Pakistan?"

"Maybe," I agree.

"You should translate it," continues Jose.

"Yeah, I will."

Jose hands me back the postcard and I put it back in the box. He picks up the piton and smiles at me. "So what is the deal with this piece of metal?" He turns it over in his hand and looks closely at the inscription.

I take one deep breath. "It is a piton, it is used for climbing to attach rope to the mountain so you can stay safe should you fall. I think this one was on Nanga Parbat with my grandfather when he attempted to climb it in the winter of 1970. He gave it to my mom." I draw another big breath, having held the last one as I was explaining.

"Nice. So what does the inscription say?"

I steel myself, worried that pinch of emotions will return. "**Aniela, this piton has been higher than I could have ever dreamed of going, but I never feel as high as when I hold you in my arms. Love Dad.**"

Nothing. I feel nothing. Jose must think I am upset, however, because he has taken both my hands in his and he is leaning in close to kiss me. I want to grasp hold of him, pull him into me, and make him make me feel something. But instead I sit perfectly still and let him kiss me. After our kiss Jose holds me for a long time stroking my hair. It feels wonderful and I am scared to say anything that will break the magic moment. Eventually I draw a big breath and sit up smiling at Jose.

"I probably need to get some sleep before work."

"Can I stay? I mean, nothing will happen, I just thought I can stay on the sofa or whatever?" Jose looks embarrassed.

"Sure," I feel giddy. "You can stay in my bed." I shrug and go into the bathroom to get into my pajamas, feeling excited and a little shy.

When I get into bed Jose wraps his arms around me and pulls me in close before almost immediately falling asleep. I lay awake listening to his soft sleeping breaths for a long time before finally falling into a deep sleep.

In the morning my head is aching from the beer and wine and I feel a little less confident than I had last night when I invited Jose to stay.

But Jose just smiles at me. "Good morning gorgeous."

All the nerves instantly dissolve. I smile back at him and kiss his nose.

"You want first shower?" I ask.

"Sure."

I watch Jose get out of bed, admiring his muscular body, not bulky, but fit. Like he could run a long way.

"You can grab a fresh towel in the second drawer," I say pointing at my closet. He gets a towel and wraps it over his boxer shorts and heads for the bathroom. As soon as I hear the shower come on I get out of bed and walk in to the kitchen. I rummage around the fridge and cupboards trying to find something for breakfast, anything for breakfast.

"Your turn." Jose is standing in the doorway to the kitchen, hair still wet from the shower.

"Oh, that was quick. I don't have anything for breakfast..."

"Why don't I pick us up something while you shower?"

"Sounds great, there is a Starbucks around the corner. Short Americano and a croissant please."

We eat our pastries in the kitchen; it feels homely, I could get used to this. The sunlight dancing in through the half-pulled blinds and the smell of coffee lingering in the air, Jose chatting away across from me.

"OK, I best be off." Jose stand up and I walk him to the

door. I am not entirely sure of the protocol, but Jose seems to know the ropes. He leans in and kisses me, placing a rouge piece of hair behind my ear.

"I will call you later." He closes the door behind him.

I do a little victory dance around the apartment, my entire body is bubbling with joy. I can't wait to tell Sonia.

***

When I open the door to Sonia's office I am grinning from cheek to cheek. Sonia is already seated at her desk, her charm lost amongst all the wood-paneled walls and neat piles of files on her desk.

"Looks like you are in a good mood, and late," she adds for effect.

"Yes." I smile. "Jose kissed me."

Sonia jumps up and gives me a hug. "That is fantastic Marta." Now she is beaming just as much as I am.

"And he stayed the night," I continue.

Sonia's smile drops. "That was quick."

"Oh no, nothing happened, we just slept... in each other's arms."

"Well that is fabulous news Marta." Back to smiling.

Sonia is in my opinion a little prude, she does not approve of my usual one night stands, which I tend to favor over relationships.

"There are a couple of things I didn't show you last night. One because I forgot and one because I wasn't ready, but I am now if you want to see them?"

"What sort of question is that? Of course I do."

I get the postcard and piton out of my bag. "I forgot to show you this postcard from my grandfather to my mom. I think he sent if from his K2 expedition, well actually I am pretty sure he did considering it is a picture of K2 and it is post stamped in Pakistan. But it is written in Polish."

"You should translate it."

"Yes. I am about to." I hand Sonia the piton. "There was also this."

"What does it say?"

"Aniela, this piton has been higher than I could have ever dreamed of going, but I never feel as high as when I hold you in my arms. Love Dad."

"Oh Marta, are you OK?" Sonia stands up and walks around her desk giving me a tight hug.

"Yeah, yeah, yeah, I am fine." I shrug, ignoring the heavy feeling in the pit of my stomach.

"Sure?" Sonia is trying to read my face.

"Yeah. I am all good. Best get to work," I reply, quickly turning around to leave before I get all soppy and emotional.

In my office I sit down at my desk, and while the computer is firing up I place the postcard on the desk in front of me. The hand writing is neat and the postcard is in great condition. It looks much more recent than it really is, still white, not yellow like you may expect from an old card. My computer screen flickers and asks for my password. I enter 'MARTATHEMOUNTAINEER' and the screen unlocks. Google pops up automatically when I open up a new web-browser, and I enter the Polish text into Google Translate;

Dear Aniela,

I have arrived at K2, it is as beautiful of a mountain as I remembered. It takes your breath away just looking at it. So far we established camp one and two. Now waiting for better weather. My dear friend Mr. Murtaza Jarwar is climbing with me. One of our high altitude porters have promised to post this card for you once he gets back to Rawalpindi. He has sadly suffered severe frostbite on his left hand (which I guess is lucky because left is considered the dirty hand by Muslims) and are therefore leaving us early. I hope to have summited and be back in Warsaw by the end of September. Miss you.

Love Dad

I hold it together just fine, no sadness. Instead I smile a little at the almost naïve optimism and how anyone could consider severe frostbite lucky no matter which hand. I pull out the article I am to translate, but decide it is too much text to tackle right now. It is surprisingly hard to copy text in a language that is not your own.

I keep checking my phone, making sure the sound is turned up loud, afraid I will miss Jose's call. But when I leave work at 6 p.m. I still haven't heard anything. By 9 p.m. I am tethering between despair and rage when my phone finally beeps. A text message from Jose;

Sorry. Shit has hit the fan at work. Will call tomorrow. Jose X

I am amazed at how quickly I am back to feeling on top of the world, he sent me a kiss. I am overjoyed. I reply;

No worries. Hope you are OK. Talk tomorrow. Marta X

***

I wake up to loud knocking on my door, the alarm clock shines 2:08 a.m. My first thought is that whoever is at the door is going to wake up the cranky old couple who live next door, so I rush out to open it. Jose stands in the doorway, he has a wild look in his eyes and he looks really upset.

"Marta, I have been told to take six weeks off work."

"What, why?" I step aside so he can get passed me into the

apartment.

"I don't know, I was translating that article you gave me when my computer locked. I was about to call IT support when the chief walked in and told me the department wished for me to take an extended leave of absence. He wouldn't even tell me why, but they asked a lot of questions about the article I was translating. Luckily I was using a photo copy. The original was in my wallet the whole time." Jose has taken his shoes off and walked into my living room sitting himself down on my sofa while speaking.

"Why do they want to know about my grandfather?" I say sitting down next him.

"Well, I guess they know more about Mr. Hawkins' murder than they let on, and maybe your grandfather has something to do with this whole mess. But I didn't say anything, I just said I was looking into Mr. Hawkins' death a little extra and that I found this article about the climb. Luckily they bought it. I am not sure if it even mentions the Americans, I didn't get a chance to finish the translation. But it must have, because they took the article and a few hours later they came back and they looked pretty pleased with themselves. They told me I needed to take some time off since I had defied orders by prying further into a case that is closed."

"Can they do that?"

"Yeah, they can. But it doesn't make sense. Officers look into closed cases all the time."

"Jose I am so, *so,* sorry."

"It is OK, this gives me time to look into this proper," he smiles.

"Oh no it doesn't. Let's just leave this one alone. It really doesn't matter."

"Marta, we can figure this out -"

"I have no doubt we can," I interrupt, "but I don't want it

to cost you your job. End of story." I stretch out my hand and Jose opens his wallet and hands over the neatly folded article like a teenage boy having his naughty pictures confiscated.

Chapter 11

When I open my eyes a sense of relief washes over me. Jose is snoring next to me and I do not have to worry about all this mess anymore. It is amazing how great it makes me feel, letting go is much easier than I had expected. I sneak out of bed, shower, and start the coffee machine. I still have nothing for breakfast so I leave, leaving a note saying 'back in ten.'

When I get back with a bag of croissants Jose is sipping coffee in my kitchen. Warmth spreads throughout my body. It is so perfect, Jose in my kitchen, drinking coffee, as if it is the most natural thing on the planet. He smiles and pulls me over for a kiss. We spend a long time eating croissants, drinking coffee, and goofing around. Both of us light as feathers, no discussions of murders, or foreign spies. Just us having a jolly good time.

"Shit, I am going to be late again." I stand up, racing around stuffing things at random in my bag.

"Are you OK to see yourself out?"

"Sure. How do I lock the door?"

"Oh, don't worry about it, just leave it unlocked."

Jose looks mortified. "Marta. Do you really think that is a good idea?"

"I do it all the time. People can't get in the front door without the code anyhow."

Jose shakes his head.

"I forget you are a cop," I smile.

"Hopefully," he replies.

I stop and stroke his cheek with my hand. "Jose, it will all be OK. It is over now, no more secret detective work."

He kisses the inside of my hand before I rush out the door.

Jogging down the hill I am justifying being late to myself, it is Friday, almost the weekend, you are allowed to be late on

Fridays. Sonia will probably be grumpy with me again. I run up the stairs to the front doors skipping every second step; at the top of the stairs I almost run straight into Sonia. She grabs a hold of me and wraps her arms around me, letting out a loud sob.

"Marta, what is going on?"

"I don't know what you are talking about. Sonia? What is it?" I pull her away from me holding her at arm's length so I can look her in the eyes.

"It is Lisa," cries Sonia.

I take Sonia's arm and lead her inside, in the reception area other staff members are gathered having animated discussions. I manage to get me and Sonia past reception without anyone paying us any attention. Once we get to my office I usher Sonia inside and close the door behind us. I sit Sonia down and place myself at my desk opposite her.

"Explain," I demand.

"Lisa is in the hospital. Someone broke into her place. I don't know all the details, but she is in the hospital."

"Fuck. We need to find out what has happened," I say handing Sonia a tissue from the box on my desk.

"Karen told us during the Friday morning meeting," sobs Sonia.

Shit. I had forgotten all about the weekly Friday morning meeting. Hopefully Karen hadn't noticed I wasn't there with all this going on.

"Apparently Lisa's mom called early this morning. It happened last night. Lisa will be OK, but she is pretty badly shaken up."

"Which hospital is she at? We need to go see her."

***

80

"Who goes to Northwest Hospital?" I ask. "Who even knows there is a Northwest Hospital?" I continue, hoping my rambling will distract Sonia as we sit in the back of the taxi travelling up Aurora Avenue. Sonia takes my hand and squeezes it.

When we arrive at Northwest Hospital, which I did not know existed until today, I have no idea where to go. Sonia and I get dropped in front of the Emergency entrance.

"I guess we just go inside and ask for Lisa?"

Sonia shrugs her shoulders and goes towards the entrance, me in tow. Just as Sonia walks through the sliding doors my phone starts ringing and I turn around. I pick up my phone, which is announcing an incoming call from Lisa.

"Lisa, how are you? Where are you? We are at Northwest Hospital, can we see you?"

"Marta, I need to speak to you. I have just left the hospital."

"Oh shit, we are here looking for you."

"I will turn around and come get you. Meet me outside Emergency in ten minutes."

"Already here waiting." I hang up just as Sonia comes back out.

"Marta, she has already checked out."

"I know," I reply. "She will be here in ten minutes."

When Lisa pulls up and we get inside her silver Prius she looks just fine to me. I am surprised. I had expected black eyes and choke marks around her neck the way the entire office had reacted.

"How are you?" asks Sonia.

"Good. Well, I am good now. A little scared, but good."

"What happened?" I ask.

"Someone broke into my apartment. When I got home the place was upside down and I was just about to call the police when this man grabbed me and held a gun to my head, asking all sorts of questions," she draws a breath. "A lot of questions about some poster that he needed me to give him, he said he knew I had it. It took a long time before he figured out I had no idea what he was talking about. He said he saw me at Vertical World. That is when I realized that it is you he is after."

"Fuck." Sonia glares at me. I know I shouldn't swear but the moment so deserves a little profanity.

"I was hoping you could tell me why my car was broken into, my apartment ransacked, and I was held at gun point?" continues Lisa while pulling into the drive-through Starbucks. "I need caffeine," she declares, and we sit in silence while she orders and picks up her coffee.

Rather than pulling back out on to Aurora she parks in the small parking lot next to Starbucks and turns towards me. I am a little annoyed that she assumes that this whole mess is my doing, but she is right so I bite my tongue. I am not sure what to tell Lisa, but Sonia takes charge explaining the whole entire mess while Lisa sips her coffee.

"He held a gun to my head. I think you need to go to the police Marta." She looks only at me.

"I already have," I lie. It is kind of true, Jose is a cop. "They say the case is closed."

"Well, then I would get the hell out of town if I were you," continues Lisa, as she turns the key in the ignition and pulls back out onto Aurora. She drives around for a while. "Someone is following me," Lisa's voice is quivering.

"Holy crap, what have we gotten ourselves into?" Sonia sounds scared.

"I am going to drive into work and drop you off at the front doors. You guys go into the office and I will drive to my parents' house. OK?"

Both Sonia and I nod.

We sit in silence while Lisa drives and it is not long before

Lisa pulls up next to the curb in front of our office.

"Thank you Lisa. I am so sorry about all of this.' am opening the car door.

"Don't worry about me. Be careful. Good luck."

Sonia and I run up the stairs. I grab Sonia's arm just as she is about to open the front door and instead we stand and watch Lisa drive away. Only opening the front door once she has cleared the traffic lights and we can no longer see her car.

In the office everything has calmed down and it seems things are back to normal, only they are far from normal for me and Sonia. Sonia fetches us coffees before we lock ourselves in my office.

"What's next?" asks Sonia looking worried.

"Shit, I don't know Sonia. I don't know what is going on. Jose got suspended from work..."

"What?"

"Well, he got asked to take a six-week leave of absence. He was translating the article about Zygmunt on K2 on his work computer, next thing his computer is locked up and the chief of police is in his office telling him to take six weeks off."

"That is bananas."

"I know right. So we decided last night to stop looking into this whole mess, the price is just too big..."

"Looks like it is too late for that," Sonia looks grim. "Where is Jose now?"

"Probably left my place a little while ago." A flutter of joyful butterflies in my stomach, and I can't help but smile.

"Crap. If he has been asked to take a leave of absence for looking into this case there may be a tail on him too."

"Bugger, bugger, bugger." I am pulling out my phone as I am cursing, dialing Jose's number in a panic.

Jose doesn't pick up. I leave a short message to call back as soon as he can and hang up.

Sonia produces the article she was meant to translate and sits down at my computer, painfully typing out the Polish words while I dial and re-dial Jose's number over and over again.

"Stop it," says Sonia. "He will call you when he can. He is probably having a nap or something."

But the look on her face is far from reassuring. I keep dialing.

"Here we go," Sonia copies the text into Google Translate. We both huddle around the computer and read it at the same time.

"Well that was disappointing." I sigh.

"Not really. Zygmunt was one of Poland's big heroes," smiles Sonia. "The first Pole to climb Lhotse."

"But there is nothing in there that helps us understand this any better."

"No, but you learned a little more about your grandfather. He was from Katowice, like you suspected, and he started climbing in his late teens in the Tatras."

I smile at Sonia's enthusiasm for my family history as I get my article out and switch seats with her. My turn to type. My article from 1970 talks of Zygmunt's winter successes in the Tatras and the Alps during the late 50s and early 60s, before he got a chance to climb in the Himalayas in 1970. While he never reached the summit of Nanga Parbat, he got higher than anyone before him on any mountain during the winter season. It quotes Zygmunt:

The bitter cold and fierce winds turned me and Murtaza around. If we had carried on the price may have been too big, I may never have gotten to see my daughter Aniela again. No mountain is worth that risk. Murtaza Jarwar was the perfect companion, he helped me come down the mountain safely and tended to my frost-bitten feet, without his care I would have probably lost a few toes.'

"Murtaza again. He must have been a close friend of my

grandfather's."

"Seems like it. I wonder if he is still alive," ponders Sonia.

She pushes me out of the way and sits back down at my computer and types Murtaza Jarwar into Google before clicking enter. It appears to be the most common name in Pakistan, and when multiple searches show up with nothing useful she shifts her focus to the Polish Alpine Association.

"I think we should call the Polish Alpine Club," Sonia declares. "What is the time in Europe?" she asks without expecting an answer as she types the question into Google. "Half past midnight. Let's call first thing tomorrow," she continues the conversation as if I am not there. She writes down the number on a Post-it note that she slips into her pocket. "It is four-thirty, let's go to your place Marta."

When we leave the office no one is around and the reception desk is empty, Lisa never came back to work. We walk up the hill arm in arm, the sun shining down as if all was well in the world. But I feel jittery and unsettled, I still haven't heard from Jose. It is making me nervous and my mind is miles away when I unlock the front door of my building. Sonia is a few steps ahead of me coming up the stairs.

"Marta, did you lock your door?" She calls back at me.

"Nah, I told Jose he could leave it unlocked."

"Did you tell him to leave the door open as well?" she says just as I catch up to her standing in front of my wide-open door.

"No. He wouldn't have left it open, he was mortified that I don't always lock it," I say and take a step into the apartment.

Sonia yanks me back, calling into the apartment. "Hello, anybody in there?"

"Oh come on," I say. "What do you think, someone will call back, 'yes we are here waiting to slice and dice you.'" I take a few quick steps inside so Sonia can't stop me again.

The place is empty. I know it even before I step inside, it lacks that distinct feeling the presence of another human being gives off. It takes me less than a minute to make sure I am right, the bonus of a tiny apartment is that it takes no time at all to search. Someone has been in here though, drawers are rifled through and all my books are strewn on the floor.

"Anything missing?" asks Sonia.

I stare at her wide eyed.

"The box."

Chapter 12

"No, no, NO." Sonia scurries around the apartment, tripping over the books on the floor and banging into the sofa, which takes up almost the entire living room. "It will be here somewhere."

"Sonia, I left it on the coffee table," I feel panicked.

Sonia encapsulates me in a bear hug. "I am so sorry Marta," she sounds defeated.

"It is OK. I didn't even know it existed a couple of days ago."

"But it did exist and it was your past. No one else's. Those bastards."

"Those bastards who? We don't know who we are up against. What we are up against? What even is this?"

"No, but trust you and me we will find out." Sonia's cheeks are flaring up hot pink with anger. Wow, my lovely level headed, always calm, angel-like, best friend colored pink with anger.

Sonia walks over and closes the front door, which has been standing wide open the entire time. The air instantly feels thicker, confined, and I gasp. The escape route has been cut off; I am more scared then I am letting on, even to myself. Sonia must have felt the same thing because she stands back up and opens the door again.

"It feels better," she says.

I nod in agreement.

"Let's go to mine."

We never go to Sonia's place. Sonia has a roommate; I hate Sonia's roommate. She is deeply religious and always lectures me about the unchristian things that I do. We once had an argument for over two hours about whether shit is a swear word or not. Me claiming it to be merely a bodily byproduct. Jill or Lill or whatever her name is, not so much. She really does annoy the crap out of me. Or shit I guess, ha ha. I swore off roommates years ago, but the thought of staying in my apartment is making my skin crawl.

I quickly pack a few things while Sonia tidies up the books, placing them back on the book shelf and closing my kitchen drawers. This time I make sure my door is securely locked when we leave, testing it twice before following Sonia down the stairs. The bus to Sonia's place is quick and I feel a little bad for visiting so rarely. I blame Jill. The small craftsman bungalow is in Wallingford, the neighborhood next to the University District, it is painted a light mint-green color and a magnolia tree obscures one half of the house. Charming is probably the word a real estate agent would use. When I step inside I am pleased to find it the same way it always is; neat, tidy, and homely.

"Doesn't look like I have had any visitors," Sonia sounds relieved.

"Praise the Lord," I laugh.

"Give it up. Jill isn't home," Sonia giggles.

"Bible study?" I ask.

"Be nice."

My phone rings.

"Jose," I call out before picking up.

"Hey babe." He called me babe. "Are you OK?" He sounds concerned.

"Yes, are you?"

"Not really, but you have lovely neighbors. That old couple, sweet really."

"Oh you have met Mr. and Mrs. Lee I see. Sweeter little old couple you will have to search high and low for." My voice heavy with sarcasm.

"Yeah, they were lovely."

Oh, he is serious. I bite my tongue, literally.

"Honestly though, you should get a spare key. I would have liked to lock up."

"Yeah good idea." My sarcasm is gone.

"I took your box with me, I hope you don't mind?"

My jaw drops. "You did what? Say that again?"

"Oh please don't be mad."

"Mad?" I am screaming, "I bloody love you."

The line goes dead silent.

"I mean that is fantastic Jose."

"I am a little confused right now. But you are not mad, is that right?"

"Yes, yes. Not mad, happy."

"Oh good, I had the weirdest feeling when I was leaving, something just didn't feel right. Maybe because I couldn't lock the door. So I thought I'd take the box with me, just for now, for safe keeping you know. I am at my parents' in Wenatchee, where I have the copy of the poster. I figured maybe they best be hanging out together for now."

"Buddy, your intuition is impeccable."

"First you love me, now you call me buddy?" Jose acts pretend hurt.

I gruff embarrassed. "Someone has been through my apartment. The door was open when I got home from work and someone has gone through all my stuff."

"I knew it!" exclaims Jose. "I thought I heard someone inside your apartment when I left the Lee's but I figured I was just being paranoid and left. I wish I had checked it out."

"Oh God Jose, I am happy you didn't check it out. The guy at Lisa's place had a gun."

"The guy at Lisa's place?" asks Jose.

"Wait. You were *at* the Lee's?"

"Yeah, they invited me in for coffee and cake when I was

leaving your place."

"Wow, I have never been invited in for coffee and cake." In fact the Lee's only speak to me when they have something to complain about; midnight showers not being allowed as the water pipes run through their bedroom wall, or mud left on the hallway carpet from my mountaineering boots. The complaints are many and colorful.

"Hey, what happened to Lisa?" Jose sounds concerned.

"Someone broke into her place, ransacked the place, and when she got home the guy was there waiting. He held her at gun point asking her about the poster, saying he needed it back."

"Wow. That is crazy."

"Yeah, she is pretty shaken up, but fine. She is with her parents. A car was following us after we left the hospital with Lisa…"

"Holy crap. Marta, I don't think you should be in your apartment right now."

"I am at Sonia's place."

"Good. Why don't you and Sonia come out here tomorrow?"

"Sonia, you want to go to Wenatchee tomorrow?" I ask, holding the phone away from my ear.

"Yeah… I guess that is a good idea."

I put the phone back to my ear. "We will be there. Text me the address."

"Leave early. It is less likely you will be followed if you leave before dawn."

"OK, see you tomorrow morning. I will text when we are on our way."

"And bring overnight stuff," adds Jose just as I am about to hang up. "Just in case it gets late."

"OK. Ciao."

***

I spend the night at Sonia's, sharing her double bed. Jill says a curt hello when she gets home before quickly locking herself in her room for the rest of the evening. Fine by me. I feel a lot better after speaking to Jose. Knowing the box is safe makes me feel safe. Maybe whoever is after the poster still doesn't know that Zygmunt is my grandfather. Sonia and I spend a long time discussing whether we should have called the police from my apartment, but we conclude that since it never occurred to us when we were there it was the right decision. Plus, I have reported it to Jose. He never said I should call the police station.

At 4:30 a.m. Sonia's alarm goes off.

"Alpine start," chirps Sonia as I pull the pillow over my head.

Sonia has breakfast ready when I get out of the shower, fried eggs, bacon, mushrooms, and avocado. I almost weep with joy. I can't remember the last time I had a home-cooked breakfast, the last time someone cooked breakfast for me. Sonia laughs at me when she sees my clean t-shirt, it is an old Ramones shirt with faded print and a hole in one armpit.

"I guess you didn't know we were going to Jose's when you packed."

I panic for a second, but my brain just doesn't care. I am so wound up with everything else going on that I simply don't care, I might as well have been naked covered in mud and I still wouldn't care.

"Well, I am guessing he didn't fall for my impeccable sense of fashion."

Sonia giggles. "Nope, that is for sure."

By 5:30 a.m. we are buckled into Sonia's car, showered, and

fed. It is still dark when we cross the 520 Bridge on our way to Highway 2. The roads are empty and as the sun starts to rise we have not seen a single car, it is almost too quiet. I want to stop at my favorite espresso hut just outside Index, it has beautiful views and the hut itself looks like something straight out of *The Sound of Music*, if they had espresso huts back then, probably not. But it is closed. Instead I have to wait until Starbucks in Leavenworth.

Leavenworth is a pretend German town, every building being in the style of Bavaria. In summer the town folk wander around in Lederhosen and pretty much every restaurant serves bratwurst or schnitzel. It is kitsch on steroids. Best thing about it is that the town has no German roots whatsoever, the town was struggling as the logging industry it depended upon faded, and to save the town the idea of making it Bavarian took root. They transformed a sleepy logging town into a tourist hub of everything Bavaria. It works pretty well as the backdrop is mountainous, making it almost believable that you are in the European Alps.

We go through the Starbucks drive through, the Bavarian Starbucks drive through. I order an Americano, it is so hot that when we arrive in Wenatchee half an hour later I still haven't been able to take one sip. The turn off to Jose's parents' farm is a little before town and we drive up a gravel road having to stop twice to open and close gates, before finally pulling up in front of a large white farm house with a wraparound porch. Jose is sitting on the steps waiting for us and when he sees us pull up he stands up to greet us.

It is still early morning and Jose leads us into a large warm kitchen where his mom is buzzing around stirring pots. She stops whatever it is she is cooking and pours us all coffee, taking my still full Starbucks cup out of my hand and replacing it with drip from her pot. I don't argue. She doesn't seem like the kind of lady you should argue with. Jose is about to protest on my behalf, but I wave my hand in the air in an *it-doesn't-matter* kind of way and he stops himself. We sit down at a large wooden farm table that is covered in scratches and dents.

"Mom, come join us."

Jose's mom turns the stove down and places lids on her pots and then joins us at the table. We sit in the kitchen for almost an hour chitchatting with Jose's mom, she is a small rotund lady with a heavy Latin-American accent and a big smile. I like her straight away, she comes across as a no-nonsense kind of woman. After three cups of coffee Jose finally stands up.

"I have some work to go through with these lovely ladies," he says, looking at his mom before leading us upstairs to what must have once upon a time been his childhood room. Remnants of childhood are still present in the form of model planes lining the shelf on the wall. But it looks more like an office with a large desk and a framed high school diploma, as well as his police academy diploma on the wall behind it. A single bed is pushed against the wall and it barely looks big enough to fit Jose.

"Wow, do you fit in there?" I ask.

"Nah, I sleep in one of the guestrooms out in the cottage," Jose is pointing at a smaller building visible through the window.

The cottage is still larger than my parents' house in Darrington had been.

"Can I use the computer?" asks Sonia, sitting down in front of it.

"Sure."

Jose moves the mouse to wake the screen up and Sonia types *current time in Warsaw Poland* into Google.

"Oh no," exclaims Sonia when the screen announces 6:30 p.m. "No one is going to answer at 6:30 p.m."

"Try anyway," says Jose.

We sit in silence as Sonia dials the number. "Hello, hello." Sonia nearly screams. "Do you speak English?"

For the next thirty minutes me and Jose strain our ears trying to hear both sides of the conversation, but end up being stuck nonetheless with only half of the dialogue. Sonia is taking notes on a single sheet of letter sized paper that she pulled out of Jose's printer without asking. I try to lean in to see what she is writing but she swats me away. When she finally hangs up, both Jose and I are seated on the edge of his abandoned single bed with anticipation written all over our faces.

Sonia smiles. "Great news Marta. You have a grandmother."

Chapter 13

"What do you mean I have a grandmother?"

"As in still alive," replies Sonia.

My jaw drops. I have a grandmother. An actual alive grandmother. Why has no one ever told me?

"The lady in the office had a quick look at their records. She didn't have much time, there was some sort of event going on. But she looked up Zygmunt and his wife Luiza is listed as still alive."

"Wow." Is all I muster to say, my head is spinning.

"She gave me Luiza's last listed address." Sonia is holding up the piece of paper she was scribbling on whilst on the phone. "It is in Katowice." Sonia stops briefly, her eyes fixated on mine. "They didn't know of your existence." Sonia's voice has gone soft, cautious almost. "The lady I spoke to was surprised when I told her. Your mom was mentioned, but all they had was that she moved to the States in 1983, five years after Zygmunt perished on K2. Maybe your grandmother doesn't know that you exist either?"

"It doesn't seem right, surely mom would have told me. Why wouldn't she tell me that her own mother is alive?" I say while the world around me is spinning. I can't get all the dots to connect and I feel dizzy.

"Oh and there was one more thing. Their records didn't mention that Zygmunt was climbing with the Americans like the webpage we found did. It just said he was soloing on K2 without a permit."

"Maybe Google Translate got it wrong," I reply. "There sure is no mention of Zygmunt in any of the American accounts."

Jose gets the last news clipping out of his desk drawer and sits down at the desk. "Maybe this article will shed some more light," he says, typing one letter at a time using only his left index finger.

God, this will take forever, I think as I watch him press key after key. One single strand of tap, tap, tap, not the clicking of a keyboard that you get from a skilled typist. After a painfully long time during which no one speaks, Jose finishes typing the article. Google Translate does its thing and we try to decipher the poorly translated article.

"Well this definitely mentions the Americans. It says Zygmunt was invited by his friend Mr. Hawkins," says Jose. "I think that for some reason someone is doing their best at covering up the fact that Zygmunt went to K2 on an American expedition, and it appears they must have some sort of power because both the American and Polish records are omitting the fact that Zygmunt was on the summit with Mr. Hawkins." Jose stops talking, waiting for me or Sonia to say something.

I am still trying to get my brain to catch up so I stay silent, leaving Sonia to dive into the discussion. "I agree. I think we need to find Murtaza Jarwar, or his relatives if he is no longer alive, and we need to contact Luiza. They may be the only people left with any clues."

Sonia pushes Jose out of the way and sits down at the computer while Jose reaches in under his old single bed and gets my box out. My heart skips a beat at seeing it again after believing it was lost forever. He places the article he has just copied in the box before handing it over to me. I open it, everything is in there. I take out the piton then close the box again and tell Jose to put it somewhere safe. He slides it back under the bed.

"I have emailed the Alpine Club of Pakistan to ask about Murtaza Jarwar and I found a number for a Luiza Pyszka in Katowice at the address we got," says Sonia.

"Wow, Sonia you are a machine," I say impressed. Sonia

hands me her phone and the number. I am about to protest but decide there is no point, so instead I dial the number with shaking hands.

"Luiza," says an old voice on the other end of the line.

"Hello, my name is Marta," my voice is shaky.

"*Cześć?*" the old voice on the other end replies.

"Yes, hello, do you speak English?"

Click. The line goes dead.

"I guess my grandmother does not speak English." I am both relieved and disappointed.

We decide to go for a walk to clear our heads. I put the piton in my pocket and we head outside in the sunshine. The sun feels warm, like proper spring sun. Not that weak wintery sun that still makes up the intermittent sunshine in Seattle. Here on the other side of the mountain range it actually feels like summer is on its way. Jose leads the way through his parents' apple plantations, and while the trees are not yet in full bloom the buds are plump and ready to explode into a kaleidoscope of white and pink at any time. A few have already burst into white flowers and petals are floating to the ground.

"It is gorgeous when it is all in bloom," says Jose.

"I can imagine," I reply.

"Marta, you need to go to Poland. She is your family. The only family you have left really." Sonia is nagging me.

"Yeah… But why has my mom never mentioned her…" No matter how I twist it in my mind the only conclusion I can come up with is that my grandmother must be an awful person.

"Marta, are you even listening?" Sonia's voice interrupts my train of thought.

"Oh sorry, no what were you saying?"

"I have always wanted to go to Europe and I have this enforced time off. I can come with you if you want?" Jose looks uncertain, almost like he is scared of rejection.

I smile. "Jose it is lovely of you to offer. But I can't afford to."

Sonia takes over. "Marta, you really haven't been listening to anything that we have been saying, have you?"

"I can lend you the money for the tickets if you like. I have a lot of air mile points, so I wouldn't really be out of pocket anyhow." Jose looks at his feet instead of me.

It makes me smile, not as self-assured as he pretends I think. "I don't know Jose. I mean, I don't know when I would be able to pay you back. It is hard to save with the payments for my mom's nursing home."

"It is OK, I don't mind. You can take as long as you need. Like I said, it is points anyway, so it really isn't a big deal if you never pay me back. Years of visiting family in Mexico have its upsides."

"Well I would imagine it has many upsides. Tacos, cervezas, sunshine, a warm ocean, beaches -" I would have kept going, but Jose cuts me off.

"Yes, yes, of course," he is laughing. "But I do have a lot of points, so really it wouldn't be a problem at all."

"Maybe. If I can get the time off work."

"I already asked Karen." Sonia chips in.

"You what?"

"I called her earlier to check, just in case. She said you have a lot of annual leave up your sleeve, so if you want to she agreed you can have a couple of weeks off starting Monday."

I want to be mad at Sonia for meddling at work. But I can't find the energy nor the will, I know she is doing all of this for me. Instead I give her a tight hug.

"Wow, no snarky reply? What have you done to the Marta I know?" jokes Sonia.

***

We spend the afternoon Googling Poland, Katowice, translators, flights, and accommodation. The mood has shifted from serious to joyful. I have never been outside the US, in fact I have never been outside the state of Washington. Sonia has many times threatened to kidnap me and take me to Oregon to climb Mt. Hood, only a little over a four-hour drive away. But we haven't made it yet. I also feel oddly proud of the fact that I have never ventured outside the Evergreen State. I protect my disposition with lines like, *I don't need to leave, everything anyone could wish for is here*, or, *I still have some 300 mountains to climb in Washington before I move on to a new state.*

Dinner time rolls around and Jose's mom has cooked us all dinner. Jose's dad joins us, he is back from a day working in the orchards. Jose's mom informs us that she has set up the guest room next to Jose's in the cottage for me and Sonia. I am not sure if she knows about me and Jose, but Jose doesn't let on, so I smile kindly when she shows us the bed in our shared room. As soon as she leaves the cottage, Jose picks up my small bag and carries it in to his room. Sonia gives me a cheeky grin and winks.

We sleep late on Sunday. We then spend hours at Jose's parents' kitchen table eating freshly baked bread and fried eggs prepared by Jose's mom, and drinking endless cups of coffee. When we finally go upstairs to check Jose's emails, he had emailed Alaska Airlines about using his points as we couldn't work out which airlines we could use or how to book using the points, it is already past 11 a.m. No email from Alaska Airlines yet, I guess it was a little much to expect that they would work throughout the night. Sonia checks her mail next and lets out a yelp of excitement.

"Murtaza. He is alive." Sonia can't sit still, bouncing up and down on the chair as she gives us snippets of information while she reads the email. "He still lives in Rawalpindi. He is 68 years old. I have his email address," she turns and looks at us smiling. Sonia had emailed the Alpine Club of Pakistan the day before to ask about Murtaza. By the sounds of things they have replied. "I think you should email him now."

I type a rather long email to Murtaza explaining who I am and that I am seeking some information to better understand who my grandfather had been, as I never got a chance to get to know him, purposely edging around his death and the mysterious photo of him on the summit of K2. I press send and feel edgy. I am impatient for a response, despite knowing it is late in Pakistan and it is unlikely I will be receiving a response before tomorrow.

We spend another few hours in the kitchen, Jose's mom buzzing around filling our coffee cups and placing an assortment of baked good on the table with regular intervals. Sunshine is streaming in through the windows and the yellow walls add to the warm homely feeling. It reminds me of being at home with my parents, spending a Sunday afternoon doing nothing in particular in the kitchen. Just the three of us enjoying each other's company. My stomach fills with warmth as I allow myself to daydream that perhaps this is my family now, imagining a future with Jose by my side.

My phone buzzes in my pocket. The screen informs me I have one new email and I open up my Gmail. Murtaza must be a night owl, or perhaps an early bird depending on which way you look at it, because it is a reply to the email I sent him a little while ago that has set off my phone. I start reading while Jose and Sonia continue to chat, unaware of my distraction.

> *Dear Marta,*
> *I am delighted to hear from you. Zygmunt, your grandfather, was a very close friend of mine and I have spent many years wondering what became of his*

daughter. He was very fond of Aniela. I am happy to learn she has a daughter and overjoyed that you found me. Zygmunt was not only a very strong climber, but also a big hearted man who touched those around him and lit up their lives with his positive energy and joyful disposition.

There are so many questions I would like to ask you and so many memories I would like to share with you. In fact, I would be honoured if you would come visit me in Rawalpindi, I know it is a big ask, but there are so many things I would like to share with you. I understand this may not be possible, but I feel both you and I would benefit greatly by meeting in person.

Best regards,

Murtaza Jarwar

"Hey, have a read of this," I say and hand my phone over to Sonia.

"Oh my, Marta, this is fabulous. You must go," she says before passing my phone on to Jose.

"I think he is trying to tell you something," says Jose.

"I had the same feeling," I reply.

"Wait, let me read it again." Sonia grabs the phone out of Jose's hand.

"You know what, I think you guys are right," she says after staring at the screen for a long time. "Even more reason you need to go."

"I can't go to Pakistan for God's sake."

"Why not?" Jose taking Sonia's side annoys me a little.

"I can't afford to. It is miles and miles away. I don't know the first thing about Pakistan. I am scared of heights." The thought of going to Pakistan is making my heart race.

Sonia scoffs, "Marta. You are not scared of heights. You

are the person least scared of heights on this planet. Flying for a really long time maybe, but heights no."

PART II – Pakistan

"The word adventure has gotten overused.
For me, when everything goes wrong,
that's when adventure starts."
– Yvon Chouinard

Chapter 14

"Kacper," says the young man who looks to be in his twenties, his cheeks are covered in pimples and long bangs cover one of his eyes.

He is waiting for us at Katowice bus station. The station is new looking, all glass and steel. It surprises me, I am not sure what I had expected.

"Nice to meet you," replies Jose stretching out his arm. "Thank you for meeting with us. We will need you to translate once we get to Marta's grandmother's house."

"Twenty US dollars an hour right?"

"Yes, of course."

Jose had found Kacper on the Internet and organized for him to translate for us. Kacper leads us over to a row of taxis parked in front of the bus station. A neat row of white cars with Echo-Taxi written in red and yellow down the side.

"Where to?" asks the driver in broken English.

Jose pulls out the piece of paper with my grandmother's address and hands it to the driver. We drive through town, it starts out with old stone buildings mixed in with new modern office blocks, but as we get further out of town the landscape changes to abandoned industrial buildings, smoke stacks shooting up towards the sky. After thirty minutes the taxi draws to a stop in front of a small cottage. It could do with a lick of paint. The current yellow paint is flaking off in big pieces like sunburnt skin. The yard is neat, cropped grass and rose bushes lining the edge along the fence with big pink flowers that have just started to droop.

My heart is racing inside my chest as I stand in front of the door. I press the doorbell and hold my breath when I hear the sound of someone slowly dragging their feet towards the door. I almost chicken out, but Jose is holding on to my hand with such force I don't think I could get away even if I tried. When the door opens I am met by an old and tired looking lady, but her eyes are bright and the same color green as my mother's.

"Hi. My name is Marta. I believe you are my grandmother." I am shifting my weight from one leg to the other as I wait for Kacper to translate.

Luiza's eyes go wide and she puts her hand over her mouth. She leans against the doorway for a while before finding her voice. "Chodź do środka." She gestures for us to step inside.

The house is small and filled with knickknacks. Almost like a museum everything is from a different era, but tidy and clean. I wonder if this is the same home that my mother grew up in, if everything is just as it was when she was a small child. Sun rays dance across the floor in the living room and a large ginger cat is sleeping on the brown velvet sofa. Luiza shoos it off before inviting us to sit down. Again, I wondered if my mom have once sat in this very spot, and I touch the brown velvet feeling its fabric, rough with age, underneath my hand.

"How is Aniela?" Luiza asks after a moment's silence.

I wait patiently while Kacper translates. "She is not doing too well. She is in a nursing home with dementia."

Luiza's eyes tear up and she dabs at them with a tissue. "I didn't know I had a granddaughter," she say's looking in my direction but not meeting my eyes.

"I would like to hear more about you and my grandfather. I understand he was quite the mountaineer?" I purposely steer the conversation away from my mother, not sure I want to hear what drove them apart.

Luiza clears her throat. "I met Zygmunt here in Katowice in 1953. He was painting the smokestacks of my father's factory. Back then many young climbers worked painting smokestacks. It made sense, they knew the required rope skills and could complete the job quickly for a decent sum of money. Money they used to fund climbing trips. I was only eighteen at the time and fell head over heels for Zygmunt, his broad shoulders, wild smile, and icy-blue eyes had me enthralled. His hair was longer than the other boys in town and it was bleached blond by the sun. To me he was different and exotic. My father, however, was not pleased. We were wealthy and my father was a member of the Communist Party. Zygmunt came from a poor family, his parents worked in the factories and got by on government rations." Luiza stops and dabs at her eyes again. "They lived in an apartment block without heating or indoor toilets. Zygmunt's father was a drunk, which was not unusual, many people turned to alcohol as the reality of everyday life was simply just too grim to bear."

Kacper is struggling to keep up, translating almost on top of Luiza talking. By now tears are streaming down Luiza's cheeks, a quiet cry, as if someone has accidently left the tap on. They show no sign of slowing down or stopping, and she lets them flow, only occasionally lifting the tissue to her cheeks. She is hugging herself as she speaks.

"I think Zygmunt turned to the mountains not only to escape the poverty, but also the fists of his drunken father. I was madly in love and couldn't believe that such an adventurous man could find me attractive. I fell pregnant almost immediately after we started dating… So we were married within the year of meeting each other. Any other solution was unthinkable. My father had had higher hopes for me, his only daughter, than a dirt-bag climber in worn clothes and no permanent address. He provided us with a small cottage at the edge of town, but he did little else for us, barely acknowledging the baby girl once she was born — your mother." Luiza stops and looks up at me. But she averts her eyes before I manage to lock on to hers.

"However, as Zygmunt's fame grew so did my father's opinion of him. Once he was hailed as a hero of the Polish people my father was quick to point out to his party friends who it was his daughter had married." Luiza stands up and disappears into an adjoining room.

We wait in silence not sure what she is doing. Jose, who is sitting next to me on the brown velvet sofa reaches over and squeezes my hand while Kacper is wriggling uncomfortably in his chair. Luiza returns with a tray full of cups and saucers with intricate paintings of violets, and a large matching pot of tea. She pours us all strong black cups of tea without asking. I watch Jose wince as he takes a sip, not accustomed to any hot drink lacking in milk and sugar. But he politely keeps sipping at the hot brew.

Luiza sits down and starts back up. "Zygmunt was smitten by his daughter and adored everything about her, spoiling her at every opportunity. But he was away for long periods of time and the job of raising the child fell largely on me. Zygmunt didn't have to witness the trials and tribulations of raising a child." Luiza wipes at her cheeks with the tissue. Her jaws tighten and she is steeling her gaze. "At times I would get so mad at the child, so mad to be left alone with all the responsibility and never knowing if Zygmunt would return, so mad that I would take it out on the child." Luiza looks me in the eyes for the first time since we arrived, her green eyes meeting my pale blue ones, perhaps to see if I will recoil in disgust.

I don't, but it does seem odd to me that she keeps referring to my mother as the child rather than by name, as if she belonged to someone else. Perhaps it is a defense mechanism to ward off the guilt. Luiza sits in silence for a couple of minutes, perhaps to give me time to react or say something, but I don't say anything, I am not sure what I am supposed to say.

"I didn't have a close relationship with my daughter to start with, and once Zygmunt died it deteriorated completely." Luiza is fingering the edge of her apron. "I think Zygmunt's death may have been my fault."

"Oh surely not," I say as soon as Kacper has translated.

"Well, my daughter thought so. She cut all ties with me after Zygmunt's death. She moved to Warsaw and never contacted me again. It completely broke my heart when I found out from a friend that she had gotten married, and once she moved to America I had no way of knowing where she was. I wasn't even sure if she was alive." Luiza again puts her tissue to her eyes in an attempt to stem the flow. "I was too proud and stubborn to try to restore the ties, I believed she would come around, so I never even tried to contact her. Then I found out it was too late, the boat had sailed and my daughter was gone forever."

"How can Zygmunt's death possibly be your fault? He was in Pakistan." I ask.

Luiza leans forward and lets out a loud sob. Kacper looks terrified and starts making motions to leave, but Jose gives him a stern look and he sits back down.

Luiza never looks back up, her eyes fixated on her lap. "Zygmunt was against the Polish regime, with the USSR puppeteering the Polish politicians. But the only way to get a permit to leave the country and receive funding for climbing expeditions was to spy for the government. It wasn't like sending U-boats into the Baltic Sea or anything, it was more a listening exercise. Befriend other climbers, preferably American, and listen to their stories from home. Maybe ask a question or two and then report it back to the Polish government upon your return. Zygmunt was never fond of this arrangement and he often complained about it loudly in the house, and maybe whilst swinging from the ropes high on the factory smokestacks with his climbing friends. But never anywhere else. As it turned out Zygmunt was great at making foreign friends. Only he actually became their friend and Mr. Hawkins was one of his most cherished friends. Zygmunt often referred to him as his American brother. I suspected that he had stopped spying and was making up stories for the government after his trips. I feared that he may have switched sides, but hoping he was not so foolish, as it may put our family at risk. But then one day I thought that if I told the government my fears and they believed he was giving information to the Americans he would never again be granted a permit to leave and he would be forced to stay at home with me and our daughter; helping me with the troubled child. So I hinted to my father, telling him that Zygmunt being invited on an American expedition seemed too good to be true."

Luiza takes a deep pained breath and whispers, "It must have worked because later I learned that five days after I hinted my suspicions to my father, Zygmunt died on K2. My father never liked Zygmunt and I guess he finally found a way to get rid of him. It was never my intention. I loved Zygmunt dearly. I just wanted him at home. I thought my father would handle it differently. Maybe I was naïve." She stops talking.

We sit for a long time, everyone in their own heads, apart from Kacper who looks like he is about to run for the door given any indication that he is allowed to leave. I stand up and Kacper leaps off his chair. He looks desperately disappointed when I sit back down next to my grandmother. I wrap my arm around her tortured figure. "I am sure it is not your fault, it is something much bigger than your talk to your father that caused Zygmunt's death."

Luiza breathes out deeply, I can almost feel the weight lifting off her shoulders. She pats my hand that is resting on her shoulder.

"We best get going Marta." Jose's voice is soft.

I stand up and Luiza leads us to the front door. We hoover in the doorway not sure of what to say.

"Please find out the truth for me?" Hope is dancing across Luiza's large emerald eyes, eyes that remind me so much of my mother's.

"I will," I reply and give Luiza a tight hug.

Kacper looks relieved once we are inside the taxi on our way back to the bus station, and right out giddy when we pay him before we board the bus back to Warsaw. Only once the bus is moving and Katowice is disappearing behind us, being replaced by fields and old farmhouses, do I realize that I never did ask if Luiza's home is the same one that my mother grew up in.

Chapter 15

"I think we are the only foreigners," I whisper to Jose as we are boarding our final flight from Dubai to Pakistan.

"Yeah, I guess Pakistan isn't high on most travelers' wish list. It isn't exactly known for its white sandy beaches or fun nightlife." He giggles.

I laugh, I am not sure what on earth I have gotten myself into.

After take-off I notice that all the other female passengers go into the bathrooms in their western clothes and exit wearing beautiful salwar kameez's. The traditional dress in Pakistan with scarves loosely wrapped around their heads.

"Jose, should I be wearing a scarf?" I ask.

He looks around. "Maybe."

"But I don't have a scarf." Panic is bubbling up.

"It is OK, we will work it all out once we get there," Jose says, and I try to settle down. But I have a nagging feeling of dread in the pit of my stomach.

When we land at Benazir Bhutto International Airport it is nothing like I had expected. It seems new and efficient. We go through customs and passport control quickly without incident and in the arrivals hall stands a man with our names on a sign. He is young, too young to be Murtaza, and when I say hello he introduces himself as Anam, the driver Murtaza has organized to pick us up.

When we step outside the air-conditioned airport we walk into a wall of hot air. It is like stepping right into a sauna. I have never experienced anything like it before. It is so hot and dry I find it hard to breath and it is a big relief once we are safely inside the air-conditioned car.

"How do people live in this heat?" I whisper to Jose.

"Hey, I am from Mexico, this isn't too bad." Jose smiles

back at me.

I look out the window as we travel through the city. It is still dark outside, but light is pouring out of apartment blocks and people are walking along the road in traditional dress. Most of the buildings are modern and I am a little surprised how modern and well developed it all feels. So foreign from the picture that the news media has painted for me before I left. As we near our hotel, Anam points out the Faisal Mosque. Its large angular dome shape and four spires are lit up and it is dominating the skyline, reminding me of something out of *Arabian nights*. Anam pulls up in front of a large iron gate and a guard gets up to pull it open. Behind the gate is a small but lovely guesthouse, flowering bushes lining the wall. The air smells of flowers and grilled meat, and something else that I can't put my finger on. It isn't an unpleasant smell, just different. I guess it is the smell of Pakistan. So different from the wet salty smell of Seattle. When we enter the foyer a breakfast buffet is in full swing in the adjoining dining hall.

"Go eat while I sign you in," says Anam.

I am thrilled to try the curried eggs and the bread, which I keep referring to as tortillas, Jose correcting me every time saying they are called rotis and are in fact nothing like a tortilla. I guess he would know. There is a plethora of tropical fruits, some I have never tried before, and the mango is so sweet and juicy I have two full plates.

"So, the driver isn't back for another two hours to pick us up. Do you want to see if we can find you a scarf before then?" asks Jose.

"Yes, but do you think it is safe outside those gates?"

"Only one way to find out," replies Jose. But when he sees my worried face he quickly adds, "I am just kidding. The hotel can probably get us a driver."

The hotel can get us a driver and we go to the Bazar. I had

imagined the Bazar to be a bustling marketplace full of noise, life, and smells. Spice vendors and copper lanterns, like something out of *Aladdin*. Instead it is a large building with small glass-fronted shops each selling a variety of salwar kameez's. There are mannequins draped in bedazzled pant suits and scarfs in every shop window.

"Jose, I am going to look like a Christmas tree."

Jose laughs and points at a particular glittery contraption in one of the windows. "What about this one? You can probably land a role in a Bollywood movie in that one."

"Not enough skin," I counter, pushing the door to the shop open.

Inside there is a jumble of salwar kameez's, rack after rack of colorful contraptions. The shop smells of incense and a jolly man eager to help is following me around as I look through the racks.

***

I am dressed in a beige salwar kameez when Anam returns to take us to Murtaza's house. The traditional pant suit hangs loose on my thin frame. Every inch of skin is covered apart from my hands and my feet, which are thankfully in airy flip flops. A thin matching scarf is draped around my head and shoulders. Anam smiles at my outfit and I am actually pretty pleased with it myself. The heat feels less oppressive in my loose clothing. I want to hold Jose's hand but he gives me a stern look when I reach for his hand, and I remember that we aren't supposed to publically display any signs of affection. So instead I stand there looking lost.

Once inside the car Jose quickly squeezes my hand before just as quickly letting go again. I appreciate the gesture even if it does nothing to settle my nerves. The drive takes an hour and

114

the scenery changes from the wide orderly roads of Islamabad to highly trafficked streets with car horns beeping and mopeds zooming past. Street stalls are lining the road, and people, hundreds of people everywhere.

"Where are all the women?" I ask Jose.

"At home cooking for their men," replies Jose, and winks at me.

"Oh," is all I manage to reply.

Anam slows down on a tree-lined street and comes to a complete stop outside a small house with a lovely garden. Outside the front door in the shade of a tree sits an old man who stands up as we get out of the car.

"Marta." He walks towards me with his hand stretched out. I shake his hand and his smile is so infectious I can't stop grinning at this joyful man that exudes positive energy.

"You have your grandfather's face," he smiles, "those blue eyes and high cheekbones."

I have always wished for my mother's big green eyes, but right now I am overjoyed at my pale blue eyes that are so light they sometimes appear colorless. Murtaza shows us to a set of wicker seats in the garden.

"We must take tea," he announces and disappears inside to fetch the teapot and cups.

He chats to Anam for a while offering him tea before sending him away, and finally sitting down with us. He pours us cups of sweet milky tea, much to Jose's relief. Murtaza asks me about my life. Where I work? What life in America is like? What did my parents do? Finally, he says, "It is such a shame your grandfather never got to see what a beautiful granddaughter he has."

"Talking of my grandfather," I intersect, "what can you tell me about him?"

"He was the most honorable man I have ever met. At the

time life in Pakistan was hard. It still is I suppose. But back then both Pakistan and Poland were poor countries and we found in each other a unity over the hard lives we were both living. Back then most climbers came from wealthy nations and saw us Pakistanis as backwards. But not Zygmunt. He came from the same poverty I was experiencing, and rather than treating me like a servant he treated me like a brother.

"Us Pakistanis were employed to carry loads, to cook food, and to set up camps, but Zygmunt wanted more. He carried the same loads as me and invited me to climb with him, where other expeditions would never have dreamt of allowing a Pakistani to come high with them on the mountain."

Murtaza pauses, but I remain silent so he takes back up. "We climbed on Nanga Parbat together in 1970. We got very close to the summit, but it was so cold, the snow was up to our waists, and we had run out of fuel. We knew that to push on was a death sentence. Zygmunt insisted that the most important achievement was to come home alive. If Zygmunt hadn't been there to turn me around I may still be a permanent fixture on the mountain. I was young and eager.

"It took eight years until I got to meet your grandfather again, when he came to climb K2. But we kept in touch via letters, hundreds of letters. We had become brothers. Most of our letters talked of the lack of trust we put in our governments and about our climbing feats and ambitions. I kept climbing with other climbing teams arriving in Pakistan. I summited Nanga Parbat, Broad Peak, and Gasherbrum 2, before Zygmunt returned. K2 was meant to be our dream come true. Finally, summiting a big mountain together. Zygmunt had been invited to join the American expedition and he had negotiated that I would be climbing alongside him. But promises made at sea level rarely hold true at altitude. On summit day I was not to partake in the first summit team, instead having to hold off in

116

high camp with two other members. We would be the second summit team. Zygmunt was furious and disappointed in the American team, many of whom he trusted and believed to be his friends. That next day Zygmunt lost his life and I never tried for the summit, instead I returned down the mountain when the second summit team pushed on up, trying their luck. I had lost my passion for climbing. It left my body the minute I learned of Zygmunt's death. I have not climbed since."

"What do you think happened?" I ask.

"I will tell you all my thoughts during our hike," smiles Murtaza. His facial expression saying it all, I can almost hear him think, *patience-is-a-virtue*.

I feel a little disappointed when Anam returns and I have learned so little about my grandfather's death. Anam takes us straight to the Alpine Club of Pakistan so we can register for our hike, and so I can pick up any documentation they have about my grandfather's climb in 1978.

The secretary sits behind a shiny dark wooden desk and the white walls are filled with photographs and maps of the Karakoram and Himalayan Mountains. His smile is stern and he goes through a long list of regulations and recommendations, giving Anam displeased looks as he explains our itinerary. Turns out Anam is not just our driver, but also our guide for the trek, and our cook. This displeases the secretary. He tries over and over again to explain that we really need at least one if not two official guides, and a dedicated cook with an assistant. But Anam stays firm and slides an envelope across the table. The secretary opens it, twists his mouth, and stamps our paperwork. Anam hands over a second envelope, again the secretary looks inside before opening a drawer. He takes out an A4-sized yellow envelope and hands it over to Anam. After the exchange of envelopes, we all shake hands and the secretary wishes us the best of luck. The stern face lights up with what looks like a genuine smile.

"That has got to be one of the oddest experiences of my life," I exclaim as we get outside. I am posing under the white sign that reads *Alpine Club of Pakistan* in blue letters while Jose is taking my picture.

Anam smiles at me and hands over both our stamped permits and the yellow envelope and says, "Let's go make photocopies of your permits and passports. It will make the trip to Skardu a lot smoother."

Chapter 16

It is 11:30 p.m. when I hear a soft knock on the door. I am awake, jetlag had seen me go to bed at 6 p.m., and then being bright awake again at 10 p.m. I nudge Jose. "Are you awake?"

"Uhu…" he grumbles.

"There is someone at the door," I whisper.

Jose groans and gets out of bed, pulling on pants and a sweater before opening the door. I can hear Anam's hurried voice whispering and Jose responding. It sounds serious, but I can't make out what they are saying. The door closes and Jose comes over.

"Marta, we need to go now," Jose is still whispering.

"Go where?" I ask.

"We need to leave for Skardu now. I didn't quite get why, but it is urgent. So get up and pack."

"OK, OK, no need to be bossy." A nervous smile decorating my face.

I swing my legs out of bed and start sorting through the pile of clothes on the floor, where I had emptied the entire contents of my duffle bag.

"This doesn't seem right Jose. We are not meant to leave until tomorrow morning. What if Anam is part of the Taliban and wants to kidnap us," I continue as I am getting dressed.

"Well, we have already chosen to put all our trust in Murtaza, and if he trusts Anam, so will we."

We sneak out of our room carrying our bags through the dark hallway. At reception Anam is speaking softly to the receptionist that looks newly woken up. I pay for our room in US dollars, as per Anam's instructions. I am still nervous and I wanted to use my Visa card, thinking that leaving a little trace, something saying *Marta-was-here* would be good. But when I got my Visa card out Anam shook his head and said, "Cash."

I am too spooked to argue and considering Jose seems calm I do as I am told. When we get into Anam's car Murtaza is nowhere to be seen, but as soon as we close the doors Anam says, "Don't worry, we are picking Murtaza up now, he will explain," before waving his hand at the guard sitting on a chair next to the big metal gates, which he now stands up to open.

The streets are dark and empty, only the street lights shed illumination. It strikes me that Islamabad is very dark and quiet at night time. No lit-up office buildings where people are working endless hours of unpaid overtime, or noisy bars with neon signs. Just a quiet darkness, like nights are intended to be. Anam slows down and I can see light spilling out behind the curtains of a tea shop. When we stop the door swings open, light pouring out the open doorway like a beacon in the otherwise pitch dark neighborhood. Murtaza is shaking a man's hand and embracing him in a bear hug before getting in the front seat of our car, a small bag tucked under his arm.

"Sorry about this." Murtaza is straining his neck to look at us in the backseat. "I didn't mean to drag you out of bed, but I had some unpleasant visitors." His earlier joyfulness is now replaced by a furrow in his brow. "The secretary at the Alpine Club called me to say that three Americans accompanied by a Pakistani army officer had visited the office shortly after you guys left. They had asked about our permits and thankfully he had said that we would be trekking to the basecamp of Nanga Parbat, camping at Fairy Meadows, leaving the day after tomorrow. He then called me asking for a bribe to stick to his story. I paid up, hoping the lie would give us a day's head start of whoever is on our tail. But then at about 8 p.m. a dark car with three westerners and a Pakistani army officer stopped in front of my house. I hid in the closet as they rang the doorbell and banged on the door. They spent two full hours by my front door before getting in their car and leaving. I packed a bag, called Anam, and told him to meet me a few blocks over. I snuck out the back door and through my neighbor's garden. Anam took me to my friend's tea shop, and after a few cups of tea we decided to leave tonight."

I can feel a chill travel down my spine. "Maybe they were from the embassy," I ponder.

"I don't think so," replies Murtaza. "The car had no number plates, and I think they were armed."

Murtaza's voice is a little shaky. I long for that infectious smile instead.

We travel in silence; I think I even doze off a couple of times. Murtaza points out the suburb where Osama Bin Laden was caught and killed as we drive through Abbottabad a couple of hours after leaving Islamabad. We are stopped at several check points, where Anam hands over the photocopies of our passports and trekking permits before being waved on through. By the time the sun is rising we are already a long way along the Karakoram Highway, and Anam pulls over at a tiny little village clinging to the mountainside high above the Indus River. A road side tea-stall serves us steaming cups of sweet milky tea and packets of stale cookies. My stomach is grumbling and I dream of the curried eggs from the previous morning. When we first sit down I am shivering in the cold mountain air, but soon the sun is high enough to reach the valley and I am yet again baking hot.

A few hours after our sparse breakfast we pull into Chilas. My guidebook describes it as an unwelcoming town, in particular to foreign women, and I am thankful for the black window shades that Anam placed in the backseat windows before we left from our early morning breakfast stop.

I am peeking through the shades looking at the dusty streets lined with men in the traditional dress of kurtas, woolen Chitrali caps, and long beards. No one is smiling, and by now I have gotten used to there being absolutely no sign of any women young or old. Jose, who is peeking out his side of the car, must have thought the same as me as he says, "I see why there are no bars in Pakistan. It would be frightfully boring since it would just be a bunch of men."

Anam is idling in front of a sign that reads 'Hotel Chilas' and a man scurries out to open the gates. Safely inside Murtaza opens the door for me and informs us we will take breakfast here. A minivan is parked in front and inside the restaurant is a group of tourists. I instantly name them *the Germans* as they are all wearing shorts with white socks and sandals. The women are in tight V-neck t-shirts and shorts, all oblivious to the displeased glares of the local staff.

I am still poking fun at the Germans, who we by now have realized are in fact Russian, when a bowl of hot steaming broth with floating bits of sinewy goat is placed in front of me. I am famished, and despite the goat more resembling chewing gum than meat I eat every last bit of it. Anam is on his mobile phone again and Murtaza has gone outside to pray.

"Jose, what do you think those Americans wanted?" I whisper.

"I don't know, but Murtaza seems convinced they are up to no good. I am sure he will explain once we are on the trail." He smiles and squeezes my hand under the table.

When we drive out of Chilas, I am pleased to leave this dusty unsmiling town behind. We are stopped at yet another police barricade and Anam spends a long time talking to the police. In the end Murtaza gets out and squeezes in the back with us. A police officer and his giant rifle sit down in the front seat, his gun leaning over his shoulder pointing straight at me. Murtaza tells us the police insisted we need an escort for this next section of the Karakoram Highway, but really the police officer just needs a ride. So no need to worry. That big gun pointing right at me does make me worry, however. In fact, I am more worried about the policeman in our car than any threat he is meant to protect us from.

About an hour out of town Murtaza points out the trailhead for the hike to Nanga Parbat basecamp. The mountain that Murtaza and my grandfather had climbed high on some forty-four years ago, forging their deep friendship. A little further on Anam pulls over at a viewpoint in response to Murtaza's insistence. The police officer looks annoyed when we all tumble out of the cramped backseat, happy to get to stretch our legs. A sign reads '*Look to your left, Nanga Parbat, height 8,126 meters, 26,660 feet.*'

Murtaza looks serious. "The sign used to say Killer Mountain Nanga Parbat, but they painted over the killer mountain bit after last year's terrorist attack at basecamp."

"Yeah, I can see why," I reply.

"What happened?" asks Jose.

"A year ago militants dressed in scout uniforms stormed basecamp at night and killed ten climbers and one local guide. They took all their valuables and passports before lining them up and shooting them."

I look across at the mountain, the scenery is breathtaking and it is hard to believe such an ugly incident plagued this stunning mountain a little less than a year ago.

We climb a small rock outcropping to gain a better view while Pakistani trucks motor by, ornate decorations covering every inch of the trucks, making them look more like pieces of art than a mode of transportation. The sun catches all the little pieces of metal making them sparkle like Christmas ornaments.

"So why was it called killer mountain?" asks Jose.

Both Murtaza and I start to respond. I stop and let Murtaza explain. "It is a fickle mountain, claiming many climbers' lives."

At the turn-off for Skardu we say goodbye both to the police officer and the Karakoram Highway. Here the world's three highest mountain ranges, the Himalaya, the Karakoram, and the Hindu Kush, are lining the sky, competing for grandeur; towering peaks in all directions.

The road to Skardu is impossibly beautiful. Stark rocky mountains with little lush oases of green where glacial-melt waterfalls tumble down towards the Indus River at the valley floor. Along these water-fed oases spring villages, clinging to the mountainside with terraced vegetable and wheat gardens. Fruit trees are plump with ripe apricots and cherries. Little rock dwellings and people milling about tending to their gardens and goats, all to a backdrop of snow-capped peaks. Here we spot women for the first time since arriving in Pakistan. Dressed in colorful salwar kameez's they are tending to the fields. We stop in one little village, sitting in the breezy shade by a creek feasting on rotis and mangoes. At one point Anam stops in the middle of the road and Murtaza and Anam jump out of the car and climb the roadside apricot trees. They pillage them for fresh fruit like two school boys and pass down handfuls of fresh sweet fruits.

When we finally roll into Skardu the mosque is calling for evening prayers and the sun is setting. Our skin is caked in dust and the longest road trip of my life is finally over.

Chapter 17

When we check-in to Hotel Masherbrum the dining hall is buzzing with activity, rugged looking mountaineers hovering over large metal buffet trays of curried meat, vegetables, lentils, and rice. Murtaza urges us to go get food while he checks us in.

I feel a little intimidated by these people, here to climb something big. Bigger than my biggest mountain for sure. But Jose, who is oblivious to anything in regards to climbing, strikes up a conversation and we find out they are a large Spanish team here to climb Broad Peak, K2's little brother. Sitting only five miles away from K2 it is the world's twelfth largest mountain. They are excited and very friendly, but speak little English. Jose switches to Spanish and translates for me, but I still feel like I am missing most of the conversation.

The Spaniards excitement is contagious, and for the first time I feel excited about our upcoming trek, rather than nervous anticipation. I sit down on the bed in the small room with two single beds and a tiny balcony and pull out the yellow envelope from the Alpine Club. I want to be alone, and with Jose in the shower this is about as alone as I am going to get in the foreseeable future. The first piece of paper is a copy of the climbing permit. It lists the names of five Americans as well as my grandfather. In a different section Murtaza is listed as a high altitude porter. I wonder if my grandfather had seen this permit, I am sure he would turn in his grave if he knew Murtaza had not been listed as an equal expedition member. I feel triumphant however, finally hard evidence that my grandfather was indeed part of the American expedition and that he was permitted to climb. The next page is a summary of the climb. All climbing parties must debrief with the Alpine Club. It is succinct, but about halfway down the page I stop reading, mouth agape. I am still sitting with my mouth wide open on the bed when Jose gets out of the shower, reading the same sentence over and over.

"Hey there, what's up?" Jose is standing wrapped in his towel in front of the bed.

I hand him the piece of paper. "Read this."

He sits down next to me. When he get to where I had stopped he mutters, "Holy shit," before continuing, "This is good news though, right?"

"Yeah I guess," I say, and take back the paper to finish reading the summary of the climb.

Jose is reading over my shoulder and my skin is crawling with a wish to be alone, but worried about hurting Jose's feelings I say nothing. I am, however, thankful when Murtaza knocks on our door and I can shake off Jose's arm that he has draped over my shoulder. I feel terrible, but I am no good without alone time. I am not used to having a constant companion. In Rawalpindi Murtaza had told us that it was best to pretend to be married. In Pakistan traveling together as an unmarried couple is not looked upon kindly. Jose loves the role-play and happily introduces me as his wife each time we meet someone, meanwhile I wince every time.

Murtaza informs us that we will be leaving for Askole promptly after breakfast, so keep our bags packed. He has organized a 4WD and a driver to take us, and Anam has been out to purchase supplies for our trek. I am impressed. As soon as he leaves I pretend to be tired and hop into one of the single beds, happy our accommodation caters for prudes. I pull the sheet over my head and enjoy the self-made little haven of solitude as I listen to Jose puttering around the room and finally turning off the lights and getting into his bed.

I wake early again, my body still plagued by jetlag. Jose is still asleep and I sneak out onto the balcony. Now in the early morning light I can see what darkness had hidden the previous night; a stunning panorama of peaks and the Indus River below. A full moon still setting, changing shifts with the sun. I sit down and read the papers from the Alpine Club again, committing them to memory. I turn my phone on and photograph both papers before signing on to the slow Wi-Fi at the hotel. I upload my images to Google Photos. I also check my emails, but there are so many I decide to ignore all of them. Instead I send a quick email to Sonia to let her know we are OK.

I want to go out and wander the streets, but I am not sure if it is a good idea as a lonely lady. Instead I wake up Jose. He grumbles at being woken up an hour before breakfast is even served, but agrees to come outside with me.

The dusty main street is lined with shopfronts spilling out on to the walkway selling vegetables and fruits, and an eclectic assortment of cookies, flashlights, screwdrivers, notebooks, tinned food, and the likes. The town is waking up and some shop owners are still opening up while decorated trucks maneuver the road, avoiding mopeds and foot traffic, and stirring up clouds of dust. We purchase a bag of fresh mangoes and I have Jose walk all the way to the climbing shop that my guidebook mentions. The small shop is closed. The window display is made up of two very old ice axes, a pair of trekking poles, and a poster advertising a tent of a brand I have never heard of. I had wanted to buy a map, but if the window display is anything to go by it doesn't matter much that the shop is closed.

At breakfast we cut up the mangoes and we feast on the juiciest, sweetest mangoes I have ever tasted. Jose, with a massive grin on his face, explains how the mangoes remind him of his childhood in Mexico. It is endearing and I feel bad for wishing him away the night before. I touch his leg under the table while sipping on my hot but terribly weak coffee.

***

The bumpy road to Askole is like driving through a landscape right out of JRR Tolkien's *Hobbit* shire. Little rock dwellings, often with a large boulder forming one wall of the building, surrounded by purple flowering potato fields, yellow canola, and a wide variety of wildflowers. Explosions of bright pink flowering rosehip bushes along the roadside, all to the backdrop of rugged peaks, many clad in snowy white. Cherry trees so heavy with ripe berries that the branches are hanging low.

In one village we stop and pick bags full of cherries, which we eat straight away, spitting the stones out of the open car windows. But best of all is that as soon as we leave dusty Skardu behind, Murtaza's worried frown changes back to his charismatic smile. He is pointing out peaks and singing as the car crosses rickety suspension bridges over fast-flowing rivers. I have to close my eyes each time, my mind making up images of our car tumbling into the icy waters as the bridge gives way. But each time we arrive safely on the other side.

In the foothills of the Karakoram life is tranquil, no loud noises, no rush, no rubbish, and the air is fragranced by rose water and rotis being baked. We stop at Shigar Fort, a 400-year-old fort perched high over a village, and when we sit in the gardens eating a basket full of cherries and sipping on hot tea Jose proclaims, "If you were ever going to write a poem this would be the place."

Murtaza chuckles. "Oh, you just wait, it gets better."

As we get closer the road starts to climb higher and soon the villages sit on high plateaus instead of the valley floor. Women in bright Sari's are working the rice paddies and we pick up a man and his two young daughters for a ride to the next village. The girls are shy, stealing quick glances and braving

128

a shy smile before quickly looking away again, unaccustomed to foreigners.

We have lunch in an apple garden where men are baking rotis in a tandoori oven and children are running around, here a little braver than the girls who had caught a ride with us. When we arrive in Askole we are met by a village made up of low rock buildings, bright green fields, and snowcapped peaks all around. Our Jeep pulls up to a larger building and Murtaza tells us this is our campsite. Behind the house is indeed a larger area made for camping. A crowd of hopeful porters already stand by the large patch of grass. Jose and I get busy putting up our tent, while Murtaza and Anam pick a crew of fourteen wiry looking porters and two mules to accompany us on our trek.

I sit down in the shade in front of the larger cooking tent, Anam is stirring a pot while Murtaza pours me and Jose a cup of tea each.

"It is beautiful, isn't it?" states Murtaza, looking out over the mountains that shoot up in every direction. Vibrant green rice paddies surround the village and the barren mountains stand in stark contrast. "I wasn't sure I would ever get to see this again. I feel so lucky to get to return, and with Zygmunt's granddaughter." Murtaza is beaming.

"I have some great news," I smile. "The documents I got from the Alpine Club confirms that my grandfather made it to the summit before he perished."

"I know," smiles Murtaza.

The debrief from the Alpine Club that I had read was with Mr. Hawkins, the only American who summited that year. In the report, he said he topped out together with Zygmunt at 5:15 p.m.; they spent twenty minutes on the summit before they both turned around to head back down to lower elevation and the safety of Camp 3.

"How did you know?" I ask.

"I was there, remember. Waiting at Camp 3 when Mr. Hawkins returned, he told us that same story. What else did the report say?"

"It gets a little strange after the summit. Hawkins says that Zygmunt was struck by falling ice just as they were leaving the summit and that he fell off the mountain. Hawkins believed the ice either killed Zygmunt instantly or at least made him unconscious as he made no sound whilst falling, for what Hawkins describes as 'thousands of feet.' But if they were on the summit, where would the ice come from? I guess it must have happened lower on the way down."

Murtaza shakes his head. "This has also always bothered me, Hawkins told us all the same story. But if it happened just below the summit he cannot have been struck by ice. Hawkins was, however, adamant that Zygmunt was hit in the head by ice. Blood had colored the snow red where Zygmunt had stood just a second before. The second climbing team got close to the summit, but they didn't see any sign of Zygmunt, or bloodied snow. So it must have happened pretty high up." Murtaza's smile fades and he is staring off at the distant mountains.

Chapter 18

In the middle of the night I wake up. Lying awake in the tent for hours, I imagine what it would be like if the Taliban stormed our tent. I can almost smell the fear in the air of those poor mountaineers a year ago at the base of Nanga Parbat. I finally fall asleep again just as the sun is starting to rise. When Jose a couple of hours later nudges me saying that breakfast is ready, I am not ready to wake up.

I am finally feeling safe and warm in the tent, but the sound of birds chirping, Murtaza singing, and Anam stirring the metal pot full to the brim of tea, lures me out of the tent and into the brilliant sunshine. Breakfast consists of cornflakes with hot powdered milk, scrambled eggs, and rotis that Anam is still busy making on the gas stove in the tent. The sugar in the tea must be doing its job because I am all of a sudden raring to go. I am ready to be on the trail after days trapped inside a car. Our porters are squirreling around trying to pack up things as we finish using them. Jose feels bad for them, so he puts down his plate of eggs and breaks down our tent mid-breakfast.

At the start of the day we hike past fields and irrigation channels, water stolen from a creek or waterfall high up on the mountainside. It is then fanned out through the valley to a variety of fields and villages, bubbling along our path. It feeds the intense green rice paddies and potato fields with their purple flowers. But soon enough all signs of habitation vanish and we hike along a hot dusty path surrounded by bare peaks.

We follow the Baltoro River with the sun beating down on our heads. For most of the day we hike alone, although we are often overtaken by porters who pass us several times. They regularly stop to take a rest from their heavy loads, at which point we will pass them, only to be overtaken again shortly after as they scurry past us calling out 'As-Salam-Alaikum.' Murtaza moves surprisingly fast for his age and Jose and I stay close to his side, asking questions about the landscape. Skillfully avoiding any questions about Zygmunt, I want him to start telling us his story when he is ready. Which I have started to fear will be never. I am repeating the mantra *good-things-come-to-those-who-wait* in my head to stop myself from blurting out all my questions. The ones that I really want to ask. Instead I am asking for peak names, flower species, cultural traditions, and words in Urdu.

We stop for lunch next to the river, I sit down in the shade provided by the rosehip bushes that are lining the river, their branches full of pink blooms. Anam starts up the gas stove to boil tea and make fresh rotis. The river is running fast and brown, and a cool breeze blows off the surface. As we wait for the tea to boil a large group sits down a little downstream from us.

"Let's go speak to the expedition while wait for the tea to boil." Jose is already standing and offering me his hand.

"Sure," I reply, and I let Jose pull me up.

As we near the group Jose's smile grows wide. "They are Mexicans."

"You don't know that."

"Yes, I do." He smiles and breaks into Spanish.

I can tell he is really excited, he is waving his arms as he is conversing in fast-paced Spanish. "Marta, they are here to climb K2." He translates before switching back to Spanish again.

I leave Jose to it and start to chat to the two Nepali Sherpas they have brought along.

"I have summited Everest seven times. Last year with these guys," says Pemba, and points towards the five Mexicans that are busy talking to Jose. "But Everest is child's play compared to K2."

I think the comparison a little harsh, but I guess the

132

statistics support his comment with every one in four climbers that attempt K2 ending up dead.

"Good luck." I say smiling at the Sherpas before Jose and I wander back to fill up on fresh rotis and milky tea.

For the rest of the afternoon we play tag with the Mexicans, who cheerfully call out *'Hola'* and *'Commo Estas?'* each time they pass. In the late afternoon we arrive at Julla camp, to call it camp is a little of a stretch as far as I am concerned. It is a grassy patch with a small rock building where a caretaker lives and a few plastic portable toilets. Murtaza scorns when I ask about the caretaker's job. "It should be to keep camp clean, but look at those toilets, they are disgusting."

The Mexicans and their small army of porters, there must be close to a hundred porters supporting their team of seven, are busy setting up a small city of tents. Murtaza thankfully leads us away towards the edge of camp, along a bubbling brook where we pitch our tents far away from the feral portable toilets and the Mexicans noisy banter. One porter who is carrying a wooden box on his back sets it down and lets three chickens out. I can't stop giggling.

"Murtaza, why do we have three live chickens with us?" I giggle.

He smiles. "For dinner of course. We will kill them once we get on the glacier where we can keep the meat cold."

I stop giggling and get my camera out.

Now it is Murtaza giggling. "You better get photos of them now, tomorrow they will have altitude sickness."

"What? Chickens get altitude sickness?"

"They sure do, they just lay on their side."

I chase the chickens around for a while, but as the sun starts to set and the temperature finally drops I sit down and happily accept the cup of hot tea that Murtaza hands me. Anam cooks up another dinner feast of curried okra, spaghetti, vegetables, rotis, and mangoes for dessert. Not exactly the lightweight freeze dried meals I am used to in the mountains. I guess having fourteen men and two mules to carry all your stuff is pretty nice after all, the food is delicious.

I again wake in the middle of the night from vivid dreams, although they are thankfully Taliban free this time. In the morning when I stick my head out of the tent there is a beehive of activity over in the Mexican camp and I pull my head back inside. Jose is already up and I can imagine him over by tent city chatting to the Mexicans. So I am surprised when I get outside and find him drinking tea with Murtaza. They look serious, but when I sit down next to them they both smile and a cup of tea is produced.

"What are you two whispering about?" I ask while blowing on my hot tea.

"Nothing much, just discussing today's hike. We think we can make it all the way to Paiju in one day. It means we have an extra day for later," answers Jose.

"Sounds good to me."

As we walk the trail narrows and in parts disappears altogether where it has been washed away by landslides or the flooding river. When the trail drops low hugging the river the temperature also drops by a couple of degrees, a welcome relief from the hotness of the day. We arrive at Paiju already at 2 p.m. making me wonder how this day could have possibly been split into two. When we arrive into camp some of our porters are in a heated discussion with a few of the Mexicans' porters. They are fighting over a camp spot, both sides claiming they got there first. Murtaza manages to quell the fight, and once again we choose a spot far away from the others, although this time closer to the bathrooms. I don't mind, although our spot lacks the shady reprieve that the trees at the sites up on the hill provide. It makes it impossible to be inside the tent while the sun is up, so I follow Jose up to our kitchen tent that Anam has set up on the roof of a small stone hut. Inside the hut the porters are busy cooking up a storm, roti upon roti being turned on the skillet placed on the gas flames.

As soon as I sit down Anam hands me a cup of tea. I have learned that in Pakistan tea must be 'taken,' no one says drink, at every opportunity all throughout the day. I nibble on a sweet cookie as Murtaza informs us that tomorrow is a rest day.

"I am feeling pretty good," I say as I smile, "actually these days are all kind of short. I am used to much longer days carrying a heavy pack, so I feel fine."

"But you are travelling with a 68-year-old."

"Oh my, I am so, *so,* sorry Murtaza. You seem so strong it didn't even occur to me you need rest," I say.

But Murtaza bursts out in laughter. "I am just fine. The rest day is so that the porters can cook all their bread for the coming weeks. They will cook most of it here to save them carrying fuel and flour." Murtaza is still laughing while my mind catches up and I realize he was just teasing me. Jose is giggling uncontrollably. I smile, relieved I wasn't as thoughtless as I first feared.

The next morning, we bid four of our porters and the mules farewell, giving them a handsome tip as they shake our hands full of thanks. One of the porters looks really young and when he meets my gaze while shaking my hand I am startled by the iciest blue eyes I have ever seen, not dissimilar to my own. They make a striking feature against his dark skin and black hair. As soon as the porters and the mules are on their way I turn to Jose, "Did you see those eyes, they were amazing."

"It is an Aryan trait," intersects Murtaza who has overheard my comment, "Aryans are an ancient Indo-European tribe of Central Asia who migrated southwards into Pakistan and Afghanistan rather than westward into Europe. That is where the blue eyes come from. Some Pakistanis also have blond hair."

"Wow. That is so fascinating. Gosh, you know a lot of things Murtaza," I say.

Murtaza smiles at me. "With age comes knowledge."

I am not sure if he is teasing me again, so I just nod.

In the afternoon we scramble up to about 14,000 feet on flanks of Paiju. It is cloudy, which means our little foray does not yield the promised views of K2. Now we have to wait till Concordia, several days away, until we will have another chance at seeing the iconic pyramid of a peak.

A large block of rock on the way make for a fun bouldering object. I spend a couple of hours climbing up and then back down, then up another route and back down, and so on while Murtaza, Anam, and Jose, sit eating cookies watching me.

On the way back down we stop at a pretty waterfall and I soak my feet while watching an eagle catch a sparrow mid-flight. For some reason the sparrow being snatched up unawares makes a shiver run down my back, it feels like a bad omen. I try to shake the feeling by literally shaking my body. It seems to work. Back in camp I wash my hair under the tap and have a wet-wipe 'shower' in the tent. Jose has a more proper wash by the taps, not being restricted by the same rules of prudence as me being a female. In fact, the only female in camp.

When we are lying in our tent after dinner reading our books the porters gather outside and start to drum on an empty water canister. Soon they are all singing, dancing, drumming, whistling, and clapping. We lay in the tent listening to the enchanting music. I unzip the tent door so we can watch them dance, slowly drifting off to sleep with the traditional Pakistani song and joyful laughter as a backdrop.

***

When we reach the Baltoro Glacier the following day the temperature drops by a couple of degrees, a thankful relief from the heat. Although it is hard to tell that we are even on a glacier, it looks nothing like the glaciers at home. Here every inch of the ice is covered with moraine and only occasionally does my foot slide, revealing ice below all the rock and gravel. I am used to glaciers covered with snow, or later in the season ice, and riddled with crevasses. It feels like we have landed on the moon, it is stark and lifeless. Barren peaks shoot up on either side of this massive boulder and rock covered glacier.

As if on cue Murtaza starts telling us the story of how he first met my grandfather. Almost as if the sheer mountain faces on either side of our slow forward movement on the glacier, which is moving at glacial pace in the opposite direction, protects his words from floating on to the air and in to unwelcome ears.

"I left my home village of Shimshal as a young man, and I was on my way to Rawalpindi in search of work when I met your grandfather in Chilas. I was breaking my family tradition of herding yaks for a chance to earn real money. My background of moving yaks to higher pastures during summer meant I was accustomed to high altitudes, and my childhood was full of forays up peaks surrounding my village. So when I met Zygmunt, fifteen years my senior, he offered me the job of carrying loads to Nanga Parbat basecamp and perhaps beyond. Neither of us spoke English very well, but we formed a bond so strong over the following weeks that words became redundant. I helped carry loads of food and equipment through the deep snow, and by the time Zygmunt started to climb there was never a question whether I should join him or not. We simply set off climbing together. Zygmunt taught me all the required skills as we went along. That was my climbing apprenticeship," laughs Murtaza, "I learned on the job, attempting to climb the world's ninth highest mountain in winter."

"Yeah, a little different from the alpine climbing course I took," I smile.

"It wasn't easy, but it satisfied all my dreams of adventure. Pushing up that mountain, icicles hanging from my mustache and nose, I asked Zygmunt why he would choose to climb this mountain in winter. It sometimes seemed like madness to me. But he explained that permits were cheaper and easier to get. He also told me that his government expected him to gather information about other nations on his climbing trips. Like a climbing James Bond. But he didn't like it, climbing in winter meant there was no one to spy on."

Chapter 19

It is still early season on the Baltoro Glacier and a boot path is yet to form on the moraine. So we rock hop between boulders avoiding any slick ice, all whilst Murtaza is still telling his story, only broken occasionally by passing porters, or the Mexicans and their Sherpas. At one point a porter walks past trailing an ox and Murtaza says, "Expedition food."

"Expedition food?" asks Jose.

"They will hike the ox all the way to K2 basecamp, then slaughter it there. Saves them having to carry the meat."

"Wow. Glacier cows," I say while fumbling for my camera to take a photo.

For part of the day we are skirting the Baltoro Glacier instead of staying on top of it. Occasionally, smaller glaciers tumble down the mountainside to join the Baltoro, having us slip and slide across their icy paths hopping over melting ice that are creating rivulets of water.

"That is a lot of mules," comments Jose when a train of sixty odd mules passes us.

"They are army mules. The have delivered supplies to the army base at Concordia," explains Murtaza.

"What? There is an army base at Concordia?" I ask.

"It is only a couple of small basic shelters. Concordia is close to India, and the disputed Kashmir."

"Aha." I reply.

"On Nanga Parbat," Murtaza turns the conversation back to my grandfather. "The cold was almost unbearable. A fierce winter storm was hitting us with all God's fury. Zygmunt could no longer feel his toes and we had run out of fuel, so we decided it was time to turn around. It was a struggle to get back down, your grandfather was suffering badly from frostbite. But we made it back to Chilas and from there we travelled together to Islamabad, catching rides in the back of trucks. In Islamabad we finally had to say goodbye. Your grandfather organized with the Alpine Club to register me as a high altitude porter before he left. He left me a lot of his mountaineering gear and wrote me a letter of recommendation. As such setting me up for a career climbing with foreign mountaineers. It is funny to think how different my life would have turned out had I not run into Zygmunt. I would have probably ended up working in a tea shop wiping tables or running errands."

As we near Urdukas, this evening's camp, it is as if a tap has been turned off and Murtaza skillfully changes the topic to the myriad of wildflowers dotting the hillside as we hike the last few steep yards to camp. No mention of terrifying blizzards and screaming winds high on the mountains. Looking at Murtaza marveling at the little yellow, pink, and white flowers, one would never guess he was once a formidable force pushing up the highest peaks of the world. The transformation is so complete it makes me shiver. A thought flashes past in my mind, *nothing-is-as-it-seems*. I at once feel uncomfortable and I escape into the tent the instant Jose and I have put it up.

"Marta, there is tea and popcorn." Jose is trying to coax me out of the tent.

"I have a headache, I am just going to rest for a while." I lie.

It starts to rain heavily while I am laying in the tent and Jose dashes inside and joins me in my refuge while waiting out the rain. When the rain subsides, so does my peculiar mood and I go outside with Jose marveling at the high peaks of Trango Tower, Paiju Peak, and Cathedral Rock, across the glacier. Clouds still swirl around the mountains, every now and again giving us a sneak peek of the soaring summits.

Urdukas camp is similar to the last camp apart from being on a grassy hillside. A little oasis of green in amongst the

140

otherwise barren mountains and rocky glacier. I wonder how this tiny hillside spot got to grow so lush while I admire the myriad of flowers. At this camp there is no rock hut and no caretaker, resulting in even grosser portable toilets than Julla camp. The toilets have been placed at the most popular camp spots along the Baltoro by some Italian NGO in an attempt to prevent there being human feces on every rock. At this altitude it never really decomposes, and despite the plastic toilets there is still an impressive amount of human shit around. I guess the porters aren't accustomed to porta-loos.

"Anam, what is the plaque on the big boulder about?" I ask.

Anam is busy baking rotis, and I sit down to watch him make the perfectly round breads. I had spotted the plaque on a house-sized boulder when I was going to the toilets.

"A few years ago the boulder cracked and a truck-sized part of the boulder came loose, rolling down the hillside crushing three porters that were resting underneath and injuring a few others. The plaque is in memory of the porters who lost their lives."

"This place is wild," I say mostly to myself as I look around for Jose. A sudden urge to feel him close by. I find him still standing on the rocks looking out over the peaks and the ominous clouds.

The next morning when I wake up I feel awful. My tummy is burning and I think I may throw up. I zip open the tent flap, it is still cloudy. Jose scampers off to get me a cup of tea and some bread. The smell of eggs makes my tummy turn. I manage to eat half a roti and drink a few sips of tea before giving up, sipping my water instead. Murtaza is grumpy, complaining about the porters not using the toilets and therefore contaminating the little stream used for drinking and cooking water. The thought of human feces in my drinking water sure does not make me feel any better, and as we start to hike I am lagging behind unable to keep up with the others. Jose stops every few minutes and waits for me, finally letting me pass and instead trails behind me, forcing himself to keep my slow pace.

The day feels long and what I had estimated should be a four-hour hike ends up taking us seven hours. It is grey, cloudy, and cold. The glacier keeps undulating up and down like a creased sheet of paper, and I am slipping all over the place unstable on my feet. We have to jump over several crevasses that appear bottomless, and when Jose throws a big rock into one, it keeps bouncing off the sides for what seemed like eternity before finally coming to rest somewhere deep inside the glacier.

The brooding feeling of doom has returned with the ache in my belly and I can feel tears pricking the corners of my eyes. What am I doing here? I have no business here amongst these giant peaks. I berate myself for being so foolish as to be talked into going to Pakistan. Pakistan of all places, I mean, I have never even been to Canada, what made me think I could survive in Pakistan? All those wistful dreams of climbing in the high Himalayas that I had dreamed up when reading Mr. Hawkins' books have vanished. I long for my Northern Cascades, smaller friendlier mountains. Not big and threatening like the ones that now surround me.

I am relieved when we finally reach our camp for the night at Goro 2. This camp doesn't have as much as a strand of green grass, just endless moraine. There aren't even any portable toilets. I guess the Italians didn't think anyone would camp in this desolate spot. I again dive straight into the tent as soon as Jose has put it up, I don't offer to help. For the rest of the evening I lay zipped up in my sleeping bag. I can hear Jose, Anam, and Murtaza laughing in the cook tent, and at one point Jose brings me over a plate of plain rice, which I barely touch.

I sleep for eleven hours and wake up at 5 a.m. feeling much better. I poke my head outside the tent and am met by thick clouds, I can barely see the cook tent only sixty feet away. When we have finished breakfast, which I manage to stomach today, big heavy snowflakes are dancing down from the sky. I put on my hard-shell preparing for today's hike, and by the time we have finished packing up the tent my hair is whiter than the ice-witch in Narnia. A thick layer of snow covers every inch. Before long the wet heavy snow has changed to hail and sleet, forcing us to set a fast pace racing towards Concordia. We pass no one today, the Mexican expedition never reached Goro 2 yesterday, and we had camp all to ourselves.

We don't bother to stop for lunch, the wet and the wind sees us pushing on until camp. It is disappointing arriving at what is known as the Thorne Room of the Mountain Gods, seeing nothing but white in every directions. It is like being inside a ping pong ball. So this is Concordia, described in all the mountain lore as the most spectacularly beautiful place on the planet, and I can see nothing.

As we entered camp we walk past a cluster of tents that Anam tells us is the Italian Rescue Centre. We stop and talk briefly to the Italians, who tells us the weather is meant to improve. It gives me some hope and I feel pretty happy and content when we gathered in the cook tent sheltering from the snow, sipping on hot tea. It makes a huge difference that I no longer feel ill, and being able to eat the chicken and vegetables that Anam has cooked up makes my spirits soar. I didn't notice when the chickens were slaughtered, but it must have been a few days ago, because chicken has featured on the menu the last few days.

The next morning, I am woken up by Anam's excited voice outside our tent shouting, "K2 is clean, K2 is clean."

I am giggling as I shake Jose awake. "Anam is saying that

K2 is clean."

"Clean?" Jose looks confused.

It makes me giggle even more. "I think he means clear."

I am so full of excitement I don't even bother to get dressed properly, I just pull on my down jacket over my base layer and slip my feet into my boots without tying the laces. I fight with the frozen tent zipper before literally bursting out of the tent.

I am greeted by K2 in all its splendor, the clouds have blown off its face leaving only a few small puffs still clinging to the side of the perfect pyramid summit. The sun glistens off the icy snow slopes and I am in total awe. It stands alone and proud, dwarfing the peaks to its sides as if to say, 'Look at me, I am the grandest.'

Jose comes out and stands by my side. We stand there staring at this the most beautiful mountain I have ever seen for over half an hour. The sheer grandeur of the landscape surrounding us steals my breath away, every direction I turn I am greeted by yet another mountain giant. K2, Broad Peak, Gasherbrum 4, Chongolisa, Mitre Peak, and an endless array of smaller peaks all still taller than any peaks I have ever seen before are piercing the horizons. I could have just stood there all day gawking at Mother Earth's beauty, but Murtaza's joyful voice breaks the spell and he chirps that breakfast is ready.

At breakfast we decide to take a rest day then spend tomorrow hiking to K2 basecamp. I am giddy with excitement and after breakfast Jose and I set off exploring, first hiking down to the others camping below us. We are camped high above the rest of the campers at Concordia, and once we get down to the other tents I realize why Murtaza chose our spot. It is the only spot with an actual view of K2. The Mexicans had arrived a few hours after us and they are also full of excitement standing outside their tents, all holding a cup of tea and pointing out peaks. We tell them about the spectacular view from our camp and we hiked back up the little hill with them as they all 'ooh and aah' at the view. Leaving the Mexicans behind, Jose and I sneak off to find a turquoise melt-water river rushing along its icy path in front of Mitre Peak. Here we sit for ages just looking around at the beauty and chatting happily about trivial things. Laughing and holding hands, I feel free, light, and happy. The mountains that had previously seemed ominous and looming now feel airy and joyful.

In the afternoon we can spot another large group hiking up the Baltoro towards Concordia. We are drinking cups of tea watching their progress and second guessing who it might be. It is obvious they are here to climb something judging by the number of porters. As they get closer I realize it is the Spanish team that we had met in Skardu. Jose and I hike down to greet them. One guy, whose name I have forgotten, starts to wave at us as they get closer and runs toward us. I am surprised.

"We must have made quite an impression," I joke.

When he gets to us he stops and stoops over, leaning on his knees as he is catching his breath.

"Hi." I smile. "In a rush to get to the views I see."

"Someone is after you," he says between taking deep breaths.

Chapter 20

The blood in my veins freezes as Jose switches to fast Spanish, a spitfire of words being fired between the two men. Jose grabs my arm and pulls me back up towards camp, the Spaniard following behind, not even taking the time to drop his pack. Jose ushers us both into the cook tent and asks Anam if we could please have tea. Murtaza is already seated in the tent and moves over closer when we all pile inside.

"OK, let's start from the top," says Jose in his best cop voice, looking at the Spaniard that introduces himself to Murtaza and Anam as Israel.

Israel isn't very good at English and he often looks at Jose for translation. While the Spanish Broad Peak expedition was still preparing at Hotel Masherbrum in Skardu, a group of three Americans and one Pakistani man arrived at the hotel. At first they seemed really friendly, if odd.

"It was strange, they wore nice clothes. Not hiking clothes, they seemed really out of place," says Israel. "They asked a lot of questions about our climb and they seemed genuinely interested. They asked about what other teams we had met and once we mentioned you guys their demeanor totally changed. They became intimidating, pushing us for information, of which we had none. The Pakistani must have been army because he kept threatening to take our climbing permit away, saying all it would take is a call to the general."

"Holy crap." Jose lets out a heavy breath as he curses.

Israel takes back up. "They didn't seem very friendly anymore, in fact they were scary. We felt so bad, we had already told them you were hiking to K2 basecamp before we realized they were up to no good. I am so so sorry. We have hiked here as fast as we could to try to warn you. We didn't even take a rest day in Paiju. Our porters almost went on strike."

After several cups of tea and lots of questions Israel finally excuses himself to go see the rest of his team; he invites us to come to their mess tent for tea in a few hours. Maybe some of the other team members have something to add. As soon as Israel leaves Murtaza starts talking. It startles me at first as he has been quiet the entire time Israel was in the tent.

"We should get going to basecamp at first light tomorrow."

"How far behind do you think they are?" asks Jose.

"Well, I don't think they are mountaineers, so they are probably slow, and unorganized getting porters together," answers Murtaza. "We should have a couple of days on them."

Entering the Spanish mess tent is like entering into a little haven. It is huge, there are tables and chairs, and on the tables sit bowls of candy and jars of olives. A smiling girl opens up one of the olive jars that I am staring at and hands me a spoon and the open jar.

"Here, eat as many as you want," she says, before reaching out her hand and introducing herself as Lara.

She is Ricardo's girlfriend and is not here to climb; just basecamp company and support. She motions for me to sit down. It feels weird sitting on a chair at a table rather than cross legged on the floor eating from a bunch of shared food bowls in the middle. Our kitchen tent seems tiny in comparison, it also seconds as Murtaza and Anam's sleeping tent. This is a mansion. It is delightful chatting to Lara, the first female I have talked to since arriving in Pakistan. It feels good discussing the difficulty of washing our hair or making sure to be modest enough not to offend anyone. I wish I could have just sat there eating olives and talking to Lara all night. But the others from the expedition start to trickle in to the tent and the discussion goes from light to heavy. Everyone agrees that the Americans and the Pakistani man had been unpleasant and clearly seemed to be after us for some reason.

Lara grabs my arm. "I would get the hell out of here if I was you."

My eyes are wide when I look at Jose, trying to motion by looks alone that we need to leave. Panic is bubbling up. Jose is also visibly upset, and when we step outside the tent he grabs me and embraces me in a bear hug unwilling to let go. I wriggle trying to release his embrace.

"The porters," I whisper as Jose refuses to let go.

"I don't give a shit right now," says Jose.

I relax and let myself be held, tears trickling down my cheeks. I hadn't realized how much I needed to be held, to know I wasn't alone, lost on what seems to be an endless sea of unknowns. I feel a wave of guilt for wishing him away when we were in Skardu. He holds me tight for a long time before finally letting go, still holding on to my hand as we walk back up to our camp.

Clouds have started to swirl back in as we crawl back into the tent. I barely touched dinner, my mind is too much of a mess. So when Jose at midnight, both of us unable to sleep, pulls a packet of cookies out of his jacket arm that he has nabbed from the kitchen tent, I scoff them all down in a jiffy. Jose watches me finish the packet before stroking my cheek and whispering, "It will all be OK."

I don't believe him, but the sentiment is comforting.

***

When we wake the world outside is covered in a thin layer of snow and the sky is crystal clear. The moon is still shining and hundreds of stars sprinkle the deep blue sky, which has started to turn pink at the edges with the rising sun. I shake the ice and snow off the tent before starting to take it down. We had sent

148

back more of our porters yesterday, now only six remain. Two of them will stay here waiting for our return with most of our food supplies, while four will join us to K2 basecamp to carry our gear and food.

I am eager to get going and am already packed up well before Anam has finished baking the rotis. Me and Jose, whom I had ushered out of the tent while still getting dressed, now sit waiting in the kitchen tent staring out through the open tent doors at the sunrise. K2 turns first pink then orange, and finally a bright yellow. As we leave camp I can see people starting to stir in the Mexican and Spanish camps below us. Murtaza takes the lead as we step onto the Godwin-Austen Glacier making our way towards Broad Peak basecamp. K2 is straight ahead of us and the glacier is leading to it like a red carpet. Peaks line either side like an army standing in salute with K2 their sergeant.

Murtaza starts talking about Zygmunt and their second encounter, the fatal K2 expedition.

"Zygmunt often talked in his letters about wanting to return, to attempt to climb the mountain of his dreams. He spoke about K2 constantly. He had seen the mountain towering higher than any other peak on the horizon when we climbed on Nanga Parbat. The perfect pyramid burned into his retinas. He could never be satisfied until he got to go climb on this beast of a mountain. I think he tried for many years to get on an expedition. But as a Polish climber it was hard to get the funds together. The other European teams didn't want to climb with the Polish climbers with their cobbled together equipment and fierce reputation.

"When your grandfather climbed Lothse in 1974 he became good friends with Mr. Hawkins, who was climbing the mountain at the same time with an American expedition. They bonded and ended up summiting together when all the other members from both teams turned around due to bad weather. Zygmunt was used to winter conditions and didn't mind the blizzardy weather. Mr. Hawkins, who was at the time perhaps the best, or at least best known, mountaineer on the climbing circuit chose to stay with Zygmunt to push on for the summit.

"Zygmunt called me his Pakistani brother and started to refer to Mr. Hawkins as his American brother in his letters to me. So when he invited me to join the American team to K2 he wrote about his joy at getting to introduce his two climbing brothers to each other. I think he was disappointed when we finally met. We did not bond like he had hoped. Pakistanis and Americans, no offense, aren't exactly known for their friendship. I distrusted Mr. Hawkins and he was never able to see me as more than the help, never recognizing me as an equal climber with the same skills. I think this was hard for Zygmunt to handle, and he seemed upset for much of the expedition, only showing real joy when looking at the mountain or climbing.

"During the days in basecamp I think he mostly just wished for it to be over, wanting to finish the climb and get back home to his family. I can't blame him. Mr. Hawkins and I didn't exactly make it easy for him, always wanting him to choose sides. He had hoped to stand on the summit with me and Mr. Hawkins by his sides, but as the expedition proceeded it became obvious that this was an impossible dream. When Mr. Hawkins announced that Zygmunt and he would be the first team to go to the summit followed by me and two of the other Americans, Zygmunt was not only disappointed but outraged. He demanded to be on the second team with me. I think he had desperately clung on to the hope that somehow we would overcome our differences and that in the end the common goal of reaching the summit would trump any petty personality differences.

"Mr. Hawkins was the expedition leader and played this card with Zygmunt, offering him to be on the first team with him or forfeiting the summit all together. It put Zygmunt in an impossible situation. This was the mountain of his dreams. When Mr. Hawkins pulled this card on Zygmunt he instantly ceased to be Zygmunt's American brother. The friendship and respect was lost; the bond that Zygmunt had talked so fondly about was severed. I think Zygmunt felt betrayed. He told me he would just go home, the summit would not be the same without me by his side.

"He no longer cared for this beautiful mountain. The expedition of his dreams had turned sour. I was the one that pushed him to go. I convinced him it would be folly to turn around now, so close to reaching his dream. I also wanted the summit, and while I wanted to be on top with Zygmunt by my side, I'd rather be on top with the two Americans than not at all. So he went on with Mr. Hawkins, but his spark was gone, he no longer trusted the person he was roped to; the person who you need to trust with your life. In hindsight, I wish I had never convinced him to go. I wish we had left the Americans to the mountain and gone home."

Chapter 21

We arrive at Broad Peak basecamp to find it empty. If Murtaza hadn't told me, I wouldn't even know this is basecamp. It sits to the side of the Godwin-Austen Glacier at the base of the mountain. There is a thick blanket of snow and through camp runs a melt river. Its icy bottom reflects through the water making it a vibrant turquoise color, prettier than any other color I can think of. Broad Peak looms above, not sharp and pointy like K2, but broad (go figure) and chunky. It feels friendly, not defiant like K2. K2 is still domineering the backdrop with its perfect pyramid shape, trying to overshadow Broad Peak, and still demanding all the attention.

"In a month's time this place will be buzzing with climbers," explains Murtaza.

We sit down on some snow-covered rocks and eat handfuls of almonds and drink water, scouting out the route up the mountain whilst listening to the rush of melting water forming rivers on the ice.

"Last year a German climber fell into a melt river," says Anam.

"Oh no, was he alright?" asks Jose.

"No, *she* got sucked under the glacier. It took the rescue team two days to retrieve her body."

"That is terrible." Jose is looking shocked.

"Yes, she was taking a photo, took a step backwards straight into the glacier river."

"Let's go," responds Jose.

No one argues, we all get up and leave.

As we near K2 things start to appear on the glacier. At first I spot a piece of cloth, thinking it is rubbish I reach down to pick it up, only to realize as I am pulling on it that it is a piece of a tent partly stuck in the snow and ice. A little further on I spot a gas canister and some old tent poles. As I look around I can see bits and pieces of equipment strewn across the glacier partly burrowed in the snow.

"What is all this stuff?" I ask Murtaza.

"This is the leftovers from climbing expeditions. Things that have been left or abandoned high up on the mountain eventually find their way back down, the glacier carrying it downhill."

"Wow. I wish they would carry their stuff back out with them." I am poking an old oxygen bottle with my boot as I notice a piece of bone next to it. "Jose, what animal do you think this is from?" I ask.

"That is a human femur," replies Jose, all the blood drained from his face.

Anam has overheard us and chirps, "Yes, whoever perishes up there also gets a free ride down the mountain courtesy of the glaciers."

I shiver and fumble for Jose's hand. "For all I know that could be my grandfather's femur," I whisper to Jose as we move over the strewn debris.

I spot a few brightly colored tents when we get closer to basecamp, and when I point them out to Murtaza he says that there must already be an expedition at K2 basecamp. I feel a wave of relief. Being all alone out here makes me feel vulnerable. I had just been thinking about how I wish I had taken the time to rent a satellite phone before we left, it is eerie being surrounded by all these brazen peaks and blankets of snow with no connection to the outside world. The sight of other people gives me a false sense of security. I know we can still just as easily disappear into a crevasse and no one would ever know what happened to us. But those tents looking like confetti strewn in the snow make my shoulders relax. I hadn't realized I have been tensing them since we left Broad Peak basecamp.

K2 basecamp sits on a flat expanse of snow and moraine in the shadow of the mountain. There are no melt-rivers here, just snow, rock, and ice. The mountain feels so close as if I could just reach out and touch it. Standing next to it peering up at the snowy slopes it feels almost attainable, the sun glistening on the snow and a plume of snow being blown off its summit.

As we get into K2 basecamp people pile out of a larger tent, which must be the mess tent, and walk over to us all happy and smiling. They are a Japanese expedition and they have been here for a couple of weeks. They have started setting up the route, but bad weather has kept them low on the mountain.

"Looks like more bad weather is brooding," says one of the Japanese. "We are staying in camp for now, there has been a lot of avalanches coming down the mountain. We need a longer weather window to go back up."

They are a jolly bunch and they invite us for tea. They laugh and sing and make us point out anything that Poland or Mexico are famous for. I feel a little stupid as I don't actually know anything much about Poland. All I can come up with is Pope John Paul, while Jose is rattling off Mexican things such as tequila, tacos, sombreros, and Mayan pyramids. I don't think Auschwitz, while very famous, is something I should bring up, so I sit in silence letting Jose indulge the Japanese with his heritage. While we are drinking tea, lovely milk and sugar-free green tea, with the Japanese Murtaza and Anam have set up our tents next to the Japanese. Now Murtaza is hovering outside the mess tent motioning for us to come outside.

"Come, there is something I want to show you," he says as he starts to walk up the mountainside. He is slow and his breath is labored.

"Are you OK Murtaza?" I ask.

"Yes, yes, this body is just not as young as it used to be."

He seems bothered or maybe sad. I realize why as we scramble higher up and are met by plaques covering the rock. There are hundreds of metal plates with names carved into them; shallow graves with mountaineering boots and pieces of bones sticking out between the rocks.

"What is this place?" whispers Jose.

"This must be the Gilkey Memorial," I whisper back, it seems inappropriate to speak any louder. I have read about it in my many mountaineering books. "These are the names of those who never made it off the mountain," I continue whilst reading the names and dates of the plates.

Garlands and sun-bleached prayer flags decorate the rocks and I recognize many of the names, climbing heroes of mine whom the mountain has claimed. Julie Tullis, Allison Hargraves, and Lilian Barrad, women I look up to, who made the summit but not the return back down. It is sobering to see how many people made the summit but not the descent, perhaps forgetting the summit is only halfway. I whisper a silent prayer out into the universe that the Mexicans and Japanese won't meet the same fate as those whose memory rests here.

Murtaza clears his throat, which makes both me and Jose jump. He is motioning for us to come over and as we get closer I can see tears in his eyes. He is pointing at a metal plate that has long ago lost its shine, but the inscription is still clear, '*In memory of my Polish brother ZYGMUNT PYSZKA July 18 1978.*' I want to reach out to comfort Murtaza, but not knowing if it is appropriate I instead kneel down beside him touching the plate with my fingertips. I want to cry a little, if nothing else to show Murtaza that I feel for him, but my eyes stay dry. I don't feel any connection to this man that had been my grandfather, this man that I have never known. The sad feeling that is encapsulating me doesn't belong to Zygmunt, it belongs to all those resting here, all these brave people who followed their dream to the very end. Tiny pink flowers are growing in amongst the rocks, the first sign of life I have seen since leaving Urdukas' camp. They seem appropriate, like a little tribute to the dead from Mother Earth. But then a morbid thought enters my mind and I wondered if the only reason they can grow in this otherwise lifeless place is because of the nutrients provided by the human bodies placed in the few shallow graves. Bodies carried off the mountain and left to rest here.

We stay silent as we scramble back down and walk over to our tents. Only when we sit down outside our tent does Jose ask, "Are you OK?"

"Yeah, I am fine. Pretty sad that so many people don't make it back hey?" I reply.

"I mean about seeing your grandfather's plate?"

"Oh yeah, no I am fine. I didn't really know him."

We sit until the silence is interrupted by a giant roar. It sounds like a jet plane taking off, but when I look up I can see snow and rocks billowing down the mountain. The mountainside loaded with fresh snow from the past few days' storm is giving way tumbling down the mountain. It peters out to the right side of camp, but we still get covered in a dusting of snow and the force of the avalanche pushing the air in front of it causes a strong wind to rip through camp. The Japanese all come out from their mess tent and are pointing and talking loudly in Japanese.

"Good thing they weren't climbing," says Jose as the dusting of snow settles.

"Indeed," I reply shaking off the coating of snow.

All through the night we listened to avalanche after avalanche roar down the mountain.

"I don't think this mountain wants to be climbed," mutters Jose when we again are woken by a giant roar.

I lay in the tent eyes open staring out into the darkness.

156

This noise is different.

"Jose, I don't think it is an avalanche," I say, panic building in my voice. "That is a helicopter."

I have barely gotten the words out when I hear Murtaza outside telling us to get dressed and get outside. As I am about to go outside Murtaza instead head dives into our tent, just as a bright light illuminates the tent. He lays half on top of Jose, who was still busy putting on his pants when Murtaza dove in.

"Who is that?" asks Jose.

Murtaza looks scared. "It must be an army helicopter; they are the only ones who fly at night."

The search light once again lights up our tent and I feel like the sparrow we had watched being snatched up midair by the eagle at Paiju. We lay dead still in our tent while the helicopter keeps circling, and we can hear the Japanese next door unzipping their tents and going outside to look at what is going on. As the sound of the helicopter blades grows fainter we also go outside, watching it fly over Broad Peak basecamp, its search light scanning the ground for a long time before finally setting down a little way from where they have just searched. It stays on the ground for only a few minutes before taking off again.

The rest of the night is still and deadly quiet, no more helicopters and no more avalanches. Almost as if the mountain is holding its breath. I can't sleep and nor can Jose. We lay silent in our sleeping bags, ears pricked ready for another thunderous sound, hoping that when it comes it will be the mountain releasing some of its load rather than another helicopter whose intentions we do not know. But it stays quiet.

Just before first light I unzip the tent on my side to go pee. As I step outside I almost bump straight into someone sitting in the dark outside our tent. A scream gets caught in my throat as I see the iciest blue eyes reflect in the bright moonlight.

Chapter 22

It is the porter we had sent back in Paiju. I could recognize those eyes anywhere. Before I can speak he puts his finger to his lips urging me to stay quiet. I retreat back into our tent, grabbing Jose's arm. "Jose, the blue-eyed porter from Paiju is sitting outside our tent."

"What does he want?" asks Jose.

"I don't know, he just told me to be quiet."

"He speaks English?" asks Jose surprised.

"No, well, he motioned for me to be quiet. I really need to pee, but I am too scared to go out there."

Jose comes outside with me, and when we exit the tent the porter is standing with Murtaza and Anam over by their tent. I can hear them whispering, a murmur floating on the slight breeze, but I can't make out what they are saying. Not that I would understand even if I could. Jose follows me to a large boulder behind which I squat, relieving my full bladder. When we walk back into camp a light is on in our kitchen tent and I can hear the gas stove laboring. Murtaza motions for us to come over and when we sit down on the ground inside the tent, Murtaza and Anam's sleeping bags still strewn across the floor, the blue-eyed porter is sitting there next to Murtaza sipping on a steaming cup of tea. Anam is stirring the pot over the stove and scoops out ladles of tea, filling two more cups and passing them to us.

Murtaza clears his throat. "This is Karim."

The blue-eyed porter reaches out his hand when he hears his name spoken and shakes our hands greeting us with a quiet, "As-Salam-Alaikum."

Those piercing blue eyes sear a hole through mine. Murtaza takes back up once the introductions are over. "He has been travelling up the glacier with the Spanish expedition, they hired him as soon as he returned to Askole. Yesterday they all hiked to Broad Peak basecamp and set up camp for their expedition. They arrived there a few hours after we passed through. Last night, they were woken by the helicopter, just like we were. Only, just outside of their camp the helicopter dropped off its four passengers. The Spanish noticed straight away that it was the Americans and the Pakistani from Skardu. They didn't come into camp but set up their own tents and went inside. Israel decided to send a porter up to warn us and Karim offered to hike through the night to reach us before first light. He woke us up when he arrived and I asked him to keep watch by your tent, and to alert me if anyone arrived into camp."

"They must have thought we were camped with the Spanish at Broad Peak," ponders Jose.

Sunrise first turns the sky a dusty pink, but soon enough it is a vibrant blue and the sun is so bright it hurts my eyes. Murtaza has looked tired and sad throughout the early morning discussion. But when it is finally decided that Karim and Anam will be taking us over Gondogoro La high pass and back out through Hushe village, hoping to avoid our followers, he looks relieved. We hope that by going over Gondogoro La rather than hiking back out the way we came we will throw our followers off. Our permit states that we will be coming out the way we came in, so fingers crossed if there is anyone waiting for us they will be waiting in Askole and not Hushe.

I had read about Gondogoro La before leaving for Pakistan. It is a 19,488-feet-high mountain pass that reportedly provides one of the most spectacular mountain panoramas, with views of all of Pakistan's tallest mountains. I know that it requires some fourth-class climbing to get over the pass, but Murtaza ensures me that the climbing is straight forward when I express concern about Jose's complete lack of climbing experience.

"The army closed down the pass to tourists last year. But there should still be fixed ropes from previous years," explains Murtaza.

I hope he is right, ropes fixed to the mountain will not just save us if anyone takes a tumble, but also help us find the way.

"I wish I had the strength to come with you Marta. I am so sorry for all of this, I should never have asked you to come to Pakistan. Zygmunt would have been disappointed in me. I have failed you."

I start to protest but Murtaza continues, talking on top of me, "I don't know why your grandfather died. I suspect that Zygmunt was giving the Americans information about the Polish regime. I believed him to be on their side. But I am almost certain that Mr. Hawkins caused his death."

My eyes are wide with surprise, but in my gut I had feared the same thing. I have been searching my mind for another explanation, not wanting my climbing hero to be the bad guy. But I have no alternative. I forget all about the appropriate customs and embrace Murtaza in a hug. He squeezes me back before letting go.

"Inshallah, I will see you back in Rawalpindi."

The constant Inshallah, God willing, have been driving me nuts the entire trip. It seems lazy or un-committing to me, always leaving it up to God. I believe that you create your own path and it is not God letting us reach camp each evening, but rather my own determination and my legs walking me there. Now however, it seems fitting.

"Inshalla," I reply before leaving to pack up our tent.

We no longer have porters, so my backpack is bulging in every direction. When I heave it onto my back it is heavy, even with Anam and Karim carrying all the food and the stove. As we hike out of camp I watch Murtaza standing next to our porters waving goodbye. I feel sad and worried. Will he be OK?

What will the Americans do to him? But he seems more concerned with us than himself. He was fussing as we left, telling Anam to carry more of our weight despite Jose and me both protesting.

We have to cross the Godwin-Austen Glacier. We figure that as soon as the Americans realize we are not camped at Broad Peak they will make their way up to K2 basecamp, in fact they are probably already on their way. To avoid running into them we cross the glacier, hiking close to the other side hoping they won't spot us. For the first time the clear skies and bright sunlight are unwelcome and I am now wishing for bad weather.

When we reach the other side of the glacier we find a snowbank next to it and we can hike on the other side, obscuring us from vision. It makes me feel safe despite every now and again fearing that all of a sudden our followers will pop up over the snowbank. They can't see us, but we also cannot see them. I make everyone stop time and time again so I can scramble up the snow to peek over, each time I am met by the endless white of the glacier. Not once do I spot another human being, despite straining my eyes to see the other side.

As we near Concordia the sun is still bright and warm, Karim drops his pack and goes ahead to see who is in camp. When he returns an hour later he informs us that camp is empty bar the Italian Rescue Centre, the Mexicans must have left for K2 this morning. I am surprised that I haven't spotted them during one of my many forays up the snowbank. But I am pleased, because if I can't spot a single person from their large cohort of porters it is unlikely anyone would have spotted us.

We walk past Concordia, not wishing to stop and chat to the Italians. We do not have a permit to cross Gondogoro La, and while the Italians may be convinced to not mention our route to the Americans, they are unlikely to not alert the Pakistani army with whom they work closely to execute any required rescues. As such we skirt Concordia, and while the Italians may have spotted us they make no attempt to contact us. We keep moving fast hoping to make it all the way to Ali Camp, so that we can cross Gondogoro La first thing tomorrow before the sun warms up the slopes sending down ice and snow.

Jose is struggling by mid-afternoon, coughing and complaining of a tight chest. Each time I bring up altitude sickness he blows it off, saying it is just a cold he has picked up. But his speech is becoming increasingly slurred and I am worried. Anam agrees we should stop to give Jose a chance to rest up and acclimatize before tomorrow's big day. Not only do we have to climb up to 19,500 feet, but we also have to do it without any mountaineering equipment. Normally one would bring an ice axe, crampons, a harness, and a helmet for this climb. But we have none. We had not intended on doing any climbing.

Murtaza and Anam explained to us before we left K2 that the porters do this climb without any mountaineering equipment, carrying heavy loads, and wearing plastic sandals, so we should be fine. It is technically straight forward and we should be OK crossing it without mountaineering gear. But it still worries me, it is a big day and Jose has never climbed before. Normally the route would be fixed, fixed ropes leading the way to the top. But last year the army closed the pass without giving any reason as to why, and as such no one has been over the pass for two years. Our plan is to get up at 2 a.m. to start climbing to the pass, hoping to reach the top of the pass by sunrise.

I crawl into the tent carrying two bowls of rice and lentils. Anam and Karim will be sleeping outside tonight, we only brought one small tent that Jose and I are sharing. Jose doesn't touch his food despite me pestering him to eat.

162

"It hurts to swallow," he complains.

Two a.m. arrives way too quickly. I want to keep sleeping, and when I peer out from the tent I am greeted by thick clouds rolling in, partly obscuring the sky. Only patches of star-studded black peeking through the clouds. Jose is laboring for breath and coughing.

"Did you get any sleep?" I ask.

"Not one wink," he wheezes. "I am surprised you managed to sleep with me coughing all night."

"I was out like a rock." I smile. "I guess the lack of sleep last night caught up to me."

I am packing up my sleeping bag when Anam calls me from outside the tent, "Marta, we better hurry up."

I prod Jose before getting outside, realizing that Anam isn't just in a rush to get going, but we are in fact in a race against time. Off in the distance I can see a row of faint lights slowly making their way towards us.

Chapter 23

I guess it was easy to follow our tracks, no one has been this way since the last snow. While we are breaking trail in the snow our followers have an easier job using our already perfect steps. The lights are piercing the otherwise pitch dark night, it almost appears as if they are floating on the wind.

"Shit," I swear. "We are basically breaking trail for them, leading them straight to us."

"Hurry, hurry," says Karim in broken English.

I have completely stopped in my tracks watching the lights bob up and down, getting closer. Jose looks terrible when he comes out of the tent. But he forces a smile, trying to appear brave.

"Jose," I say, tears threatening in the corners of my eyes. "We don't have to go on. We can stop here. Call it quits and see what these guys want."

"No, no, I am fine."

Jose's voice is hoarse and his lips are blue. By now tears are no longer threatening they are tumbling down my cheeks, and the icy wind that has picked up freeze them in their tracks halfway down my cheeks and on my chin.

"Don't cry," says Jose as he shoulders his pack, his voice merely a croak.

I walk over to Jose and take both his hands buried somewhere deep inside his mittens. "We should stop. You don't look well," I say. What I had hoped to come out as strong and determined gets swept away in the strengthening wind and instead ends up sounding weak.

"I am fine, really." Jose pulls his hands back and turns away from me, walking towards Anam and Karim.

I feel helpless and scared. Scared of pushing on and terrified of stopping. My mind is craving more oxygen so I can think clearer. But where we are headed there will only be less, less oxygen and more cold.

It is 4 a.m. when we reach the bottom of the pass. We can no longer see the lights behind us, not because they have fallen further behind, but because the clouds have moved in in full force. I can barely make out Jose only a few feet in front of me. Karim is digging in the snow looking for buried ropes from previous years, but unable to find any, he starts up breaking trail relying solely on memory. Karim has crossed Gondogoro La twice before, but it has been a few years and we now have to attempt it in a whiteout with no mountaineering equipment or fixed ropes.

Dread is encapsulating me as we push up, sometimes in waist-deep snow, the wind ripping at our faces. My nose has gone numb a long time ago and I have to keep turning around to yell at Jose to keep moving. Each time finding him slumped over, his head resting on his forearms. Luckily it seems my urgent calls get him back on his feet each time. But it is exhausting. My own voice has become hoarse as we have gotten higher and my head has started to pound. If I am suffering, Jose already unwell at the base must be in hell I think to myself, as determination alone makes me put one leg in front of the other. Anam is just in front of me and I believe Karim just in front of him, but I can't see that far. Anam regularly turns to make sure I am there behind him, but we never speak. I look at my altimeter, 18,687 feet, only 800 feet to go. I turn around again. I can't see Jose.

I call out to Anam, he turns around, but my hoarse voice mixed with the strong winds means he can't hear me. I point behind me. Before I manage to try to speak again Anam disappears in the white in front of him, and all of a sudden I am alone in the whiteness. Panic is creeping in and I stand frozen in place unsure of what to do. I am calling Jose's name in the brewing storm, knowing it is futile. The wind steals my words before they can travel any length of distance. Just as I decide to start down to look for Jose, Anam returns holding on to Karim by his jacket arm, shouting over the wind.

"We have to hold on to each other."

I grab Anam's jacket as Karim leads the way back down from where we had come. It is disorienting and I can't make out where the snow ends and the sky starts, it is all just a canvas of white. I can't even spot the track we must have just made, the wind is so strong it fills in our steps just as quickly as we step out of them. We find Jose only fifty feet below curled up, sitting on his hunches, arms wrapped around his knees and his head resting on top of them. I get down next to him and shout.

"Jose stand up. NO SITTING DOWN." He waves me away with his mitten. "We have to move Jose. Come on, GET UP."

I am fighting back tears and my nose is running, causing an icy layer to form on my upper lip. Anam is helping out, actually pulling Jose by the arm.

"Must move. Almost there," he shouts. "Only a few more hundred feet. GET UP. GET UP."

Jose stumbles to his feet and Anam put his shoulder under his arm. Looking at me and Karim Anam shouts, "GO, GO, GO."

Too scared of losing Jose behind me again I step aside and let Anam and Jose follow behind Karim as I take up the tail. I am breathing heavily, my mouth is dry, and my tongue feels like a piece of leather. I have already reached for my water bottle several times, each time realizing it is frozen solid and wondering why I keep doing the same thing over and over. Until next time my mouth feels so dry it hurts to breathe and I again reach for the bottle. The same disappointment each time.

In front of me Jose is swaying like a drunk, the only reason he hasn't fallen off this mountain back down the pass that we are ascending is thanks to Anam's iron grip around his waist. Both holding him upright, stopping him from falling, and forcing him to move forwards. I look at my altimeter again, 18,792 feet. I let out an audible groan, we have only come another 100 feet. It feels like we have been moving for hours. How are we ever going to get Jose up and over this pass? I am not even sure I can get myself over safely, let alone someone with acute altitude sickness.

My toes have joined my nose in the land of the numb. It at first feels like a blessing when they go from piercing pain to all of a sudden nothing. But I know it means frostbite, so I try to wriggle them inside my ill-equipped hiking boots. I wish I had my insulated mountaineering boots that are parked inside my closet at home, in my little apartment on Queen Anne Hill. All of a sudden the memory of home is so vivid I can smell the salty sea breeze coming in through my open window, heavy with the musty smell of seaweed. It is peculiar, the smell is so strong I am sure these bitterly cold winds on top of the world so far from the ocean are in fact travelling directly from Puget Sound to me. I smile as I move on, comforted by the smell of home, until it dawns on me that I am breathing through my mouth. I am not smelling anything. My oxygen deprived brain is playing tricks on me. The wonderful salty sea breeze escapes me just as quickly as it had arrived and I feel overcome with hopelessness.

As if on cue Jose slumps over again, Anam unable to keep him upright. He is lying face down in the snow and Karim and Anam roll him over. Jose curls up into a fetal position and refuses to move. I scream as loud as I can, "STAND UP JOSE. I MEAN IT, YOU HAVE TO FUCKING STAND UP."

But he just lays there, eyes fixated straight ahead of him, seeing but not seeing. I wonder if his mind is playing him a wonderful movie of home and if he can smell the sea breeze, or the apple blossoms of his family farm. I lay down next to him wrapping my arms around his body facing him. The cold snow is biting my cheek that is resting against it. My shouting has turned to a pleading whisper, as I am begging him to please get up in between loud sobs as my tears catch in my dry raw throat. He lifts his arm and I feel a flicker of hope, but it dies when he places his snow and ice caked mitten on my cheek and whispers with much effort. "This is as far as I go Marta."

"No, no, no, no. NO," I cry.

Jose is staring at me with his icy mitten on my cheek. "I. Love. You." Each word a major effort, before closing his eyes.

"JOSE." I am shaking him as hard as my frozen hands will allow.

Anam and Karim both grab me and pull me off Jose.

"There is no point Marta."

I know that Anam is trying to be comforting, but the necessity to scream over the wind makes it sound more like a barking order. I feel anger flush on my cheeks and I can almost feel my icy tears defrost as anger races up.

"I am not going. I am not leaving Jose here to die," I scream.

"Marta, we have no choice. We can't stay here. We will all die."

Karim is watching us scream at each other as he pulls out Jose's sleeping bag from his pack and tries to get him inside it.

"He is NOT dead," I cry.

Karim says something in Urdu and Anam goes over to help him get Jose inside the sleeping bag and on to a little ledge that Karim had flattened out in the snow. They roll his listless body onto a Therm-a-Rest.

"Karim will get help after we are safely on the other side," says Anam as he pulls me upwards by my arm.

I allow myself to be dragged up the mountain. I no longer feel anything. I feel no anger, no sadness, no loss, no nothing. My feelings are as numb as my nose and my toes. I no longer care if I make it back to safety.

Chapter 24

At the top of the pass we are above the clouds and all I can see in every direction is a blanket of clouds intercepted by soaring peaks piercing through. Had my brain, body, and emotions, not been numbed by the altitude and shock, I am sure I would have been blown away by the dramatic beauty. Instead the warmth from the sun up here thaws my icy cheeks and I realize that I am still crying.

I can't really remember how I have gotten from Jose to the top of the pass, it is all a blur. The sun above the clouds makes everything seem safer, and my first instinct is to turn back down the way that we have come, go back, and find Jose. My altitude-altered brain is telling me that if I can only get him up here in the sunshine everything will be fine. But Anam is ushering me to follow him down the other side. I have too little energy left to take initiative, all I can do to stand on my feet is to do as I am told.

It is terrifying heading back down into the clouds and whiteout conditions. I want to stay up above the clouds in the endless sunshine. A world so different from this one we are entering into. The visibility once again drops to pretty much zero and I am stumbling along. Staying so close to Karim I can reach out to touch him. Anam is right behind me. Big snowflakes have started to fall and as they land on my eyelashes they become heavy. It is so easy just to close my eyes, let go, and give in to my tiredness.

"MARTA, get up!" Anam is yelling at me.

I hadn't realized I sat down. It is so comfortable sitting in the soft snow, big snowflakes dancing all around me. I don't want to keep moving. I close my eyes again.

A big tug on my jacket wakes me from the wonderful dream I am having, me and Jose running through his parents' apple farm holding hands. Sonia's laughter is just behind us. SONIA. My brain shoots back to reality. I have to get out of here, I have to get back to Sonia. I may not have much left, my dad is gone, my mom doesn't know who I am, and Jose is frozen to a mountainside. But I have Sonia, I cannot let her down.

A new found determination and a longing to be back with Sonia gets me back on my feet. I try to keep the image of Sonia's laughing face in my mind to keep me pushing forward. As we get lower we are below the clouds and our field of vision opens up a little, and with the increasing oxygen as we drop elevation my mind becomes clearer. It is like lifting a curtain. The look of Jose's body curled up on the snow as we climbed further and further away lights up in my memory so clear it physically hurts. I have to stop to grasp for breath, loud sobs escaping me.

Anam comes over and sits me down on a rock. I can't speak and I am crying loudly. Pained screams burst out of my chest. Karim and Anam communicate by looks alone, and Karim starts up the stove brewing tea. I had previously laughed at how Pakistanis think everything can be fixed with a cup of tea. But now as Karim hands me a cup of steaming tea, his icy blue eyes looking straight through me into my soul, I feel comforted by this hot milky liquid. There is something about Karim and his blue eyes, something that I can't put my finger on. But right now those eyes are willing me to be OK and they make me feel strangely calm. I drink my tea, feeling it fill my body with warmth. My nose comes back to life and with it a searing pain. My toes return from numbness. They hurt so bad that when we stand up to leave I wobble before falling over flat on my face. Karim shoulders his own pack before heaving mine on top and Anam puts his arm under my shoulder. We hobble on down.

We move so slowly it seems impossible we will ever get away from this mountain pass that I have come to hate. But eventually the snow and ice and barren rocks give way to a lush green valley. While the barren mountains are still surrounding us, they seem less oppressive when I am standing on green grass, something else living. The grass smells like paradise and I lay down feeling it against my cheek. A small sandy babbling brook flows next to where I lay, and the sound of trickling water is like conditioner to my ears. Karim starts to set up my tent while Anam is boiling water. I think both of them realize that no amount of coercion will see me leave this place today. It feels like heaven. I lay on the grass for a long time before Anam comes over and asks me to take my boots off. He has a kitchen pot full of hot water with him. Removing my boots results in intense pain, and once I peel my socks off I can tell my toes are badly frost bitten. They are completely white with black spots at the tips. The skin looks shiny and Anam baths them in the hot water, trying to rewarm my toes. I have watched many climbing documentaries and I know that rewarming of frostbitten tissue is extremely painful. But my heart is so full of pain, my chest so tight with suffering that I don't feel my toes thaw in the warm water.

I sit bathing my feet as Anam resupplies warm water and Karim makes me rice and lentils. I don't want to eat but Anam is barking at me to finish my plate, so I mechanically put fork to mouth over and over again. More hot tea, more warm water on my feet, more pain in my heart as I replay Jose's last labored words to me. I didn't reply. I didn't tell him I love him back. I had just kept screaming at him to get up.

The thought of him slowly freezing solid while I sit here sipping hot tea makes me feel nauseated and I vomit the rice and lentils back up. I am not sure how I get into my sleeping bag, but I have a night full of fitful nightmares. I dreamed that

172

we left Jose behind to die, only to wake up and realize that we did. My survivor's guilt is so strong that I long to be there with him, freezing into human ice cubes together. How can I go on knowing I left him behind? Sweet supportive Jose. The man who never wished to climb any mountain, who had come here for me. To help me find out the truth about my grandfather, a grandfather I never knew nor care about. I toss and turn and go from shivering from cold to bathing in sweat.

I sit up and start to rifle through my bag, finding my first aid kit at the bottom of my bag. The yellow prescription vial read *Hydrocodone, 1-2 tablets as needed for pain.* I had brought them along in case one of us sprained an ankle or hurt ourselves some other way. Now I empty the contents into my hand. A neat pile of twenty pills, I look at the pile wondering if these pills will silence my pain. *As needed for pain* I think, and bring my hand to my mouth.

The pills fill my mouth, they taste bitter. Just as I am about to start swallowing the picture of Sonia's laughing face shoots back. Gathering all my willpower I spit the pills back out. They are covered in saliva and I pick out two, put them on my tongue, and swallow. The other eighteen, now moist pills, I place back in the vial, not ready to throw away my escape route quite yet. My head falls back onto my Therm-a-Rest. Finally sleep arrives, a drug induced, dreamless deep sleep.

When I wake the sun is pricking my eyes through the thin tent fabric and I can hear Karim and Anam chatting outside. It all feels so normal that I turn over, half expecting Jose to be laying there next to me, expecting it all to be a bad dream. But all I find is the yellow medicine vial. Reality once again sets in. I close my eyes, wishing I had never woken up.

Anam comes to the tent. "Marta. Would you like some tea?"

"No."

"You should come out in the sunshine, it will make you feel better," continues Anam.

Not even a thousand burning suns could make me feel better, of that I am sure. But I struggle out of my sleeping bag knowing it is pointless staying in the tent. If anything we need to get moving, Jose's death will be a complete waste if we don't get out of here before our followers catch up. Actually I am a little surprised they haven't caught up to us. *I hope they freeze to death,* the thought escapes before I can stop it. I am not normally a malice person, but right now I wish death upon them with my entire being. Outside the world is basking in brilliant sunshine, the creek sparkling in the sunlight and flowers have sprung up at its edges. The beauty makes me furious. I want it to storm, and rain, and snow; this world does not match my devastated soul. But when I sit in the sunshine, warmth dancing on my skin and a freshly baked roti on my lap, I can feel little stiches starting to form on my splintered heart. Maybe I can survive this, I think to myself, as I nibble on the roti and drink cold water directly from the creek.

My toes have turned a worrying black color and have swollen up into large puss-filled blisters. It is excruciating and the thought of walking makes me feel sick. Anam is telling me that he can't see anyone coming down the pass behind us, and with any luck yesterday's bad weather has turned our followers around.

"I think we can make it all the way to Hushe today," says Anam.

But once we start moving his optimism sinks. My vision had turned black when I squeezed my battered toes into my hiking boots, I nearly passed out. Now, every step sends shooting pain through my toes and feet. It hurts so bad it makes me gag, and I regularly have to sit down when the pain turns my vision yellow then black, dots dancing around in front of my eyes. I am willing my body forward, telling myself I deserve the pain, and that I am not allowed pity. I do not deserve to be pain free when Jose has perished without me telling him I love him back. Me abandoning him, when he had so selflessly come here with me. Part of me is enjoying the torture I am enduring, somehow reasoning that I am paying my dues for surviving. I refuse Anam and Karim's constant offer of taking my pack. I don't want to get away easy, I want to suffer. But even with me pushing myself to the brink, I can't move much faster than a snail's pace. Each time I try to go a little faster everything starts to spin and I have to sit down to avoid passing out. "Slow and steady, slow and steady," I whisper to myself.

The sun's rays start to dull in intensity and the afternoon glow is basking the peaks around us in a golden hue. K6 and K7 shoot up towards the sky in defiance, taunting climbers with their sheer rocky faces. The beauty is mesmerizing, and despite all the pain inside I can't help myself to marvel at the splendor of Mother Earth. How can life be so ugly and so incredibly stunning all at once?

Signs of life start to appear, first a field filled with purple potato flowers, then the trail widens and we can hear a rooster call. Little rock walls surrounding fields fed by irrigation channels start to appear. Water rushing down from the mountainsides is channeled on to the parched soils. Soon women clad in colorful Saris tending the fields emerge, as well as men sitting in the shade of apricot trees eating the fruits. The giggles of young children escape the small rock buildings lining our path, and a goat bleats as we pass. The sounds of civilization overwhelm me, and I sit down right there on the dusty hot trail and cry.

Chapter 25

We don't make it to Hushe. Once I sit down on the dusty trail, tears of relief at being back in the land of the living and leaving all those brazen lifeless peaks behind, I can't bring myself to get back on my feet. The searing pain is too much to bear. I want to stay here listening to the sounds of human beings going about their day. None of Anam's coaxing works. This is as far as I can go.

I finally let Karim take my backpack and he goes off to find us a spot to camp. Karim returns and picks me up, carrying me to a barren field on which he has set up my tent and the stove. I am surprised at the ease with which he picks me up. One of the villagers has given us permission to camp in his field. A field that has been laid to rest for the summer. Here things are done the old way, no fertilizers or mono-cultures. Each field is tended like a precious gold mine, giving the soil time to restore itself between crops. That is what I need, I think, time to restore myself, be laid to rest for a while to nourish my withered soul.

Anam has sweet talked our gracious host into giving us a few eggs and potatoes, and he has fried up the most delicious meal I have ever tasted. Eggs and potatoes. I want for nothing else. My belly full for the first time in days, I lay down on the lumpy soil while Anam examines my toes.

"Marta, your toes aren't looking so good. You sure you can walk to Hushe tomorrow?"

"Do I have a choice?" I reply.

"We can probably get a mule."

"No," I say a little harsher than I intend, "I can walk."

I fish out two of the slimy hydrocodone pills from the yellow vial and swallow them before even attempting to sleep, wishing for that deep dreamless sleep. It seems to work as my eyelids grow heavy and I drift off to sleep quickly.

At three a.m. I wake with a start. A disturbing dream has left me feeling uneasy. But all I can remember is Karim's icy blue eyes staring into mine. It makes me shudder. I lay awake in my tent trying to work out what it is about those eyes that keeps me on edge. Searching my brain I try to remember the rest of the dream that has so spooked me. Karim never smiles, I have never seen his eyes glint with joy. Always deeply focused, like a hawk that nothing ever passes. I can't switch my brain off. I consider taking another two pain pills. More to be able to sleep, to escape my aching heart and jittery nerves, than to relieve the searing pain in my toes. Physical pain I can bare; it is the heart wrenching emotional pain I find harder to endure. If only Sonia could see me now. She always tells me I am emotionally switched off, trying to get me to play with her nieces or swoon over a cute puppy. I don't tend to get attached to things, whereas Sonia instantly pours all her love over anyone that comes her way.

"Look where baring my soul has brought me?" I whisper into the empty tent.

Opening up and letting Jose in has brought me nothing but pain. I long to be in my mother's arms, not my current mother, the mother of my childhood. The one who remembers my name, the one who I scolded for packing me kopytka, potato dumplings, for school lunches instead of sandwiches or pieces of cheese like the other kids in school. The same one who held me, and blew on my bleeding knees when I fell over racing the boys in our neighborhood. God I miss her. When the sun hits the tent fabric I am surprised at how quickly time has passed, it seems like I have only been awake for a few minutes, but I must have been laying here dreaming of a mother that no longer exists for over three hours.

When I unzip the tent I am startled by Karim's blue eyes.

He is sitting just outside my tent staring straight at my tent door. A shiver runs down my back. Has he been in my tent? Had I actually seen those eyes when I woke at 3 a.m.? I rub my eyes trying to clear my brain of any residue of the drugs. No more pills, I think as I greet Karim before hobbling over to where Anam sits brewing tea. Anam smiles and it instantly eases my nerves. I have grown very fond of Anam. In contrast to Karim his eyes constantly light up with laughter, or darken with concern. He is easy to read and I enjoy his openness and friendly demeanor.

"Let me look at your feet," demands Anam after handing me a cup of tea.

He presses a finger on one of my swollen blistered toes and I am impressed by his touch. I know from the little research I did before leaving home that in Muslim culture touching someone's feet, even when shoed, is a big no-no. I feel overwhelmed with gratitude that Anam is ignoring not only his custom of never touching someone's feet, but also touching a woman's feet. A woman that is not his wife. Tears well up in my eyes.

"Oh I am sorry, I am hurting you."

"No, no. It is OK," I reply while drying my eyes.

Anam again tries to convince me to get a mule. But I yet again refuse. Something I regret a little later when we start our final hike. I am hissing with pain, cautiously placing one foot in front of the other. I stop over and over again when the pain brings me to the point of being physically sick. But I embrace the pain, the physical pain, and the struggle to keep on moving forward keeps my mind from wandering into more unpleasant emotions.

"Look," says Anam, and points off in the distance.

All I can make out is a row of mules stirring up a cloud of dust further down the path. I strain my eyes, and as the dust

178

settles I can make out buildings and movement. There are rock dwellings spread out ahead of us, a deep chocolate-brown river flows through the valley and green rice paddies dot the river banks. People are milling around and we can hear children shriek.

"Hushe?" I ask.

"Yes. We better send Karim ahead to see what awaits us before we wander on in," says Anam.

"Good idea," I reply, although I no longer care what awaits me.

Nothing can be worse than the pain in my heart and my toes. I just long for this to be over with, no matter what comes next.

We wait in the searing sun. I can feel my skin burn but I can't be bothered to get my sunscreen out. What does a little sunburn matter in the big scheme of things, I reason, while Anam is busy with his Dhuhr, midday prayer. I watch him prostrate over and over, wishing I have something to believe in. To be able to pass off the responsibility I feel for Jose's death to some greater force would be such a relief. But I have no such faith. I know there is no reason for Jose's death, there is no bigger plan, nor will he be in a better place. He will just remain forever frozen to the mountain. The image of his slumped-over body, cloudy eyes, and blue lips, returns with such clarity it sends a shiver through my body. I suddenly feel cold in the blazing midday sun, almost like I am back there begging Jose to stand up. I pull my down jacket out of my bag and put it on. Anam, who has finished with his prayer, gives me an odd look but doesn't say anything. Soon sweat is dripping down my brow, but I still feel cold.

"Marta, you are going to get heat stroke," says Anam as he hands me his water bottle full of sun-warmed water.

I remove my down jacket feeling my clammy skin, the

jacket is wet with sweat. It feels like I am outside my own body watching myself from a distance. I wonder why I am sweating when I am still shivering with cold. Maybe over heating is like freezing. When you are close to freezing to death you start feeling warm and get undressed. Maybe this is the same, when you are close to a heatstroke you start feeling cold. I finish Anam's water bottle and he sets off to refill it in a trickle of a creek a little way away from where we are sitting.

Karim returns, telling us everything is normal in Hushe. There are no other foreigners and none of the villagers have seen anyone from outside the village for days.

"OK then, let's go," says Anam.

After sitting still it is agonizing to once again stand on my feet and I wince with pain. Karim comes over to give me a shoulder and I pull away. He looks at me showing no emotion, instead he remains standing, waiting for me to accept his help. But I know he has noticed my recoil. I don't know whether to feel ashamed or scared. I let Anam take my pack. While I still believe that I deserved to suffer I am not sure I can actually take any more suffering. It takes every ounce of will power just to hobble on the last mile into the village.

At the edge of the village a small crowd of people are gathered, they are talking amongst themselves, their body language is animated and they are standing next to a new-looking Jeep.

"Was that Jeep here when you came in earlier?" Anam asks Karim.

But Karim doesn't reply, instead his grip around my shoulder tightens.

"Karim?" persists Anam.

I can make out two figures, a man and a woman. They look like they are wearing suits, and they are most certainly not Pakistanis. The flight instinct in my body is intense. I have to stop to draw a breath. I know there is no escape. I can't run, my feet won't carry me. Instead I sink to the ground where I remain sitting, watching the man and woman get into the Jeep, which is now speeding in our direction.

"Marta run," screams Anam as he is running towards me.

PART III – Pacific Northwest

"It is not the mountain we conquer but ourselves."
— Sir Edmund Hillary

Chapter 26

"I am sorry but we could only save five of your toes." The doctor looks matter-of-factly as he tells me the news.

He has pulled the light green curtain part open and through the gap I can see another hospital bed on the opposite side of the room. But I can't make out if it is empty. I don't know what I am meant to say, so I reply with the first thing that comes to mind.

"Which ones?"

"You still have most of both your big toes, and your right foot only required partial amputation of all toes apart from the little toe, which is completely gone. The left foot fared a little worse and only your big toe remains," he looks pleased with himself as he continues, "we managed to save the nails on both big toes."

Who cares about nails, I think to myself. I'd rather have more toes, less nails. I had been admitted to Harbor View Hospital as soon as my plane landed back in Seattle. It was obvious I would lose some tissue, but I hadn't realized quite the extent of my frostbite until now.

"We have to keep you for a few days. But you should be able to leave pretty soon. Do you have someone that can take care of you?"

"Take care of me?"

"You will be in a wheel chair while your toes heal."

"Oh, OK." My brain is still catching up, slow and confused from the anesthesia.

"We realize your mom is in no position to take on the role of caregiver."

Tears are pricking my eyes and I wish for this doctor to leave me alone. Let my brain clear before bringing these questions to me.

"My friend Sonia," I answer.

"And where can we reach this Sonia?"

"Listen, I don't know where my bag is, or any of my stuff. I had a phone but for all I know it is still on some mountaintop in Pakistan. So I don't know how you will get a hold of Sonia."

The doctor's eyes soften. "Yes, sorry. I understand you have been through a lot. But maybe if you could tell us where she works we could get a hold of her there?"

"Second Chance Women's Shelter," I reply before closing my eyes and letting my fussy brain go back to sleep.

When I drift off to sleep my mind goes back to Pakistan. The Jeep is speeding towards us, Anam is pulling me by my arms, trying to get me to stand up, to run, and to try to escape. But my body is done. There is no more escape, no fight left in me. The two Americans exit the Jeep and I can hear their voices loud, so loud, but I can't make out what they are saying. Why don't I understand what they are saying? I feel myself being lifted as black dots are dancing in front of my eyes. It is over, is my last thought before I lose consciousness.

Next thing I am bouncing around in the back of the Jeep as it moves over rough terrain. But then nothing until I wake up in a bed in a barren room, an IV line in my arm, and ice packs stuffed in my armpits. A floor fan is facing me and cool air is blasting me in the face. It feels good, but my mouth is parched. My tongue feels like a piece of leather and I long for icy cold water. I can hear someone enter the room but my vision is blurred. I am expecting the Americans but instead a Pakistani nurse changes out the empty fluid bag attached to my IV for a full one. When she turns towards me she looks surprised.

"Oh, hello there. Good to see you are awake." She smiles.

"Wa," I can't get the words out, I try again. "Water," I manage.

The nurse looks indecisive like she is about to break some

sort of law, but my pleading eyes must have done the trick because she leaves and returns with a glass of water. She holds it to my lips and I drink it in small sips, letting the water wash over my dry tongue and gums. I am greedy for the moisture and I try to take over the glass so I can hurry the water down faster, but my hands are fumbling and unwilling to follow my commands. Instead I knock the glass and some of the water runs down my chin.

"Careful," says the nurse, who keeps holding the glass to my mouth allowing only small amounts at a time.

I finish the entire glass, but as soon as the nurse leaves I vomit it all back up. Slimy water mixed with stomach acid leaves a foamy patch on the sheet next to my head. I didn't manage to lean over far enough for it to hit the floor. A while later the door opens again and I can hear the nurse talking to someone in English.

"She is awake. I just gave her a glass of water."

"Oh good. Did she keep it down?" asks the mystery person.

They are standing out of my field of vision. Before the nurse can answer I croak, "No."

***

Someone is tapping on my shoulder and I slowly opened my eyes, struggling to keep them open and to focus. My eyelashes are fluttering like a pair of butterflies.

"Hello dear," says a plump elderly nurse as she leans in over me.

It takes a few seconds before my mind catches up and I realize I am at Harbor View Hospital, back in Seattle. Not in Pakistan like I was just dreaming.

"We spoke to your friend dear," continues the nurse, "she

is on her way to see you."

"Sonia is on her way?"

I am not sure I believe what she has just told me. A lump is forming in my throat and tears start to pour down my cheeks.

"Oh dear, no need to be upset dear. Your friend will be here shortly. Can I get you anything?" she smiles at me.

"Coffee?" I enquire.

"How about some apple juice instead?" she asks without really asking. Leaving to fetch me the juice.

Apple juice. My mind brings back memories of wandering through Jose's parents' apple orchards. The trees bursting with flowers, white petals falling to the ground like snow. Big heavy snowflakes falling on Jose's frozen body. Panic starts to bubble up. I am home. I have to tell Jose's parents I left him to die. I have saved myself while Jose was left to freeze to death. I can't breathe. It feels like someone is closing their fingers around my throat, tighter and tighter, until only short wheezes of breath can escape. I am clawing at my chest gasping for air when the nurse returns. She drops the juice on the ground and runs over to press the emergency button before telling me to take deep slow breaths, grabbing my arms, holding them down by my side. The doctor returns and puts something into my IV drip. The world turns black as my eyelids turn to lead.

I am back in Pakistan. The mystery person in the room walks over to my bedside in response to my barking no. A woman leans over me. Why is my vision still blurry? I think. I can make out the pale skin and brown hair, but the finer details remain a mystery. I can hear her chewing on a piece of gum, the smell of spearmint mixed in with the heavy scent of her perfume. When she speaks her voice has the accent of a New Yorker.

"Hi Marta, can you hear me?" she asks.

I nod, it hurts too much to speak. My throat is burning

188

from the acid of the vomit.

"You need medical attention for your feet. We think it is best you receive this treatment back in the USA."

I am shaking my head.

"The treatment there will be better than what you can get here and the damage is already done. There is no benefit in doing the surgery here." She goes on to explain. Mistaking my insistent head shaking for me wanting to tend to my frostbitten feet here instead of the USA.

But I can't leave. How can I make her understand that I can't leave while Jose's body is still out there in the mountains? I have no intention of leaving Pakistan without it. Even if it costs me my entire legs, I am going to get Jose's body home with me. I try to speak up, but trying to speak makes me cough. Tears are streaming down my cheeks as I am coughing up blood.

"Can you give her something to calm down?" asks the mystery lady.

"This should put her to sleep," says the nurse.

"No. Please." I manage to whisper between coughs. I can feel cold travel through my veins and my brain lights up as if it is on fire. It feels like acid is being poured over my insides. My last feverish thought before I fall back asleep is, *I am dying.*

When I next wake up I can feel the presence of someone in the room before I open my eyes. I crack open one of my eyelids. I quickly open the other one. I feel disoriented and I can't figure out what is going on. My vision is still blurry but something is off. I can feel my heartbeat quicken as I try to sit up looking around the room. Someone who is sitting in the corner of the room stands up and walks towards me. This is not the same room, I think. I have been moved. This room is green. The last room was white. Where am I?

"Good," says the person from the corner of the room.

That New York accent again, "I was hoping you would have woken up half an hour ago. They must have given you a lot of drugs. Sorry about that. The plane is waiting for you. I will help you get dressed."

"No, no, no, please," I manage through my raw throat.

"Shhh…" says the woman putting a finger over her lips to show me to be quiet.

I shake my head and whisper, "Jose."

The woman looks concerned as she takes my hand. "There is nothing you can do for Jose right now."

As if in a trance I let the woman dress me. After which she calls for a nurse, a different nurse, to come take out my IV.

"You have been given morphine for the pain," says the New York accent, "so you may feel a little bit groggy. I will travel with you to Dubai. From there you will be on a direct flight to Seattle. I have arranged for an ambulance to meet you upon arrival."

I am too tired to argue, but inside my brain I am pleading for this to be a bad dream. I am wishing to wake up and still be in sun-soaked Concordia, Throne Room of the Mountain Gods, with Jose by my side.

***

I can feel sunshine dancing over my closed eyelids. It feels marvelous. I imagine the bright white of the snow outside. The thin green fabric of the tent heating up as the sun's rays intensify. Water is trickling somewhere nearby. A small stream formed by the ever-melting glacier. Someone touches my hand and I am imagining Jose next to me. But somewhere deep inside my drugged brain I know this isn't real, I am just cheating myself, playing cruel tricks with my ravaged brain. I force myself to open my eyes. When I do it almost feels as good as

190

my dream. There she is, beautiful and supportive Sonia. Sonia that loves me no matter what. She smiles at me and I can't compose myself, tears are gushing down my cheeks. Sonia holds me for an eternity. Not saying anything, no questions, just a big embrace of support. When she finally starts to pull away I am not ready. I mustered all my strength and hold on to her for dear life.

"Don't leave," I whisper.

Sonia releases herself from my grasp and takes my hands.

"I am not going anywhere Marta."

We sit in silence holding hands until I drift back to sleep. I don't dream of Pakistan this time, it is a deep dreamless sleep. When I wake up Sonia is gone. It makes me feel panicky and I press the button for a nurse. The elderly nurse comes rushing in.

"What is up dear?"

"Where is my friend?" I inquire.

I must look horrible, because the nurse gives my arm a compassionate stroke. "She is just outside speaking with Jose's parents, I will get her for you."

Bile reaches my throat and I have to swallow hard not to vomit.

"Jose's parents are here?" I more confirm than ask when Sonia pulls the light-green curtain aside and sits down on the chair next to my bed.

"Yes, they would like to see you."

I am crying and snot is running down my lip but I can't be bothered to wipe it away, instead it bubbles out of my nose as I whisper, "I can't face them yet..."

"It is OK," says Sonia, "they are with Jose right now anyway."

Chapter 27

"How did they get his body home?" I ask so shocked my tears, which have been running non-stop every waking hour for days now, stop flowing.

Sonia looks at me. "His body? Marta, you do know that Jose is going to be fine right?"

Going to be fine. I don't understand. I had seen him die. His cloudy eyes and frozen lips. The ripping storm, the wind, the snow and the altitude. His body giving up, Jose sitting down to die.

"He is alive?" I am terrified as I utter my question. Knowing the answer will disappoint me, but hope is a cruel thing, it just never gives up.

"Yes," laughs Sonia, "he is just a few doors down the hall."

I sit up in bed, ripping at my IV line, swinging my legs over the side of the bed.

"Hey, hey, Marta, hold up. I don't think..." Sonia is trying to stop me.

But I am already at the door on wobbly legs, a trickle of blood escaping the hole in my arm where seconds ago the IV line had been attached. I make my way down the hall as quickly as my legs will bear me. With each step pain is shooting up through my legs from the missing toes. I don't care. I am tracing the wall with my hand for support, showing my bare butt in the open hospital gown to anyone in the hall way. But all I can think is that *Jose is alive.*

I must be a terrifying sight, because both of Jose's parents gasp and place their hands over their mouths when I enter the room. Unsure if I am welcome I stop in the doorway, swaying from side-to-side. My hair is standing on end and blood is running down my arm. My cheeks are hollowed and what I don't know is that my wind and sun burned face is peeling off in large chunks of leathery skin. I look like a crazed animal.

"Marta," Jose calls out, and he waves at me to come over.

Jose's dad finds his feet and rushes over to support me to Jose's bed. He doesn't mention my bare backside. Jose's mom pulls a chair close to Jose's bed and helps me to sit down before going to fetch some hand towels from the bathroom to put over my bleeding arm. I take Jose's hand and lay my head down on his chest, again tears are flowing. Jose pats my hair.

"Everything is OK Marta. It is all OK."

Before I find my voice Sonia enters the room with the nurse and doctor in tow. I have so many questions, but before I can ask any of them I have been put in a wheelchair and am being wheeled back to my room. None of my pleading to stay with Jose helps. But as I am leaving the room against my will I finally call out, "I love you too Jose."

The plump nurse helps me back into bed and puts the IV line back in my arm. The light green curtain around my bed is drawn shut so I can't see what else is going on in the room. The doctor standing next to Sonia looks cross. "You mustn't walk on your feet. This little stunt may cost you more of your toes if you are not careful."

My feet are throbbing but I don't want any more drugs. I want my brain to be clear so I can make sense of it all. No more of that terrifying morphine. Sonia can tell I am in pain, she knows me better than anyone. But she bites her tongue until the doctor and nurse have left the room.

"You should get something for the pain Marta," she says.

"No, no more drugs. It is hard to keep track of what is real," I reply.

They must have given me something though, because I keep drifting in and out of sleep, and each time I wake up I am unsure if I have dreamt that Jose is alive. Each time Sonia is sitting there holding my hand confirming that Jose is indeed alive and in the room down the hall. She never once scolds me for asking the same question over and over. But as night creeps closer and darkness finally encapsulates the room she whispers, "Marta, what happened over there?"

I don't know what to reply. I am not sure of what actually happened. I still feel a tremendous amount of guilt over leaving Jose, despite him being three doors down the hall in what I have come to understand a much better condition than me.

"I am not sure," I whisper. It feels dangerous to even mention our misadventure. Like the hospital walls have ears. Maybe the drugs are still carousing through my blood. I feel paranoid. "I thought that Jose had died. That I left him behind to die," I continue, unable to steel myself enough not to cry.

"You almost died," responds Sonia.

"No, just frostbite."

Sonia takes my hands, "Marta, you almost died from heat exhaustion." She squeezes my hands so hard it hurts.

"How can I be suffering from frostbite and almost die from heat exhaustion?" I inquire.

"Ironic isn't it?" says Sonia.

I close my eyes and breathe hard.

***

The next day Sonia wheels me down the hall to see Jose, finally feeling a little less groggy. Sonia brushed my hair before we left.

"You look a little rough," she said.

When I get to Jose he smiles. He is sitting up in his bed and a small TV attached to the ceiling is on, but muted. The room has three other beds, one is empty, the other two have the same color green curtains as in my room drawn around them. Jose looks well. It is hard to match this version with the one I left in Pakistan.

"You look like you caught a bit of sun," Jose winks at me.

A laugh slips out before I can stop it. It feels good, I can't remember the last time I laughed. On closer inspection I can tell that Jose's lips are cracked and his skin looks rough.

"So do you. Are you OK?" I ask.

"Yeah, I am mostly fine. A little bit of frost nip on my toes and fingers, but no tissue loss."

I breathe a big sigh of relief.

"I was hypothermic when they got to me. But they managed to lower me down. I don't remember much of the rescue. I was in pretty bad shape from the altitude. But my condition improved as soon as we got lower."

"Jose, I am so sorry. I should never have left you. I tried to turn back," I whisper, riddled with shame and guilt.

But Jose just smiles. "You had no choice Marta."

Jose is looking at me, not allowing me to avert my gaze, "I didn't allow you to stay. This is on me, OK?" When I don't answer he repeats, "OK?"

"OK," I whisper, mostly to please Jose.

"Well, it looks like I get to go home today," says Jose.

"Wow, that is great," I say, but inside I feel a pang of sadness. I want Jose to be close by. To never let him out of my sight again. "Will you be going to Wenatchee?" I ask.

"No, I think I will stay in the city until you are out of here," he smiles.

I feel overwhelmed with gratitude and selfish all at once. "You don't have to Jose."

"I know, but I want to."

I don't argue. We don't get a chance to talk for long. I am wheeled back into my room and my feet are re-dressed. The pain is overwhelming, but I bite my lip and smile while the doctor examines my feet. I have never ever in my entire life felt so happy before. Jose is alive.

The next few days pass much the same, either Sonia or Jose is always at my side from when I wake up until I go to sleep. At one point I ask Sonia if they sleep here too, half joking. But she brushes off the question saying they just want to make sure that I am not alone. One night I wake at 2 a.m. and find Jose dozing off in the chair next to my bed. I guess they do sleep here. The plump nurse tells me in a rare moment that we are alone.

"Those are some good friends you have there."

I can't agree more. But both Jose and Sonia skillfully avoid any questions about our time in Pakistan. At first I think they do it for me. To let me heal before I am confronted with reliving the last few days in Pakistan. But as the days pass, and I feel stronger and happier, it occurs to me that maybe they don't want to discuss it here.

Eventually I can't bear it anymore and I say as firmly as I can, "Jose, when are you going to tell me the whole story?"

Jose squirms in his chair. He looks at me with pleading eyes, but I stay staring at him, demanding an answer.

"Jose, I need to know. I am racking my brain here to make sense of all of this. And I just can't."

"OK," says Jose, staring at me, urging me to listen closely.

"The Americans that were following us…" He stops and walks over to the open door looking down the hallway before returning to the chair next to my bed. "They were actually there to help us."

"Help us?" I ask.

"Well, they are from the FBI."

"FBI?"

"Yeah, crazy isn't it. Anyhow, they were trying to get a hold of us to let us know we may be in danger."

"In danger from who?"

"Well…"

"In danger from who?" I push.

"Murtaza," Jose replies.

I shake my head.

"He is affiliated with the Taliban. The FBI had him on some watch list and when the FBI picked up that we were travelling to see him they soon followed, at first they believed that we were also in some way involved with the extremist group, and as such it started out as a mission to observe our intentions. But soon they realized we were just tourists, so they set out to help us before anything horrible happened. Apparently that is why I was suspended. They thought I was part of some terrorist group."

"But that doesn't make sense," I argue. "We didn't contact Murtaza until after -"

Jose puts a finger over his lips and mimes 'I know.' My skin is crawling. Something is off, but Jose obviously can't tell me here.

"I believe they will be here to speak to you soon," finishes Jose.

***

I can smell the perfume before the lady enters the room. It brings me back to the white room in Pakistan, the empty IV bag next to my bed, and my blurry vision of a lady with a New York accent. When the lady now enters the room I can see her clearly. She is gorgeous, trim with shoulder-long brown hair. She smiles at me and rows of perfect white teeth reveal themselves to me. The smile however, never reaches her eyes.

"Hi Marta, I am Special Agent Bollinger."

She reaches out a hand towards me and I almost laugh. How could this perfect looking, yet intimidating woman be called Bollinger? Such a joyful almost silly name. I doubt she will appreciate my giggles, so I keep it together and take her hand.

"Hi."

"I am happy to see you are recovering well. That was a pretty close call."

"Yeah, so I have been told," I say.

"I have spoken to Jose and I understand you guys were on a pilgrimage to honor your deceased grandfather. But considering who you ended up hiking with, it would be very helpful for our continued investigation if you could tell me everything from the top."

I feel nervous and the palms of my hands are sweating. I haven't even started telling my story, the story I intend on telling this lady, and already my cheeks are flaring up bright red.

"Well," I have to stop to regain my composure, my voice is shaky. I try again more firmly, "Well, it started when I found out I had a grandfather that I never knew about. I don't really have any family left. So I did my own investigation and learned that he was a mountain climber, just like me."

"I understand climbing is a *hobby* of yours," she corrects.

"Yes, I am not a professional climber like my grandfather was. But nonetheless it made me feel like we had a connection," I say, cheeks burning again, but this time from being corrected. Why was I feeling like a child being reprimanded? "I wanted to learn more about him and found out my grandmother is still alive. So Jose and I came up with this trip to go see my grandmother and then hike to the Gilkey Memorial by K2 to see my grandfather's memorial plate."

"That is a big trip for a dead grandparent you never knew," says Special Agent Bollinger.

"Well, with my *hobby* of climbing I have always wanted to visit the Himalayas. So it seemed like a nice way to kill two birds with one stone."

Bollinger looks displeased. "But the Karakoram's aren't the Himalayas, are they?"

"No, not really, but it is close enough and it has several of the world's highest mountains. *And* this is where my grandfather came to finally rest."

"Don't go anywhere, we may need to speak to you again."

I point at my feet. "I won't be *going* anywhere." Adding, "*Thank you very much*," as she is about to leave. She does a double take, detecting the sarcasm in my voice. But I smile at her sweetly so she shakes her head and leaves the room. Her perfume lingers for a long time.

Chapter 28

When I am finally allowed to leave the hospital Jose and Sonia take turns at wheeling me out to the car, stopping to hold doors open, and poking fun at my annoyance at being unable to make any of my own decisions.

"Yes, yes dear," says Sonia, "I know you want to get a coffee, but the nurse said it isn't good for you," as she wheels me straight past the hospital coffee shop.

"Liar," I scream.

A couple of minutes later while Sonia and I are still waiting for the lift Jose hands me a piping hot Americano.

"*Thank you.* Now that is a true friend," I tease.

"I have been over to your place to pick up a few clothes." says Sonia when we are all buckled into Jose's car.

"Why?" I ask. "Where are we going?"

"To my parents' place," answers Jose. "I am pretty strong, but getting a wheelchair up and down those stairs in your old building may prove too much even for me." He winks.

"Oh, of course."

I had forgotten about my wheelchair and inability to walk. I feel a little disappointed. I had looked forward to finally being back in my own space, sleeping in my own bed.

"Are your parents OK with this?" I ask.

"Why wouldn't they be?"

"Well, because I left you. I abandoned you. I left you to die," the words tumble out before I can stop myself.

Jose looks at me, "You did no such thing Marta."

"But I did. I cut the rope." Tears are threatening in the corners of my eyes.

"Cut the rope? What are you talking about?"

"Normally you are tied to each other with a rope when you are climbing," intersects Sonia, "but Marta, sometimes it is OK to cut the rope."

"No. No it isn't," I say. "You never ever cut the rope on your buddy. Rather slit my throat than cut the rope."

"Well, there was no rope. So you're fine." Jose looks sincere.

"I will spend the rest of my life making it up to you." I am still on the verge of crying.

"You will do no such thing." Jose sounds mad.

But I know that I will. I will be forever tied to Jose by an invisible rope of guilt.

"So what really happened anyway?" I say.

"Not now Marta," says Jose a little harsher than what seems necessary.

The word guilt floats back up to the surface and I stay silent.

The atmosphere has gone from cheerful to dark. Sonia is fumbling to fix it. She tells me how wonderful it will be for me to heal out in the countryside, and how she has shopped for all my favorite foods. I reach my arm back behind me and Sonia squeezes it. Sweet wonderful Sonia. By the time we get to Wenatchee the mood is almost back to joyful.

The air is hot when we step outside the air-conditioned car. Baking hot. The cool spring breeze that had been so refreshing last time I was here has been replaced by suppressing heat. My butt and the back of my legs are sticking to the wheelchair and it feels like I have wet myself, but I don't want to seem ungrateful so I don't say anything. There it is again, guilt.

"Mom has set up the cottage for us. Separate bedrooms of course," winks Jose.

"Of course," I smile.

I remember how well that worked out when we last stayed here. I am feeling a little nervous about being with Jose again, so much has changed. Sonia is piling bags of groceries out of the car, throwing a package of Theo's dark chocolate peanut butter cups at me. I smile and rip the package open.

"Will you stay for dinner?" Jose asks Sonia.

Before she can answer I cut in, "Staying for dinner? Aren't you staying here too?"

"I am sorry Marta." She really does look distraught. "I have been taking a lot of time off work. I can't take any more time off. But I will be back on Friday night."

"Yeah, fair enough," I say trying to not sound as disappointed as I am. "Do I still have a job?"

"You are fine. They will have you back when you are out of the wheelchair."

Sonia does stay for dinner. In fact, she cooks dinner. She is standing over by Mrs. Johnson's large stove looking into the oven while I sit in my wheelchair at the end of the table happily chatting to Jose and his mom. Sonia brings over a big plate of nachos draped in melted cheese, guacamole, and sour cream. Mrs. Johnson is horrified.

"You call that Mexican food?" she asks.

"No." Sonia smiles. "I call this Marta's favorite American-Mexican food."

Mrs. Johnson is cursing in Spanish under her breath. I feel a little embarrassed, but any embarrassment disappears when I bite into the part crunchy, part chewy, corn chips. This is heaven.

After dinner Sonia drives Jose's car out of the driveway. I try to fight the feeling of abandonment, wondering if this is how Jose felt when I left him in the snow. But I know they don't compare. Jose wheels me over to the cottage where he has placed two planks of wood up the three front steps. He pushes me up while grunting.

"Are you sure you are strong enough for this?" I ask.

"Sure, it will be good for me. I need to build those muscles

202

back up."

"Yeah, you look thin."

"I look thin. Have you seen yourself?"

"Just a few more meals by Sonia and I will be back to normal in no time." I giggle, referring to the mounds of sour cream on my nachos.

Standing inside the little cottage Jose pauses. "So, would you like to stay in the room my mother prepared for you or in the one she prepared for me?" He looks insecure.

"I guess in whichever one you are sleeping," I smile.

"Oh good," is all he says as he pushes me into the bedroom his mom has prepared for me. I know it from last time. This room has a double bed; Jose's room is smaller with a single bed. While I had been excited about the thought of spending a night in my own bed alone, I feel a pang of excitement at being able to share this bed with Jose. Jose reaches down to lift me out of the wheelchair.

"Oh come on Jose. I can get myself to bed." I smile as I wobble out of the wheelchair walking on my heels. It hurts, but less than my pride would had Jose carried me to bed.

It feels nice, safe, to be falling asleep in Jose's arms. Jose caresses an unruly lock of my hair and whispers, "It is all over."

But when I wake a few hours later Jose is missing. I reach my arm out and find the space next to me empty. The mattress is still warm from his body. A sliver of light is shining in under the door and I can hear whispering voices out in the living room. Oh, caught by Mrs. Johnson I think, and almost giggle out loud. After a while the voices die down and I can hear the front door groan as Mrs. Johnson is leaving. Soon after the light under the door goes out and a floor board creaks as Jose slowly opens the door to our room and sneaks back in under the sheets, placing an arm over me. I pretend to be sleeping. I don't want to embarrass him.

I feel less kind in the morning when we linger in bed.

"So did we get caught by your mom last night?" I tease.

"What do you mean?"

"I heard you talking last night. Did your mom catch us sharing a bed?"

"Oh, yeah, ha, ha. Caught red handed," laughs Jose. "Let me fetch you some breakfast in bed," says Jose, bouncing out of bed and heading for the main house before I can protest.

When he opens the door to the living room a waft of air rushes into our room. A shiver runs down my spine. I know that smell. The lingering aroma of perfume.

Chapter 29

Sun is bathing the large yellow-painted kitchen in light and coffee cups are littering the worn farm table. Sonia has come for the weekend and we are listening to Jose's mom tell us stories of Jose as a young boy and all the trouble he used to get himself into.

"So, I was thinking of taking Marta into town. Maybe look in some of the shops and get a coffee," says Sonia.

"I'll come," says Jose.

But his mom cuts in, "Let them have some girl time."

Saved by Mrs. Johnson. Not that I really want to be away from Jose, if anything I am willing to do anything he wants me to. The guilt is always there next to me like an invisible companion. But if Sonia wants me to herself, I am not going to argue. I crave Sonia time.

I hobble into the car while Sonia is folding the wheelchair and placing it in the backseat.

"You sure you girls don't need a hand?" Jose is hovering by the car.

"Nah, we will be fine," says Sonia.

We can see him waving as he watches us drive down the access road.

"Wow," says Sonia, "protective much."

"Yeah, he has been great. Sometimes I wonder if he feels as guilty as I do."

When we get into Wenatchee we drive down the main street, little low-rise brick buildings line either side of the road, an eclectic assortment of shopfronts in each building. It reminds me of an old cowboy town. Sonia parks right on the main street.

"Street parking is a little easier here than in the city." She smiles.

"Thank God." I giggle.

"What first? Shops or coffee?"

"Coffee. Always coffee," I reply.

"Let's get them to go and drink them by the river," Sonia says as we are ordering at the counter.

"Sounds good to me."

The path down to the river is gravel and both coffees spill over into my lap.

"Hey, easy on the off-roading," I call out.

"Sorry," giggles Sonia.

Bushes and small trees that look newly planted line the grassy waterfront and statues are strategically placed along the shore. The park looks new. We stop by a bench facing the river and Sonia wheels me up close so we can sit next to each other. She liberates me of one of the coffees.

"Are you happy?" she asks.

"Yeah, I think so. I am happy I am alive. I am happy Jose is alive."

Sonia looks around then sticks her hand in her pocket. "I found this in Jose's car." She holds her hand out and I can feel the cold of the metal as I take the piton from Sonia.

My piton. Or rather my mother's piton, given to her by her father, my grandfather. I had kept it in my pocket our entire time in Pakistan. I fiddled with it, placing the cool metal against the palm of my hand as I am doing now. I can't remember if I had told Jose I had it with me. But I guess he would have seen me play with it, turning it over to look at the inscription, and imagining my grandfather's love for his daughter.

"Why do you think it was in Jose's car?" asks Sonia.

"I don't know. As far as I am aware it lived in my pocket. I assumed it ended up wherever my clothes ended up when I was captured." Sonia gives me a peculiar look. "I mean rescued," I correct, but it still feels like I had been captured.

"So why is it in Jose's car?" she asks without expecting an answer.

"Maybe he got it back and was keeping it safe for me."

"But why hasn't he given it to you?" presses Sonia.

"Maybe because you had the car?"

"I left it there all weekend. He has had plenty of opportunity."

"They spoke English," I call out louder than intended.

"What?"

"They spoke English. I couldn't make out the conversation but I heard that they were speaking English. Jose speaks Spanish to his mom." I can feel the jitter in my nerves returning.

Sonia looks confused. "What are you talking about?"

"Special Agent Bollinger was in the cottage. I am sure of it."

Sonia still can't make sense of what I am saying.

"The other night I woke up and Jose was in the living room talking to someone. In the morning I thought I could smell perfume, the same perfume Special Agent Bollinger wears. But Jose said it was his mom he spoke to, and that she caught us sharing a bed. Something has been bothering me about it but I couldn't work it out. But now I know. They spoke English."

Sonia's eyes go wide. My hands have started to shake and I have to place my coffee cup on the ground, still holding on to the piton, unwilling to put it down.

"Something is not right," I say.

"OK, but we don't know what. So let's just bide our time and figure things out."

"What? Sonia, I am sure there is a reason for all of this."

"Yes, I agree," says Sonia, "but let's just play it safe until we know more."

"You know I can't tell a lie. How can I look Jose in the eyes and keep this from him?"

"Please Marta, let's just wait. Give him a chance to come to you. If we haven't learned anything more by the end of next week we can talk to him."

"OK." I finally surrender. "One week."

***

After two days of trying to act normal around Jose, trying to not pull away when he touches me, Jose sits me down, well figuratively, I don't do anything but sit down these days.

"What is going on Marta?"

"What do you mean?"

"You seem jumpy and distant," he is looking straight at me.

I reach into my pocket and pull out the piton. "Jose, *I* should be the one asking *you* what is going on."

"Oh."

"Why did you have my piton? And why was Special Agent Bollinger here the other night?"

Our eyes are locked in a staring competition.

"It is a long story."

"Well, I have all the time in the world."

"OK then," Jose is breaking away from my stare, losing the competition.

He stands up and walks over to the kitchenette filling the kettle with water and placing it on the gas stove. I am not sure if he is buying time or actually thinking I will need a cup of tea for this.

As if he can read my mind he turns to me and says, "You will need a cup of tea for this."

After the kettle has whistled Jose sits down on a chair

facing me, handing me a cup.

"When I got suspended from work the FBI contacted me."

"What?"

"Please let me finish before you judge."

"OK, sorry. Go on."

"The FBI contacted me and said they had been looking into the case of Mr. Hawkins. That their investigation was the reason that our department dropped the case and let the public believe it was a heart attack. The lady who phoned me, Special Agent Bollinger, works for the Joint Terrorism Taskforce. She needed information about Murtaza. I don't know how she knew we were in contact with him, but I guess they must have hacked into my computer. It is way over my pay grade and I was excited to be involved in such important work. She was the one insisting we should travel to Pakistan."

"What?" I can't stop myself.

"Marta, please hear me out."

I remain silent.

"I thought it would be a good idea. Not just because of my career but because you would get a chance to see your grandmother in Poland and visit Pakistan. In the process learning a little more about your grandfather. I insisted on going to Poland. Bollinger had no interest in your grandmother. But I told her it was a deal breaker."

"Wait, was it the FBI who paid for our airfares?"

"Yes. But I would have. I would have paid for you Marta." Jose looks distraught.

"Go on."

"She told me it would be an intelligence gathering job. We would hike with Murtaza and I would try to learn as much as I possibly could about him. I would then report back once we got back to the USA. A little like a paid vacation, courtesy of the FBI. It sounded too good to be true. I guess it was." Jose pauses, taking a big sip of his tea. "It all went wrong when the FBI decided to pay Murtaza a visit before our hike. He got suspicious and fled, and from there on started our race against the FBI. The people I was actually working for."

"Wait, what, why didn't you just tell me what was going on?"

"I was under a confidentiality agreement. Still am. I figured everything could still go ahead as planned, just at a faster pace."

"Where was Special Agent Bollinger in all of this?"

"Hot on our tail. She has explained to me that when we started our journey in the middle of the night and they lost track of us, they believed we were in danger. The FBI decided it was time to pull us out. But we didn't know this. So the wild goose chase began."

"So when you were dying on the mountain, you weren't really dying?" I feel confused and mad.

"I was in pretty bad shape. But I knew rescue was behind us. I couldn't tell you, we were on the mountain with what could be the Taliban. I had to stay quiet and let you go ahead."

"You sent me off with the Taliban." I can feel the rope of guilt untying its hold of me, setting me free.

"No, no, Karim, he was also working for Bollinger."

"Karim?"

It makes sense, those blue eyes following everyone's every move like a hawk.

"Yes, they recruited him when he returned to Askole. He hiked back in with the Spanish expedition hoping to catch up to us. He told me the Americans had sent him and that they were right behind us."

"But he doesn't speak English."

"Well... actually he does."

I feel stupid. Like I have somehow been on a different trip to the one Jose is describing. How could I not have noticed all of this?

"When you left me I actually feared they wouldn't find me and I would die right there. The weather was so bad. But I had a locator beacon, so I set it off and a few hours later I was lowered down the mountain. I was in a pretty sorry state, but the rescue was swift. I was picked up by a helicopter the next day and flown to Islamabad."

"You had a locator beacon? Why didn't you just set it off the night at K2 basecamp when the helicopter was circling?"

"Because by then I wasn't sure if I actually believed that Murtaza was in any way involved with the Taliban. I wanted to find out more."

"OK. But how does Mr. Hawkins fit in to any of this?"

"I am not actually sure. But for some reason the FBI believes his murder is related to the Taliban."

"And my grandfather?"

"Haven't got the foggiest. Bollinger has never mentioned Zygmunt, so I guess he has nothing to do with the case." I breathe a sigh of relief. "And Jonny?"

"I don't know. Probably just a drug deal gone wrong."

"What happened once you got to Islamabad?"

"I was in the hospital for a couple of days. I had pulmonary edema and a touch of hypothermia. They wanted to send me back to the USA, but I refused to leave until I knew you were safe. Once they had gotten you to the hospital in Skardu, with a scheduled transfer to Islamabad, I finally agreed to leave the country. I didn't want to Marta, you must believe me. But I was under a lot of pressure.

"You were first treated for heat exhaustion and your frostbite in Skardu. But as soon as a flight was leaving, the weather grounded you for a couple of days, they transferred you to Islamabad and then on to Seattle. The rest you know."

Jose looks at me. We sit in silence for a long time.

"So now what?" I ask.

"Bollinger was here the other night. They no longer need me. The case is closed. I don't know if they will continue to investigate Mr. Hawkins' murder. But... Murtaza is dead."

"What? No, no, no."

"It was a heart attack."

"Yeah right. Just like Mr. Hawkins," I reply.

I can tell Jose doesn't believe it either.

"I know. But there is no way we will ever know."

"So in the hospital when you started telling me the story..."

"Yes, I wanted to tell you everything, but I couldn't get my head around it. There is something that bothers me, but I don't know what. Then Bollinger came here to tell me the case was closed and that Murtaza is dead. I figured that was it, end of story. I was going to tell you parts of it when the right time came. But I could tell you had lost all your trust in me. So here we are, the full story is out. I don't know how many laws I have just broken."

Jose leans in to touch my cheek.

"Don't touch me," I say.

Chapter 30

Jose stands up and leaves the cottage. I sit alone with tears running down my cheeks unable to work out if my crying is because of Jose's betrayal or out of relief that I no longer have to carry the burden of guilt. It is still there though, but smaller than before, I had still left him behind. I didn't know he would be rescued, so a little of the guilt is still mine to carry. But it is smaller now, more like a sack of rocks than an entire mountain. Finally, I wheel myself over to the bedroom and pick up my phone.

"Second Chance Women's Shelter," answers Lisa.

"Lisa. Could you please put me through to Sonia?" My voice is thick.

"MARTA. How are you?"

"Good, good. I can't chat, sorry, Sonia please."

She must have picked up on my mood because she doesn't press, instead she puts me straight through.

"Sonia."

"Sonia, you have to come and get me now."

"OK. I will leave right now."

When Jose walks back into the cottage I am fighting with my wheelchair trying to wheel myself around the cramped bedroom to pack my things. Jose doesn't say anything, instead he takes the bag from me and goes around the room placing all of my things inside it. When he hands me the bag back I can tell that his eyes are red rimmed. He must have been crying too.

"Marta, please believe me, I never meant to hurt you..." He looks so sad I have to fight back the instinct to throw out my arms and embrace him.

"But you did. Both physically and mentally."

"I am sorry. So, so, so, sorry," he whispers as he again leaves the cottage.

I feel bad for not easing his guilt, like he had tried to ease mine. For not letting him get away with it. But not bad enough that I let my own bag of guilt get any larger. I have already carried too heavy a load for too long, I think, as I sit waiting for Sonia to arrive.

It seems like an eternity has passed when Sonia finally bursts into the cottage out of breath.

"Marta, I have broken every traffic rule there is to get here. What is up?"

"Jose was working for the FBI."

Sonia doesn't look as surprised as I had expected.

"You knew?" I ask.

"No. But I guess I suspected as much when you told me that Bollinger was here."

"Murtaza is dead."

"No way. What happened?"

"Heart attack."

"Yeah right."

"That is what I said. Seems like an odd coincidence that both Murtaza and Mr. Hawkins died the same way."

Sonia nods in agreement.

"I need to get something to thank Jose's parents before I leave," I say changing the subject.

Sonia doesn't reply. But she gets up and wheels me out to the car. She is still driving Jose's car.

"Give me a minute," says Sonia after I have already buckled in.

She is off before I have a chance to protest. When she returns she is looking sad, but she doesn't say anything. We drive past what seems like endless apple orchards, small green apples, not yet ripe, hanging from every branch. Only when the red brick shopfronts of the main street pass outside our windows does Sonia speak.

"So, what are you after?"

"Flowers?"

"Sure."

Sonia pulls up next to a shopfront with a sign that reads *Bloomers Flower and Garden House*. I had hoped we would just go to Safeway, I could pick up a ten dollar bouquet of flowers and a box of Lindt chocolates and we would be done. But no such luck.

Inside Sonia takes charge, clearly used to getting fancy flower arrangements, something I have never done before. Inside the shop the air is pungent with the smell of flowers. Buckets full to the brim with blooms line the walls, and little decorations used for weddings sit on the shelves. I look at a little ceramic tray, one side read *Mrs.* and the other *Mr.*

"Sonia what are these?" I whisper while the lady behind the desk is busy with our arrangement, flowers of every color laying on the bench in front of her.

"They are for weddings. For the rings I guess."

"Odd," I whisper back.

A large, rather extravagant, flower arrangement rests on my lap when Sonia pushes me out of the shop. Instead of driving back out to the main road Sonia makes one more stop, pulling up in front of the coffee shop we had previously visited. I stay in the car, but I can spy on Sonia making our order through the large shopfront windows. The barista makes two Americanos and boxes three large slices of chocolate cake.

"You got one for Jose too?" I inquire.

"Yes. It wouldn't look very good if I didn't would it?" she asks without expecting an answer.

I can tell she is feeling sorry for Jose. But this is Sonia, she feels sorry for everyone.

I watch the apple trees speed past in a blur as we drive back, and when we pull up outside the white farmhouse Mrs.

Johnson is standing on the porch. She embraces me in a spice-scented hug when I hand her the flowers and tuts at me in Spanish, patting me on my head, and I am truly sad to be leaving her behind. While nothing like my own mother she does feel like *a* mother, caring and good natured. She insists we have a coffee before we leave, and Sonia wheels me inside the large bright kitchen. I am squirming in my wheelchair as Mrs. Johnson pours me a cup of filter coffee, thinking about my lovely Americano getting cold in the car cup holder. Mr. Johnson is out on the farm somewhere and Mrs. Johnson promises to pass on my thank you. I have no idea where Jose has gone.

"See you soon." She smiles when we finally escape the kitchen, unaware that I have no intention of ever coming back.

"God, I feel awful," I say to Sonia.

"I am sure she has lived through worse," replies Sonia, making me feel sheepish rather than the intended lighter.

When we drive down the access road it feels like a book closing. A story reaching its end.

Chapter 31

The white walls make me feel uneasy. The smell of rubbing alcohol and powder-free gloves is pricking the inside of my nose. Had I heard him right? No more wheelchair? Rather than euphoria I feel an urgent need to leave this barren white room and the creaky bed with its paper sheet that tore as soon as I sat down on it. This doctor isn't the same one that had done the surgery, but he seems equally uninterested as he is rattling off instructions. "Got it?" He looks at me.

"Sure."

When I hobble out of the hospital my legs feel unsteady and a dull pain is thumping away where my toes once were, the sheet with 'after care' instructions is fluttering in the wind. I feel relieved to be outside again, leaving the hospital and its sharp smells behind, and excited to be walking on my own. I hate to rely on others. I haven't told Sonia I was going to the hospital today. I wanted to be alone. Making my way down Madison Street from First Hill I think about getting a taxi, but I can walk.

By the time I reach the International District I am sweating profusely and the dull pain has increased to agonizing. I try to remember if the doctor had mentioned that this might happen. I have to sit down on a park bench for a good twenty minutes before I gather up enough grit to push on. I start back up the hill, the way I just came from. I have decided to visit my mom. Going uphill is less painful as my toes are not pushing against the front of my shoes. I feel proud of my effort when I sign-in at the nursing home and push the double doors to the common room open.

"Marta," Mom's voice is shrill with excitement.

I hobble as fast as I can to reach her before her memory fades.

But her eyes stay clear and she starts to tell me about all the

217

mundane things in her life. The nurse that is getting divorced, the meatloaf she had for lunch, and the itchy rash that has developed on her arm. I never want her to stop. Listening to her trivial day-to-day pattering feels wonderful. We sit on the veranda in the sunshine, it is hot outside, but after my week in Wenatchee it feels positively frosty. A refreshing sea breeze tugs at my hair.

"Mom, look what I found," I say on impulse as I pull the piton out of my pocket.

"Oh dear. Oh dear."

She turns the piton over and reads the inscription in Polish out loud; a smile plastered over her face.

"Marta, I wish you could have met your grandfather. He was such a strong man. You two would have gotten along famously."

"I think so too," I smile.

I can feel mom's grip on my hand soften and I realize she has fallen asleep. I am pleased when the nurse I find is not Patty, but rather a sweet looking girl. Maybe she is working during her school holidays, she looks awfully young with her blond hair and big blue eyes. She promises me to make sure that the piton that my mom is still holding onto won't end up in the trash.

I walk back on to the veranda and kiss my mother's forehead before calling a taxi. I wait outside the nursing home for the cab to arrive.

"Where to?" asks the driver as I get into the backseat.

"Second Chance Woman's Shelter on First."

***

God, she is like a puppy, I think to myself when Lisa literally bounds towards me arms stretched out and a big smile on her

218

face. Her blond ponytail swings from side to side as she scoops me up in a hug before I even make it halfway across the entrance area of our office.

"Marta, it is so good to see you," she gushes.

"You too," I lie, instantly feeling guilty.

Why can't you leave me alone? I want to scream at the guilt that seems to have infested my every fiber, like a disease. Sonia must have heard Lisa's puppy-like yelps because she is now coming down the corridor wagging a finger at me and laughing at the same time.

"You didn't tell me?" But Sonia doesn't look disappointed, just happy.

"Sorry."

"Don't be sorry. Be happy." The words coming out in sing song, half singing, and half speaking.

"We should celebrate," shouts Lisa.

She has her back to me so I put my finger to my head indicating to Sonia that I'd rather shoot myself.

"Maybe a little later," says Sonia.

"Holy crap, she is like a kid on Kool-Aid," I mutter as soon as Sonia closes the office door behind her.

"A friendly lovable kid," corrects Sonia.

"So no more wheelchair?"

"Nope. Free like a bird and these pegs still work just fine." I smile pointing at my legs.

"I am going to talk to Karen next, I think I can come back to work on Monday."

"That is great. I guess you will be moving home toady then?"

"Yup. Headed home after this."

I don't know who is more relieved, me or Sonia. I know Sonia will do anything for me. But my constant bickering with her housemate Jill, and having to drive me to physical therapy and the doctors, and cooking and cleaning after me for the past few weeks must have been tiring, even for someone with a heart of gold and the patience of a saint.

I step into my own office. It is neat, an unusual state for my space. I had tidied before I left for Pakistan, tying up any loose ends and filing away all the clutter on my desk. The wild smiles of me and Sonia on top of Rainier in the frame behind my desk catch my attention. I wonder when I will climb again. Rainier seems so small now, friendly and easy. I can't imagine what it will be like, climbing it now after all of this. Maybe I should teach at the Mountaineers next year, I have a pretty kick-ass story to tell, I smile to myself and close the door.

I walk to my apartment after speaking with Karen, it is all uphill so my toes do fine. I do, however, get slightly out of breath as I walk up the thick carpeted stairs of my apartment building. I have to hold on to the banister and I curse at myself, unhappy about being out of shape.

Musty air hits me in the face when I unlock and open my door. I open all the windows allowing salty air to rush in between them, forcing the staleness of my two-month absence away. I sit down on my worn sofa and drink in the happiness of being home. The creaking of the wooden floor when you step into the kitchen, although the place is so small it is more like transitioning into the kitchen, it isn't really its own room. The bookshelf overfilled with mountaineering books, tales of heroic feats, and factual instructions on how to improve your mountain prowess.

I reach for the pile of mail that I have brought up from my mailbox downstairs. Sonia had offered to get my mail, but I had insisted there was no need. I barely ever get any mail and when I do it is only bills, most of which I pay online anyhow. No junk. How odd. I have always had a *no junk mail* sticker on my box, but junk mail always clutters it up nonetheless. Guess they finally got the message.

Like I suspected there isn't much mail, maybe eight or nine envelopes—all bills. Mostly from the hospital, but also two bank statements, an offer for a new credit card, the water bill, and one with information about new recycling regulations. I open one at a time and lay them down in order on the coffee table. I haven't placed them like this on purpose, but when I look at the envelopes it seems peculiar that they are all sorted. I had opened them from the top of the pile as they appeared in my mailbox. They are not in order of postdate but rather organized by category—hospital, bank, utilities. Someone has been through my mail.

I stand up.

Someone has been through my mail.

I walk through the apartment, inspecting every detail. It has been two months since I was here, I can't remember how I left it nor work out if anything is out of place. Just as I am about to sit down on my perfectly made bed I notice that someone has sat here. The duvet has a dimple in it. I put my hand to it. It doesn't feel warm, not that recent. I wonder how long it takes for a duvet to fluff itself back up. I move to the other side of the bed and sit down.

My heart almost stops when I hear the key turn in my door. My body tenses up readying itself for fight or flight.

"Howdy," Sonia's voice fills the hallway and I breathe a sigh of relief. "I got some groceries and your stuff," Sonia says, dropping off two Trader Joe's paper bags in the kitchen before placing my bag in the bedroom.

"NO. STOP."

Sonia freezes with her arm midair.

"Don't touch the bed, or put anything on it. I am conducting an experiment."

Sonia places the bag on the floor instead.

"What experiment? How long you can keep it made?" She laughs.

"I know, it is pretty isn't it?" I giggle. "Someone has been in here and I am trying to work out how long ago."

"By not touching the bed?"

"There is an impression on the bed where someone sat down. I made my own impression on the other side of the bed to work out how long it takes before it is no longer visible."

"You're an idiot. That will never work. What if the other person was a fatty? Or what if they sat down for an hour longer than you? What if it never fluffs back up?"

I can see that she has a point, but I am too attached to my ingenious detective work to simply abandon it.

"Yeah, maybe I will give up on that experiment," I lie.

Chapter 32

I stand over the bed inspecting my impression, then I move over to the other side inspecting the one made by someone else. They both look the same, showing no signs of disappearing. My neck is sore from sleeping on the sofa and I long to be in my bed. I have been dreaming about it for weeks now, so why am I sleeping on the stupid sofa, I think to myself and pull the duvet off the bed before I can change my mind. Sonia was right, again. It is 10 a.m., but I don't care. I slip into bed rolling around stretching out my arms and legs like a starfish, taking full advantage of the new found space.

The cotton sheets feel cool against my skin and the smell of clean laundry tickles my nose. My favorite smell on the entire planet is clean laundry. Sonia once told me that for someone who relishes the smell of clean laundry as much as I do, I do laundry remarkably seldom. My big toe is touching something; I stretch a little further. Reaching my hand down only once I realize I don't have any toes to grab it with. A small ball of tin foil. I unfold it carefully. A chewing gum wrapper, I can still smell the spearmint on the white inside of the foil. I don't chew gum, and I had made the bed fresh before leaving. My mom always said you never leave a dirty home when you go away, which is funny because we never went anywhere, but the words have stuck with me. I place the piece of foil on my bedside table.

I hear knocks on the door.

"I am coming," I shout as loud as I can.

When I pull the door open I almost gasp.

"Oh, hello."

"Sorry. Can we talk?" Jose looks thin, I guess he never regained those pounds after all.

Looking at him now I realize he is suffering the same

disease as me, only worse. I hope it isn't fatal, I think as I open the door wide allowing him to step in. He bends down to untie his shoes but I stop him.

"It's OK. This won't take long."

I regret the words when I see Jose's disappointed face. But it is true. My anger has faded; I haven't seen him for almost three weeks now. I am no longer mad, but the feeling of betrayal still stings. Millions of tiny wasps stinging all over my skin, their venom pulsating through my veins.

"Marta, I am so sorry. I feel really bad, and I miss you."

I do miss him as well, it is true. Despite it all, I miss him. I miss rolling over in bed and feeling him there next to me, knowing that he is breathing only an arm's length away. I miss seeing his eyes light up with laughter, and his slightly accented cursing when he gets mad. But each time I miss him the image of those same eyes clouded over by death knocking on the door pulls me back to the surface gasping for air.

"I never meant to hurt you and I never wanted to go behind your back," he continues when I remain silent. "You must believe me, I thought I did what was best for you. For us."

"Jose, I do believe you. I believe you when you say you never meant to hurt me. But you did. No matter how hard I try I am never going to be able to forget what happened. It very nearly killed me. It very nearly killed you. I can't just go back to the way things were. But I can forgive you. No more guilt Jose." He looks at me, searching my eyes to see if I mean it. Heck, I am not even sure I mean it. But I continue, "Jose let it go. It is OK, it is in the past now. You deserve to be happy again." I smile, it feels good.

I take Jose's hand and he smiles, stroking the back of my hand with his thumb. I feel like Jesus curing the blind.

"Marta, can I still be your friend?" he asks.

"Jose… I don't know that I can be your friend. Maybe in the future, but now I need to heal."

"I see you are walking again, that is great," says Jose changing the subject and smiling.

"Yes, it is great. But I was referring to my brain. My brain needs healing too."

Jose looks confused. "Do you mean soul? You mean soul don't you? Only you would think of the two as the same thing."

"Yes, my soul if you prefer." I smile. "Jose, I think it is best if you leave now."

Jose looks hurt, but hurt I can handle, it is the guilt that worries me.

"One more thing," I say as Jose is walking out the door. He turns around, hope dancing over his eyelashes. "Do you chew gum?"

The instant disappointment is palatable.

"No," he says, before closing the door behind him.

Chapter 33

"Are you sitting here again?" My neighbor is laboring past me up the stairs with bags of groceries. Her rotund bottom is brushing up against me as she turns sideways to get passed. She is wearing a dark blue dress with tiny orange and purple flowers, which stops between her knees and ankles. An old ladies dress. I am sitting on the thick carpet that covers every inch of the stairs and hallways in our building. It is meant to look old, to fit in with the faux Tudor design of the building. I think it is hideous, all dark and demure.

"Just waiting for the postman."

"I am sure he will come whether you are here to greet him or not. By the way, I let your friend into your mailbox when you were away."

"What friend?" I ask a little too quickly.

"The lady, ummm, what was her name…. The smart looking one," she looks concerned like maybe she has done something wrong.

"Aha, yes, that is OK."

What is wrong with me these days, I think, I am turning into a saint. Allowing her to feel OK about letting a stranger, someone I in fact distrust, into my mailbox. It is the third day in a row I am waiting in the stairs, looking out for the mail and looking out for anyone else coming to check on my mail. But maybe the case is really closed, I have not seen anyone hanging around and it doesn't feel like anyone is watching me. Everything just feels like normal, like Pakistan never happened, just a bad dream. If only, I think looking down at my bare feet, big scars where there were once toes. I had cried when I realized I could no longer wear flip flops. I have no toes to hold them in place. Sonia had laughed and promptly bought me a pair of Birkenstock sandals.

"I look like a German tourist, or maybe an elderly housewife," I had squealed displeased. But when I tried them on they were really quite comfortable, and they don't require toes.

My phone rings and when I look at the display it announces an incoming call from Sonia.

"Talking of the devil," I answer.

"Hey, want me to come over after work?" Sonia sounds cheerful.

"Yes. Wine?" I reply.

"Sounds good, let's go to the park, it is glorious out."

It really is, the sun is hot and bright in the sky. I walk back up to my apartment, giving up on my mission to catch the postman, to instead get ready for our picnic. I make a quick trip to the supermarket to pick up supplies, and by the time Sonia comes over the sun is low in the sky and less intense, instead spreading a golden hue. I am already waiting for her in the foyer of my building, picnic bag in hand.

"What have you got?" Sonia asks as soon as I get into her car.

I don't know when she and Jose switched cars back, but I suspect that she sometimes sees Jose. I don't mind and I don't want to know.

"Sushi, Pinot Grio, coconut water, strawberries, and chocolate," I rattle off.

"Perfect. Gas Works or Madison?" Sonia asks.

"Gas Works," I reply without hesitation, going to Madison will mean watching everyone else swim in the lake while I am stuck on shore. The risk of infection is still too high for me to get into the lake, and I long for nothing more than to submerse myself in water.

"People will still be swimming at Gas Works," says Sonia reading my mind.

"Yeah, but I don't mind that so much. They will probably all end up with deformities, growing an extra head." I am referring to the signs warning people that the sediment around Gas Works Park may contain toxic contaminates, and as such swimming should be avoided.

"Perhaps you could grow a few new toes," jokes Sonia.

"Wohoo, under the belt." I giggle.

We drive through Fremont and along Lake Union before parking in the large lot by the park. The picnic basket is swinging on my arm as we walk over the large grassy expanse, the old gasworks buildings rusting behind a tall fence. We choose a spot close to the water next to a stand of blackberry bushes. Sonia laughs at me when I spread a big beach towel on the grass, I don't own a picnic blanket. I never really saw the need for a specific blanket just for picnics. I pull a beer out of my basket.

"Hey, I thought you said Pinot Grio?"

"I did." I smile and get the wine bottle out for Sonia.

While I had remembered to buy a bottle with a screw top, I had forgotten that I broke the last of my wine glasses before I left for Pakistan. Instead I now hand Sonia a water glass that I had grabbed last minute, and she gives me a look of *that-would-be-right*. But she doesn't comment.

"How did your experiment go?"

"Not so well, I gave up on that." I smile.

"How many nights did you spend on the couch?" asks Sonia.

"Two."

"I am impressed, I thought you would still be curled up in your living room," she laughs.

"Nah, but I have been watching out for my mail."

"Anything?"

"No."

"That is good." Sonia looks serious.

I sip on my beer. "Yeah, maybe it really is over. But it doesn't feel over to me. There is still so many questions."

"Right. So we *know* that Mr. Hawkins was murdered. We *believe* that Jonny was paid to do it, and then was himself murdered, not a drug deal gone wrong. Right?" She looks at me for confirmation.

"Right," I reply.

"And Murtaza was murdered, not a heart attack. Right?" Sonia again pressing me for confirmation.

"Right."

"I am willing to bet my left leg that they were all killed by the same person or persons."

"I am not betting on any body parts," I smile, "I have already lost too many. But I agree. Somehow it all links back to my grandfather. I just don't quite understand, he has been dead for over thirty years. Why now?"

"I think it all started with that poster. Someone doesn't want the world to know he was on the summit with Mr. Hawkins."

"But who cares, it was an age ago?"

"I don't know." Sonia looks deep in thought. "But I think Mr. Hawkins wanted the world to know. He must have chosen that picture. And remember that last talk, he was eluding to someone being there with him. The same in his book if you read between the lines."

"Guilt."

"Guilt what?" Sonia looks confused.

"I bet he was riddled with guilt. Keeping secrets will do that to you."

"I would call it lying. Secrets are fine, lying is not."

"Whatever. I think he was coming clean and someone desperately didn't want him to."

"I think you are right. But I don't know how we can find out," replies Sonia.

"Me either. Guess it is just going to be one of those mysteries we will never know, like Stonehenge."

Sonia giggles at me holding out her glass for me to pour her more wine. "Yes, just like Stonehenge."

***

On Monday morning the sun is still shining and I feel joyous as I walk down the hill in my Birkenstocks singing to myself, '*Hi Ho, Hi Ho, off to work I go.*' I don't think I have ever been this happy about work. I woke early and have been ready for hours, drinking way too much coffee willing the clock to move faster, wanting it to be work time.

Despite my best efforts to make time pass I still turn up before anyone else. I unlocked the office door, surprised my key still works. It feels like it has been years. I turn on the computer in my office, listening to it labor to warm up, wondering if we will ever get new computers. I am going through my endless email list when I hear someone else come in the front door. I had started through my work emails the other day, logging in remotely from home. But I got overwhelmed and stopped after a couple hundred. Most aren't important, but I still need to go through them all.

Karen pops her head in my door.

"Welcome back." She is beaming at me. "I made cake and the coffee is brewing."

"Wow, thanks Karen," I say. "It is great to be back."

"Great to have you back. Coffee in ten."

She closes my door behind her and I look at the clock in the lower right-hand corner of my computer screen, 08:30 AM, I have already been in for an hour and a half. Just another 683 emails to go, I sigh, my initial excitement at being back at work has already started to fade. Coffee and cake it is.

Karen is in mid breath blowing up a balloon as I walk into the large office kitchen, tables and chairs scattered throughout the space almost like a cafeteria.

"I said ten minutes."

"Oh, sorry." I look around, the room is decorated with *Welcome Back* banners and balloons.

On the table sits a large cake of unknown variety, it looks homemade.

"Oh, is this all for me?"

"It was meant to be a surprise," smiles Karen.

"It is." I am choking up, overwhelmed by the gesture. "Thank you."

"The others will be here soon. They are a little better at following instructions than you are," she says, giving me a smile.

It is festive, all of us drinking cup after cup of coffee and eating way too much cake, lingering, hoping to stay a little longer. Finally Karen orders us all back to work. I sneak another piece of cake, carrying it into my office on a napkin. I argue with myself that the sugar will help me see through the long list of emails. I wait while my computer whirls, waking up from its slumber. *Shit.* The email count has gone up to 687 emails while I was having coffee. I browse through the headings. No subject line, I look closer. *Shit.* It is from Jose. I click to open the email, worried it will ruin my good mood.

> *Marta,*
> *I need to talk to you. Please pick up your phone, or*
> *call me back. Please.*
> */Jose*

But I don't want too, I think to myself. It is hard. Hard because I miss him. Hard because I know I wouldn't trust him enough to let him back in. Annoyed at the effect the email has on me I delete it. Maybe later, I think before yet again turning my attention to the list of emails.

By the end of the day I have whittled my email list down to a respectable twenty emails left in my inbox, all read, but these still need my attention. *Nice work,* I congratulate myself before turning off the computer. Stepping out of my office I almost bump into Sonia.

"Want to grab dinner?" she asks.

"You know what, I am exhausted. First day back has taken it out of me. I think I just want to go home and crash."

"No worries. You want me to drop you home?"

"Nah, I will walk," I say pointing at my feet.

"Nice shoes," giggles Sonia before grabbing me by the arm walking me down the hall, waving me goodbye as I start my walk home.

I stroll up the hill in the sunshine, feeling happy and content. Halfway up the hill I turn around and look out over Puget Sound below, its surface sparkling in the afternoon sun. I take in the view before turning back around and walking the last bit to my apartment building.

"Hey wait," my neighbor calls out as I am unlocking my door. "I thought I heard you," she continues.

I stop, my key still in the door.

"I got this for you," she hands me an envelope. "I saw the postman put it in your box and I thought I would bring it up for you."

"Thank you. That is very sweet of you."

Mrs. Lee looks pleased with herself and she gives me a small nod before closing her door. I turn my key and open the door, turning the envelope over. I had expected another hospital bill, so when I find my address written out in neat handwriting I am intrigued. I look closer while stepping into my apartment, the door still open behind me. I freeze, staring at the stamp. It is postmarked Rawalpindi.

Chapter 34

I set the envelope down on the coffee table, sitting down in front of it. I look at it, nervous about opening it. Finally, I stand up and walk into the kitchen, grabbing a knife. I am scared that if I rip open the envelope, this is how I usually treat my mail, I will tear whatever lies inside.

I sit back down looking at the envelope again before finally putting my kitchen knife to it and carefully slitting it open. Inside are several lined sheets of paper filled with neat and slightly shaky handwriting in blue ink, single-sided. I let my eyes flit to the end of the letter before reading it, confirming what I have already suspected.

Inshallah we meet again. All the best,

Murtaza

I guess it wasn't God's will that we meet again, I think before returning to the first page sitting back in my couch to read.

Dearest Marta,

I am so sad I never got a chance to see you before you left for home. I am however, pleased to know you got out safe. It took me a long time to hike back out from K2 after you left for Gondogoro La, and by the time I had found my way back to Rawalpindi you were long gone. Anam confirmed you got proper treatment for your frostbite and I hope you didn't lose any toes. The mountains can be a cruel muse. I have so much more I wanted to share with you but I never got the chance. Time wasn't on our side. I fear it still isn't, so I am writing you this letter to tell you the rest of my story.

Where was I? Like I already told you, our expedition did not get along. Mr. Hawkins did not appear to be the kind-hearted man that Zygmunt had told me about. I think that Zygmunt also felt this and that he was disappointed by the entire expedition. But we all had one thing in common, the desire to climb K2. The pull of that mountain cannot be underestimated. We all hungered to stand on the summit. In the many letters Zygmunt and I shared over the years between Nanga Parbat and K2, we discussed our displeasure with our governments and the poverty and hardship of life in our countries. Zygmunt often expressed his disgust over fellow Polish mountaineers who had taken the lure and was spying for the Polish government. They were treated to supplies of good climbing gear and were the first names on the lists for government funded climbing expeditions, both to the Alps and the Himalayas.

After Zygmunt went on the expedition to Lothse, where he met Mr. Hawkins, the tone of his letters changed. He talked of taking a stand, and of freeing his people from the USSR. Finally having a truly Polish government and not one that was a mere puppet for Russia. He didn't come straight out and say it, but he alluded rather heavily towards the fact that he had decided to work for the Americans. Something he confirmed when we finally met again in Islamabad. During a whispered conversation at my friend's tea house he confirmed that he was gathering information about the Polish government for the Americans. That he had grown tired of being a bystander not taking a stand for his country and its people. In reality I think that what was driving him was Aniela. He wanted a free Poland for his daughter, for her to have the opportunities he never did. He was excited and triumphant when we met in Islamabad, like change was just around the corner. But his excitement died when Mr. Hawkins arrived. I heard them having heated arguments in basecamp, but Zygmunt never elaborated. I think he wished to keep me out of any trouble he had gotten himself into. But it was obvious that Mr. Hawkins and Zygmunt no longer saw eye to eye.

I can't say for a fact, but I believe that Mr. Hawkins must have been the go between for the American government and Zygmunt, and that something in the plan had gone sour. Zygmunt was distant and ill-tempered for the rest of the expedition, often seeking out solitude, or spending the days with me. I think he felt like he had betrayed me, he would often apologize for the Americans to me. But I was used to being treated like a porter, I often was a high altitude porter. Zygmunt was outraged however, and bitter, accusing the Americans of bigotry and being just like Hitler.

A life is a life no matter what, he would often say. I could tell he was ready to be over with this mountain. I wish we would have just left, but for both of us getting on an expedition to climb K2, any expedition, was no small feat. The mountain had cast its spell on us and there was no turning back until our bodies had been forced to their outermost limit and we had tried our damndest to reach that summit. So we plodded on making trips up the mountainside, acclimatizing and carrying loads to the higher camps. We separated ourselves from the others by going up as everyone else was coming down, choosing to carry loads when the snow was falling and high winds whistling, and staying in basecamp during fair weather when the others went up to higher camps.

It worked well, we hardly ever saw the rest of our team. This is why it was such a big surprise when the summit teams were picked and Zygmunt was placed with Mr. Hawkins and not with me. We had fully expected the Americans to put themselves together in the first summit team, and then letting me and Zygmunt try second, scrambling for leftovers. It wasn't just us who were surprised, the other Americans were also surprised and disappointed, I think. They didn't necessarily want to go with me. Zygmunt tried to change it, offering to switch with the other Americans, letting them go first. But Mr. Hawkins was adamant and unmoving. In hindsight I know there was never a choice. I believe that Mr. Hawkins had been given a task to carry out, a task that would only be possible if he climbed with Zygmunt.

Marta, I am sad to tell you this, but I believe, no I am pretty certain, that Mr. Hawkins killed your grandfather after they had stood on the summit together. I also think he was truly sorry for it. He looked distraught when he got down to us, he was shaking and couldn't stop rambling. At first I thought that the altitude, they had spent an entire night high on the mountain before reaching the summit, and the drama of losing a friend was making him mad. But after some time I realized that there was more to his incoherence and shaking, it was guilt. I noticed a smear of blood on the pick of Mr. Hawkins ice axe and he saw me noticing. We locked eyes and he wiped it off with his glove not saying a word.

It wasn't until about a year ago that I received a letter from Mr. Hawkins. A letter of regret and apologies. He didn't really admit to killing Zygmunt, but he told me he was racked with guilt and deeply saddened that he had stabbed his friend in the back. Not providing the same friendship and support that Zygmunt had so graciously given to him. I know it wasn't meant to sound literal, but I think it was. I think he stabbed Zygmunt with his ice axe as they were leaving the summit and then pushed him off the side. But I guess we will never know for certain.

Once the Americans had left Pakistan and the news of a successful summit started to circulate, it was as if I and Zygmunt had never been there. Our presence had been erased from history. I guess that was easier than explaining a death. More wholesome for the families at home, reading of the success of their hero rather than smearing the good news with blood. Me, who cared, I was just a Pakistani; no one even gave me as much as a mention. Easy to erase a poor local, no one was going to trust a backwards Pakistani over the strong muscular American heroes.

I was disillusioned and sad, I gave up on climbing and worked in my friend's tea shop while I earned a primary school teacher's diploma. I worked in a local school for boys until 1989 when the SOS orphanage opened in Rawalpindi. Ever since I have dedicated my life to teaching the children here in English and math, skills I initially learned from Zygmunt and then fine-tuned during my diploma. This is my way of paying back, I couldn't help Zygmunt, and even more regrettably I could not help Aniela once

Zygmunt was gone, but I can help these children who have been left with no families of their own.

That is my full story Marta. I am not sure why Mr. Hawkins was murdered and I don't know who was following us on the trail, nor why someone is watching me. There is a car parked outside my house at all times. I thought this old sad story was long buried. But perhaps Mr. Hawkins' guilt was too big to carry and he opened an old can of worms that would have been best left alone. Had it not been for the immense pleasure of learning of your existence and getting to meet you, I would say Mr. Hawkins was foolhardy to try to repent for his sins much too late. Better to let old bones lie. It was a pleasure to meet you Marta and to learn that Zygmunt's love for the mountains lives on in his granddaughter. I wish you nothing but happiness and good fortune.

Inshallah we meet again. All the best,

Murtaza

I turn back to the first page as soon as I finish the last one, reading it all again.

I pick up my phone.

"Sonia."

"Yes, hi, what's up?"

"I just got a letter from Murtaza."

"Murtaza?"

"Yes, he must have posted it before he was kil… Before he died."

"Oh. I am at my parents' place for dinner, you want me to swing by on my way home?"

"No, it is OK. I will see you at work in the morning."

I hold onto the phone for a while feeling uneasy. Goosebumps are covering my arms so I stand up and close the kitchen window. There's a sharp knock on my door.

"We need to talk," Special Agent Bollinger is staring at me, the previous fake friendly is gone.

Chapter 35

Instinct makes me slam the door, but Bollinger already has a foot in the door. She pulls it open and pushes in to my narrow hallway. She is pushing me backwards with one arm. I am surprised at her strength, she doesn't look that strong. I stumble over some shoes that are littering my hallway, but regain my balance. Bollinger's eyes are dark and narrowed into tiny slits and her jaws are clenched. She is pointing a gun at my chest.

"Sit down," she orders me when we get to the living room.

I am in no position to argue. So I sink down on the sofa, my legs feel like jelly and I am actually thankful to be seated. The room is spinning around me and I think I may pass out.

"Where is the letter?" Bollinger looks straight at me. Her perfume that is filling the room is making me gag before I can speak.

"What letter?"

"The letter from Murtaza."

I stand up to walk over to the bookcase. I don't want to die. I remember reading somewhere that if you are being mugged you just give them what they want and your life will be spared. I hoped this works the same way. Although I can't say I ever read anything about how to save your bacon from a government agent, I slide the letter out from between the books where I had placed it.

"How did you know?" I ask as I hand it over, her gun is still aimed at me.

"I have been keeping my eyes and ears on you."

Aha, I think, my phone call to Sonia. She must have tapped my phone or something. This is starting to feel too much like a movie. *Nikita*, or *Bourne Identity* maybe, I had liked both. This one however, I am not so fond of. Bollinger pulls the coffee table back and sits down on it facing me on the sofa.

"Open it," she demands.

I slide the sheets of paper out and hand them to her like an obedient dog. She starts reading, glancing up at me every few seconds. It is becoming a pattern. Read for ten seconds, look at me for two, back to reading for ten seconds, and then look at me for two. I count, one, two, then leap.

I take her by surprise. The gun slides across the wooden floor, I can hear it coming to a rest somewhere close to the bedroom door. Bollinger is flailing under me, yet to take stock on what has just happened. I don't have a plan and I struggle to stay on top of her, not sure of what to do next. A knuckle connects with my cheek and I see stars. *Bitch*, I think and scramble to get away from her, to reach the gun. I am almost there, arm stretched out. But as my fingertips reach for the gun a hand closes firmly around my ankle and yanks me backwards. Sharp pain is shooting up from the bottom of my feet. The still sensitive scars on my left foot have hit the coffee table. Sick is rushing up my throat and I swallow hard.

I turn around swinging my arms, fists clenched. I haven't been in a fight since I was a child, fighting with the neighborhood boys. This is different, Bollinger is good. The neighborhood boys had all been a bunch of pansies. My fist connects with hard bone and Bollinger lets out a swear word, but my lucky hit seems to only drive her on harder and she is grabbing for my wrists, pinning me down hands over my head. I am kicking with my feet. The pain whenever either of my feet hits its target is so overwhelming it makes my vision go black. *I am hurting myself more than I am hurting her*, I think and finally give up.

Bollinger is sitting on my chest, pinning me down and breathing hard, catching her breath.

"That was a really, *really*, dumb idea," she pants.

I can feel the blood drain from my face. I can't focus or

think of what to do next so I just lie there. It doesn't look like Bollinger knows what to do either. I am stuck, but so is she. She can't get to the gun any more than I can. We stare at each other trying to work out our next move, trying to work out each other's next move.

"You are hurting me," I wheeze, trying to sound small. Which isn't hard with her weight pressing down on my lungs.

"Good." She smiles.

Bollinger switches one hand out and is now holding down both of my arms with her one, leaving one arm free. She looks pleased but unsure of what to do with her new found free arm. She looks at her hand then at me, a smile darting across her face before she clamps it down around my neck.

My legs are kicking and I am twisting hard, Bollinger is buckling on top like a cowboy at the rodeo. But her hand stays firm around my neck. I can still draw little breaths, turns out strangling someone with one hand is quite the challenge. I think about just lying there taking little breaths and not wasting any more energy or precious oxygen on fighting back. But I can feel my fingers and lips start to tingle. I am getting air, just not enough.

Panic is lacing my body with adrenaline and I give one last big buckle. Bollinger topples over, her hand around my neck letting go and the one on my wrists loosening. I gasp for air and kick with all I got at her chest and she lets go of my wrists, sliding a couple of feet away from me. Sick makes its way all the way up into my mouth this time and the sour stomach acid burns when I swallow it back down. My doctors will not be happy, I think while trying to get up, pain again shooting through my legs as I stand on my feet. Blood is smearing the wooden floors and I can see blood soaking through my sock. I can hear Bollinger move behind but I am too scared to look back, just get to the gun, I'm thinking. Everything seems to be

243

in slow motion.

"Don't move."

The voice and command takes me by such surprise I freeze in place. So must have Bollinger because everything goes deadly quiet.

"Marta, are you OK?" Jose's voice is steady.

"Yes. I think so," I whimper.

"On your knees now," shouts Jose, and I start to lower down to the ground.

"Not you Marta."

"Oh, oh, OK." I rise to standing again, having stopped somewhere in between standing and kneeling.

"Hands behind your back."

I put my hands behind me, I am still facing away from Jose, the direction of Bollinger's gun, only a few feet in front of me on the wooden floor.

"Marta," Jose's voice is sharp.

I bring my hands back in front of me. I hear movement behind me, quick steps. I match the steps moving further away and cover my head with my arms. Why do humans do that I think, how are my arms going to protect my precious brain from a bullet? Stupid.

"Marta, it is OK."

I turn around. Bollinger is kneeling on the floor, her arms handcuffed behind her back, and Jose is pointing his service weapon at her.

"Why didn't you call me?" Jose looks at me. "When the police tell you to call them, it is generally a good idea to comply." He looks angry.

"Sorry," I whimper.

Soon the apartment is a beehive of activity. Police are milling in and out, Bollinger is carted off in a police car, and Jose leaves without saying goodbye. I feel a little hurt. Once the

244

scene has been documented, gun picked up, and letter sealed in an evidence bag, two uniformed police sit me down at the kitchen table.

"Do you need medical attention?" asks policeman A pointing at my cheek.

I lift my hand to my face and wince as my fingers connect with my swollen face. I hadn't even realized.

"Probably," I say, and instead point at my sock that is by now completely soaked in blood. "But, it can wait."

"OK, good," says policeman B looking at policeman A for confirmation.

They spend over an hour asking me questions about what has transpired tonight, but also some background probing. They finish up with, "It has come to our attention that Ms. Bollinger is not who she says she is. You are lucky we got here in time."

"So who is she then?" I ask.

"We can't go into that now. But we would like you to come down to the station tomorrow for a proper statement and we can discuss it further then." Policeman A smiles a warm smile at me. "Are you going to be OK here alone for the rest of the night? Or is there someone we can call for you?"

"Yes and no," I reply. "But you could give me a ride to the hospital."

"Oh, of course," he looks embarrassed for having forgotten about my bleeding foot.

Chapter 36

It is close to two thirty in the morning by the time I limp into the emergency room at Swedish Hospital. It is quiet, all that can be heard is a low hospital hum in the dimly lit waiting room.

"You're lucky, it looks quiet," comments policeman A before sauntering over to the reception desk.

Policeman B is waiting outside in the police car, which they have parked in the Ambulance bay.

"This lady here has been assaulted," he says in a strong voice, and the lady behind the desk snaps to attention.

I know the drill; *I* am usually the one who brings battered women to the hospital or to the police. It feels strange being on the receiving end. Policeman A explains the situation to the now wide-eyed receptionist, who quickly types into the computer as she listens.

"Can we leave her with you now?" inquires policeman A.

"Yes. Let me get you a wheelchair," she motions for me to wait.

I am wheeled into a room and before I know it I am back in a hospital gown feeling like I have never left. A nurse pulls back my bloodied sock and gasps.

"What happened to you?" The words spilling out before she can stop herself.

I chuckle.

"It is OK." I smile. "I lost my toes to frostbite, they had only just healed, well almost. Now this." I gesture down at my foot. It isn't actively bleeding, but blood is smeared all over my foot, a gaping wound stretches from the base of my big toe almost to the very edge of my foot.

"I hope you got the bastard good."

"Not really." I smile. "But the police have *her* now."

"Oh!" The nurse had clearly expected the culprit to be a

man. "I better get the doctor to have a look at this before I do anything," she says before examining my swollen cheek and the now angry blue bruises around my neck.

They clean up my foot and put in new stiches before wrapping it up. I am given crutches. I am sick and tired of not being able to walk freely, it feels like a massive defeat to be on crutches. But I quickly remind myself that at least I am not sprawled unbreathing on my living room floor.

The sun has started to rise when I finally hop out of the hospital, a small paper bag with painkillers and antibiotics in yellow plastic vials inside. I wave down a taxi and go into work. I am first in, again. I look at my watch, six a.m., no surprise then. Rummaging through the kitchen cupboard I find a brown banana and a few stale saltines. I set both down on one of the tables while I start the coffee machine. Breakfast of champions, I think as I bite into the soft banana. Sonia literally bursts into the room.

"MARTA. I have been worried sick," she slaps my hand like you would a naughty child and the half eaten banana falls on the floor. "And don't eat that. That's gross."

"What?" I look at my breakfast now smeared on the floor.

"Why didn't you call?" she continues while walking over to the kitchen bench grabbing some kitchen towels and wiping up the mess of the banana.

"I am sorry, I never got a chance to. I only just got in," I say in explanation.

"And you thought eating a half-rotten banana was more important than calling your best friend?"

"It wasn't rotten, just brown," I start out, but when I see Sonia's face I think better of it. "I am sorry. I was hungry and I didn't want to wake you up."

"Oh God, Marta. I have been running all over town for you."

"How did you know?"

"Jose called me. I raced to the hospital and when you had already left I went to your place; I panicked when you didn't open. I didn't have your spare key on me, so I rushed here to pick it up, and here you are feasting on bad bananas," she says.

"This has got to stop, one of these days I will have a heart attack from the worry."

"I think it is over. They have Bollinger."

"Bollinger?"

"Yes, she is the one who attacked me."

"What the…" Sonia stops herself before swearing, she always does. "But why?"

"I don't really know. I don't think she is with the FBI after all. I hope the police will clear things up when I go into the station."

"You want me to come?"

"Yes." I am surprised at how calm I feel.

***

Policeman B hands me a cup of hot coffee as I sit down at the table. The room is light grey and barren, the kind of room that makes you feel guilty even when you have not committed the crime. But the atmosphere is friendly and policeman A brings in pastries, making the mood seem almost festive. Same questions as last night, but this time a recorder is placed on the table. I answer each question again, policemen A nodding in approval as I speak clearly and without fuzz.

"So, who is Bollinger if she is not working for the FBI?" I finally ask.

"Ms. Bollinger works for the CIA. She was working on the Cold War team, investigating the renewed tension between Russia and the US. Russia has been increasing its military aggression in Europe, and here in the US, Russian fighter jets have been flying over Alaska. I believe Ms. Bollinger went a little rogue however, she was emotionally invested in the Cold War. Her grandfather, much like yours, was a spy during the Cold War. He was an American spy that was captured by the Russians when his plane was shot down. He never made it out of Russia. She is under investigation by the government for aggression against a civilian."

"What about murder?" I chip in.

"Yes, that too." Policeman B squirms in his seat.

"What about Jose?" I ask.

"Ms. Bollinger used him to get to you. I think it started out innocent enough. But you can add obstructing an officer to the list of charges."

He stands up, indicating that the questions are done, both theirs and mine. We shake hands and both A and B wish me good luck.

Sonia is no longer sitting in the waiting room.

"Have you seen my friend who was waiting here?" I gesture towards the blue plastic chairs.

"She went to see Officer Johnson. Third door down the hall."

I already know it is the third door down the hall.

"Thank you…" I pause to look at her nameplate, "Alex."

I poke my head in through Jose's open office door. Jose is sitting at his desk with a large window behind him, it makes it hard to make out his features. The office is neat, there is no paperwork on the desk, only a computer and keyboard, nothing else. Sonia is seated opposite Jose in one of the visitor chairs.

"Hello."

Jose stands up but Sonia remains seated.

"Hi. Come in." Jose looks better, relieved, and maybe even happy.

His cheeks are flushed and I can tell the pounds have started to come back. I sit down next to Sonia, facing Jose on the other side of his desk.

"How did you know I was in trouble?"

"I thought it was all over when you left Wenatchee. Not just you and me, but this whole sorry mess. The story had ended. But then Sonia told me that you thought someone had been in your apartment, and that someone had been checking your mail."

Sonia looks at me worried I will be mad, but I wave my hand indicating I don't care.

"So, I thought I'd just look at it a little more. I didn't quite trust Bollinger. Well, at first I did, but as time went on there were little inconsistences that were nagging me. I contacted the Terrorist Task Force and they had never heard of Special Agent Bollinger. It was peculiar because I did receive a paycheck from the government after all. Not knowing who Bollinger was or who she really worked for made me nervous, and from what Sonia had told me I worried you may be in trouble. I tried to call you, and I emailed you. But you weren't taking my calls," he quickly adds, "I don't blame you," before going on. "But it really freaked me out. I had your neighbor look out for you, collecting your mail and watching out for Bollinger. Last night she called me in a panic saying that she had just seen a woman force her way into your apartment. I quickly gathered a team and we went straight to your place."

"Wow."

"Yes, Judy has been a great help."

"Wow." I am still lost for words. Judy, I have never known my neighbors first name, nor appreciated her, but now gratitude for this grumpy little lady is washing over me. I look at Sonia.

"You better help me pick out some flowers for her."

"Sure," Sonia giggles.

"Turns out Bollinger works for the CIA and went above and beyond her job description. I think she was trying to cover up old American Cold War crimes. I believe that the government somehow had Mr. Hawkins kill your grandfather. By 1978 the Cold War was drawing towards an end and both sides were eager to clean out their cupboards, to make everything look neat. If, like Murtaza said, Zygmunt had been an informant for the US, they wanted to make sure there were no traces left behind, and a lowly Polish climber was easy to get rid of.

"I don't believe Mr. Hawkins was a willing participant, but he must have been involved pretty deeply himself. I also believe that in his old age he wanted to come clean, to tell the world the real story. His timing was off, however. The recent friction between Russia and the US means that the government is desperate to keep old secrets untold. If Mr. Hawkins came clean now the whole country would be up in arms, there would be mistrust towards the government, and Russia would have fuel for their fire. Somewhere in all of this we got caught up, and Bollinger went rogue. It appears she has been researching old Cold War crimes, and has been taking justice into her own hands. Bollinger is deeply patriotic and harbors a strong hatred for Russia. I am guessing that Mr. Hawkins wanting to tell the world of what America made him do to someone who was on our side didn't sit well with her."

"Holy shit."

Sonia looks at me, unpleased about my swearing.

"Jose. Thank you so much. You certainly saved my bacon. I don't know how to repay you."

"Let's just call it even." He looks hopeful.

"Even," I say and stand up.

Jose extends his hand across the table to shake mine. But I walk around the desk and throw my arms around him, clinging to him, like you would someone who is about to leave on a long journey. He squeezes me back hard, holding on to each other for dear life. Tears are threatening, and when I let go my voice is choked up.

"Even," I repeat, and walk back around to where Sonia sits looking the other way trying to give us privacy.

I take Sonia's arm and when we walk out the door I turn around.

"Goodbye Jose."

"Goodbye Marta."

My sincere thanks

There are many factors that played in to me being able to write this book. The first and foremost was the undying support of my husband Kristian. Who encouraged, not so gently nudged, and supported me to take a year off work to complete this book. His constant praise, cheer, and love made this not just possible but also fun. He was the first person to read this book, soon followed by Charlotte, Michelle, Linda, Jessica, and Alex who all gave me constructive feedback and helped me improve my story. Michelle also agreed to paint the beautiful cover for my book, and for this I am forever grateful, it is simply stunning. I received endless support and encouragement from all my friends and family during this process and while the names are too many to mention, just know that I love you all and couldn't have completed this without you in my life.

About the author

Ida Vincent is a mountaineering marine biologist from Sweden who moved to Seattle six years ago after spending ten years in Australia. She loves spending time at high elevations in the mountains, or below the surface of the sea scuba diving. She is passionate about conservation and enjoys writing as well as photography. A lot of her spare time is dedicated to teaching and leading alpine climbs for Seattle Mountaineers. Ida have previously published scientific work, and magazine articles about mountaineering. This is her first novel.

Made in the USA
San Bernardino, CA
22 September 2016